"It is estimated that if only two grams of anti-matter struck our planet the result would be to send the earth, with all life immediately extinct, spinning into the orbit of the sun."

"A wonderfully entertaining story."
—*Chicago Tribune Book World*

"High-pitched excitement. . . . The action bobs at machinegun pace."
—*Dallas Times Herald*

"The action never lags. . . . MacLean is up to his usual high standards."
—*Indianapolis Star*

"Alistair MacLean has an international reputation as a superb storyteller. . . . *CIRCUS* is an espionage tale that should send his admirers rushing to the bookstores. . . . The action never slows. . . . An enjoyable thriller."
—*The Columbia (S.C.) State*

Fawcett Crest and Gold Medal Books
by Alistair MacLean:

H.M.S. ULYSSES
THE GUNS OF NAVARONE
SOUTH BY JAVA HEAD
THE SECRET WAYS
NIGHT WITHOUT END
FEAR IS THE KEY
THE BLACK SHRIKE
THE SATAN BUG
ICE STATION ZEBRA
WHEN EIGHT BELLS TOLL
WHERE EAGLES DARE
FORCE 10 FROM NAVARONE
PUPPET ON A CHAIN
CARAVAN TO VACCARES
BEAR ISLAND
THE WAY TO DUSTY DEATH
BREAKHEART PASS
CIRCUS

Alistair MacLean

CIRCUS

A FAWCETT CREST BOOK

Fawcett Publications, Inc., Greenwich, Connecticut

CIRCUS

THIS BOOK CONTAINS THE COMPLETE TEXT OF THE ORIGINAL HARDCOVER EDITION.

A Fawcett Crest Book reprinted by arrangement with Doubleday and Company, Inc.

All the characters in this book are fictitious, and any resemblance to actual persons living or dead is purely coincidental.

ISBN 0-449-22875-4

Dual Selection of the Literary Guild, August 1975
Selection of the Contempo Book Club
Selection of the Doubleday Bargain Book Club

Printed in the United States of America

10 9 8 7 6 5 4 3

to

Juan Ignacio

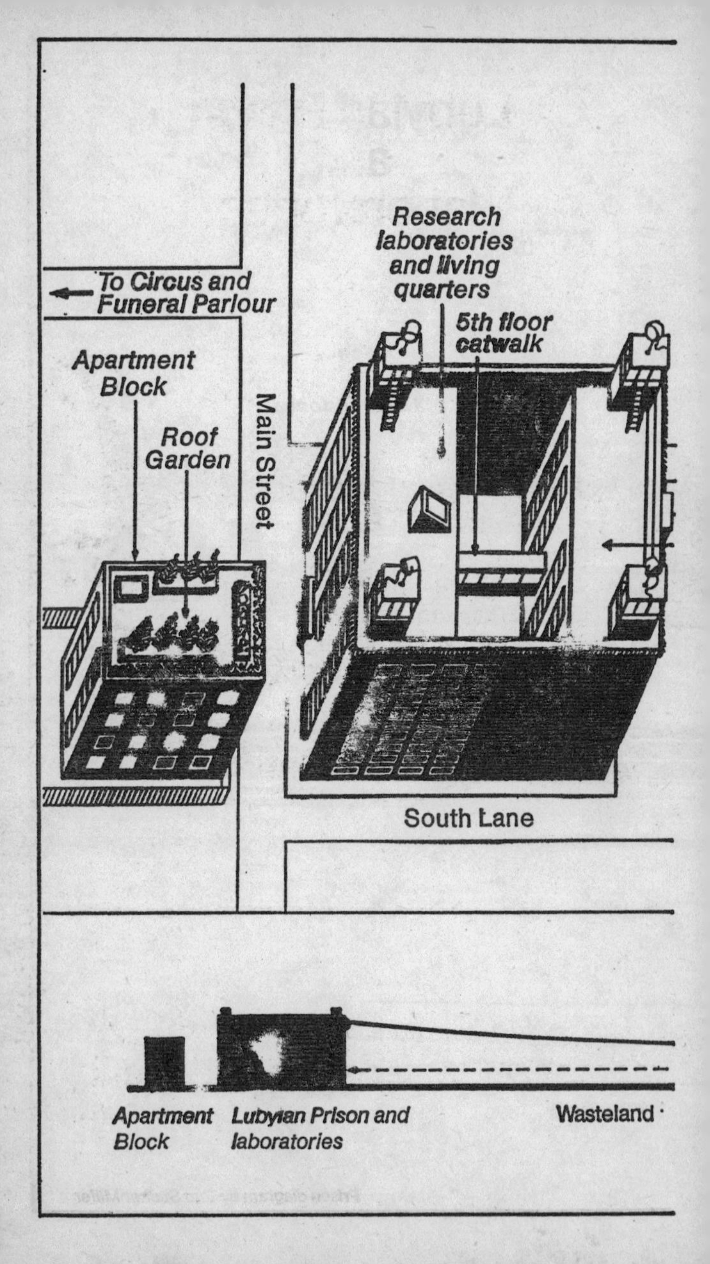

To Circus and Funeral Parlour
Research laboratories and living quarters
5th floor catwalk
Apartment Block
Roof Garden
Main Street
South Lane
Apartment Block
Lubyian Prison and laboratories
Wasteland

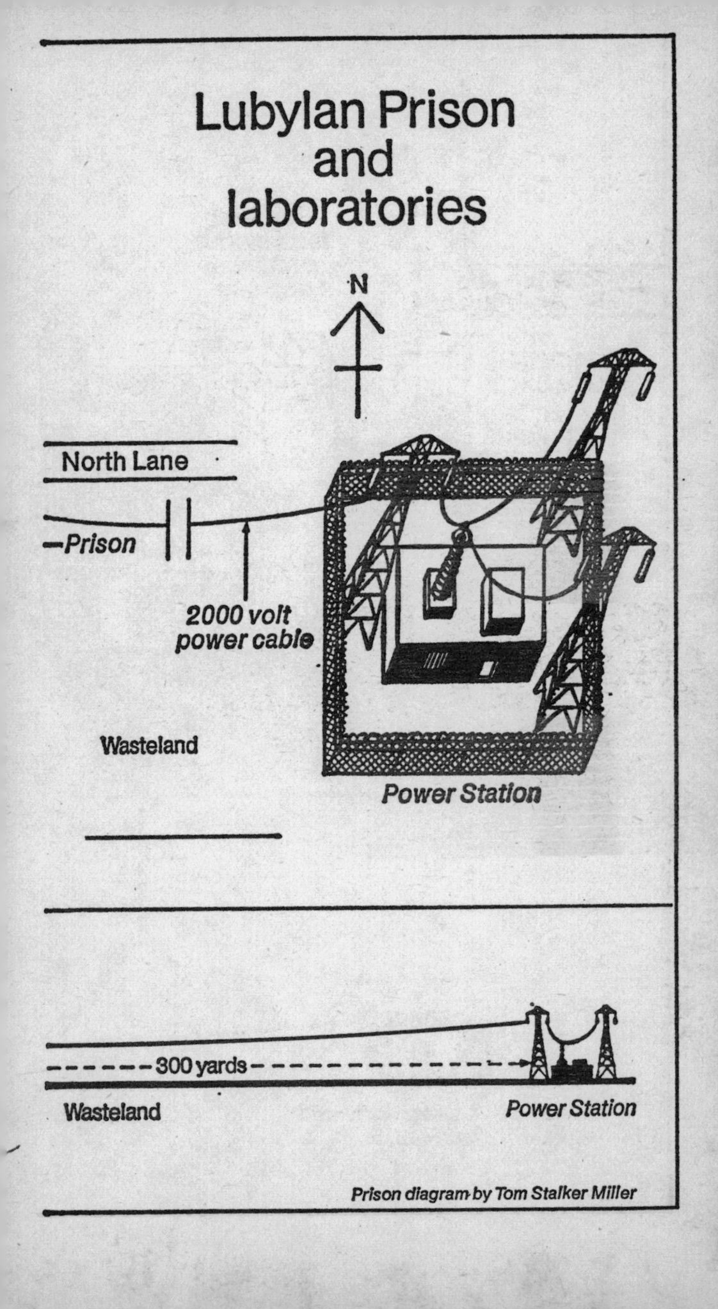
Lubylan Prison
and
laboratories
N
North Lane
Prison
2000 volt
power cable
Wasteland
Power Station
300 yards
Wasteland
Power Station
Prison diagram by Tom Stalker Miller

1

"If you were a genuine Army Colonel," Pilgrim said, "instead of one of the most bogus and unconvincing frauds I've ever seen, you'd rate three stars for this. Excellently done, my dear Fawcett, excellently done."

Pilgrim was the great-grandson of an English peer of the realm and it showed. Both in dress and in speech he was slightly foppish and distinctly Edwardian: subconsciously, almost, one looked for the missing monocle, the old Etonian tie. His exquisitely cut suits came from Savile Row, his shirts from Turnbull and Asser and his pair of matched shotguns, which at four thousand dollars he regarded as being cheap at the price, came, inevitably, from Purdeys of the West End. The shoes, regrettably, were hand-made in Rome. To have him auditioned for the screen part of Sherlock Holmes would have been superfluous.

Fawcett did not react to the criticism, the praise or the understated sartorial splendour. His facial muscles seldom reacted to anything—which may have been due to the fact that his unlined face was so plump it was almost moon-shaped. His bucolic expression verged upon the bemused: large numbers of people languishing behind Federal bars had been heard to testify, frequently and with understandable bitterness, that the impression Fawcett conveyed was deceptive to the point of downright immorality.

Half-hooded eyes deep-sunk in the puffy flesh, Fawcett's gaze traversed the leather-lined library and came to rest on the sparking pine fire. His voice wistful, he said: "One would wish that promotion were so spectacular and rapid in the CIA."

"Dead men's shoes, my boy." Pilgrim was at least five years younger than Fawcett. "Dead men's shoes." He regarded his own Roman foot briefly and with some satisfaction, then transferred his attention to the splendid collection of ribbons on Fawcett's chest. "I see you have awarded yourself the Congressional Medal of Honor."

"I felt it was in keeping with my character."

"Quite. This paragon you have unearthed. Bruno. How did you come across him?"

"I didn't. Smithers did, when I was in Europe. Smithers is a great circus fan."

"Quite." Pilgrim seemed fond of the word. "Bruno. One would assume that he has another name."

"Wildermann. But he never uses it—professionally or privately."

"Why?"

"I don't know. I've never met him. Presumably Smithers never asked him either. Would you ask Pele or Callas or Liberace what their other names are?"

"You class his name with those?"

"It's my understanding that the circus world would hesitate to class those names with his."

Pilgrim picked up some sheets of paper. "Speaks the language like a native."

"He is a native."

"Billed as the world's greatest aerialist." Pilgrim was a hard man to knock off his stride. "Daring young man on the flying trapeze? That sort of thing?"

"That, too. But he's primarily a high-wire specialist."

"The best in the world?"

"His fellow professionals are in no doubt about it."

"If our information about Crau is correct, he'd better be. I see he claims to be an expert in karate and judo."

"He has never claimed anything of the kind. I claim it for him—rather Smithers does, and as you know Smithers is very much an expert in those matters. He watched Bruno having a work-out downtown this morning in the Samurai Club. The instructor there is a black belt—they don't come any higher in judo. By the time Bruno had finished with him—well, I understand the instructor disappeared with the general air of a man about to write out his resignation on the spot. Smithers said he hadn't seen Bruno chopping people around in karate: he has the feeling he wouldn't like to, either."

"And this dossier claims that he is a mentalist." Pilgrim steepled his fingers in the best Holmes fashion. "Well, good for Bruno. What the devil is a mentalist?"

"Chap that does mental things."

Pilgrim exercised a massive restraint. "You have to be an intellectual to be an aerialist?"

"I don't even know whether you have to be an intellectual—or even intelligent—in order to be an aerialist. It's beside the point. Practically every circus performer doubles up and does one, sometimes even two jobs in addition to his speciality in the actual arena. Some act as labourers—they have mountains of equipment to move around. Some are entertainers. Bruno doubles as an entertainer. Just outside the circus proper they have a show-ground, fair-ground, call it what you will, which is used to separate the arriving customers from their spare cash. Bruno performs in a small theatre, just a collapsible plywood job. He reads minds, tells you the first name of your great-grandfather, the numbers of the dollar bills in your pockets, what's written or drawn inside any sealed envelope. Things like that."

"It's been done. Audience plants and the hocus-pocus of any skilled stage magician."

"Possibly, although the word is that he can do things for which there is no rational accounting and which professional conjurers have failed to reproduce. But what interests us most is that he has a totally photographic memory. Give him an opened double spread of say, *Time* magazine. He'll look at it for a couple of seconds, hand it back then offer to identify the word in any location you select. You say to him that you'd like to know what the third word in the third line in the third column on the right-hand page is and if he says it's, say, 'Congress' then you can lay your life it is 'Congress.' And he can do this in any language—he doesn't have to understand it."

"This I have to see. *À propos,* if he's such a genius, why doesn't he concentrate exclusively on stage work? Surely he could make a fortune out of that, much more than by risking his life turning somersaults up there in the low cloud?"

"Perhaps. I don't know. According to Smithers, he's not exactly paid in pennies. He's the outstanding star in the outstanding circus on earth. But that wouldn't be his real reason. He's the lead member of a trio of aerialists called 'The Blind Eagles,' and without him they'd be lost. I gather they are not mentalists."

"I wonder. We can't afford excessive sentiment and loyalty in our business."

"Sentiment, no. Loyalty—to us—yes. To others, yes also. If they are your two younger brothers."

"A family trio?"

"I thought you knew."

Pilgrim shook his head. "You called them The Blind Eagles?"

"No undue hyperbole, Smithers tells me. Not when you've seen their act. They may not quite be up in the wild blue yonder or hanging about, as you suggest, in the low cloud, but they're not exactly earth-bound either. On the upswing of the trapeze they're eighty feet above terra firma. Whether you fall from eighty feet or eight hundred, the chances of breaking your neck—not to mention most of the two hundred-odd bones in your body—are roughly the same. Especially if you're blindfolded and can't tell up from down, while your body can't tell you exactly where up is and most certainly can't locate down."

"You're trying to tell me—"

"They wear those black silk cotton gloves when they take off from one trapeze to another. People think there may be some advanced electronic quirk in those gloves, like negative poles attracting positive poles, but there isn't. Just for better adhesion, that's all. They have no guidance system at all. Their hoods are entirely opaque but they never miss—well, obviously they never miss or they would be one Blind Eagle short by this time. Some form of extrasensory perception, I suppose—whatever that may mean. Only Bruno has it, which is why he is the catcher."

"This I have to see. And the great mentalist at work."

"No problem. On the way in." Fawcett consulted his watch. "We could leave now. Mr. Wrinfield is expecting us?" Pilgrim nodded in silence. A corner of Fawcett's mouth twitched: he could have been smiling. He said: "Come now, John, all circus-goers are happy children at heart. You don't look very happy to me."

"I'm not. There are twenty-five different nationalities working for this circus, at least eight of them Mid- or Eastern European. How am I to know that someone out there might not love me, might be carrying a picture of me in his back pocket? Or half a dozen of them carrying pictures of me?"

"The price of fame. You want to try disguising yourself." Fawcett surveyed his own colonel's uniform complacently. "As a lieutenant-colonel, perhaps?"

They travelled to downtown Washington in an official but unidentifiable limousine, Pilgrim and Fawcett in the back, the driver and a fourth man in the front. The fourth man was a grey, balding anonymity of a person, rain-coated, with a totally forgettable face. Pilgrim spoke to him.

"Now, don't forget, Masters, you better be sure that you're the first man on that stage."

"I'll be the first man, sir."

"Picked your word?"

"Yes, sir. 'Canada.' "

Dusk had already fallen and ahead, through a slight drizzle of rain, loomed an oval, high-domed building festooned with hundreds of coloured lights that had been programmed to flicker on and off in a preset pattern. Fawcett spoke to the driver, the car stopped and, wordlessly and carrying a magazine rolled up in one hand, Masters got out and seemed to melt into the gathering crowd. He had been born to melt into crowds. The car moved on and stopped again only when it had reached as close to the building entrance as possible. Pilgrim and Fawcett got out and passed inside.

The broad passageway led directly to the main audience entrance of the big top itself—a misnomer, as the days of the great canvas structures, at least as far as the big circuses were concerned, had gone. Instead they relied exclusively on exhibition halls and auditoriums, few of which seated less than ten thousand people, and many considerably more: a circus such as this had to have at least seven thousand spectators just to break even.

To the right of the passageway glimpses could be caught of the true back-stage of the circus itself, the snarling big cats in their cages, the restless hobbled elephants, the horses and ponies and chimpanzees, a scattering of jugglers engaged in honing up their performances—a top-flight juggler requires as much and as constant practice as a concert pianist—and, above all, the unmistakable and unforgettable smell. To the rear of the area were prefabricated offices and, beyond those, the rows of changing booths for the performers. Opposite those, in the far corner and discreetly curbed so as to minimise the audience's view of what was taking place back-stage, was the wide entrance to the arena itself.

From the left of the passageway came the sound of music, and it wasn't the New York Philharmonic that was giving forth. The music—if it could be called that—was raucous, tinny, blaring, atonal and in any other circumstances could have been fairly described as an assault upon the eardrums: but in that fairground milieu any other kind of music, whether because of habituation or because it went so inevitably with its background, would have been unthinkable. Pilgrim and Fawcett passed through one of the several doors leading to the concourse that housed the side-show itself. It covered only a modest area but what it lacked in size it clearly compensated for in volume of trade. It differed little from a hundred other fair-grounds apart from the presence of a sixty-by-twenty, garishly painted and obviously plywood-constructed structure in one corner. It was towards this, ignoring all the other dubious attractions, that Pilgrim and Fawcett headed.

Above the doorway was the intriguing legend: "The Great Mentalist." The two men paid their dollar apiece, went inside and took up discreet standing positions at the back. Discretion apart, there were no seats left—The Great Mentalist's fame had clearly travelled before him.

Bruno Wildermann was on the tiny stage. Of little more than average height, and of little more than average width across the shoulders, he did not look a particularly impressive figure, which could have been due to the fact that he was swathed from neck to ankle in a voluminous and highly coloured Chinese mandarin's gown, with huge, billowing sleeves. His aquiline, slightly swarthy face, crowned by long black hair, looked intelligent enough, but it was a face that was more pleasant than remarkable: if he passed you in the street you would not have turned to look after him.

Pilgrim said, *sotto voce:* "Look at those sleeves. You could hide a hutchful of rabbits up them."

But Bruno was not bent on performing any conjuring tricks. He was confining himself strictly to his advertised role as a mentalist. He had a deep carrying voice, not loud, with a trace of a foreign accent so slight as to make its source of origin unidentifiable.

He asked a woman in the audience to think of some object then whisper it to her neighbour: Without hesitation Bruno announced what the object was and this was confirmed.

"Plant," said Pilgrim.

Bruno called for three volunteers to come to the stage. After some hesitation three women did so. Bruno sat all three at a table, provided them with foot-square pieces of paper and envelopes to match and asked them to write or draw some simple symbol and enclose them in the envelopes. This they did while Bruno stood facing the audience, his back to them. When they had finished he turned and examined the three envelopes lying on the table, his hands clasped behind his back. After only a few seconds he said: "The first shows a swastika, the second a question mark, the third a square with two diagonals. Will you show them to the audience, please?"

The three women extracted the cards and held them up. They were undeniably a swastika, a question mark, and a square with two diagonals.

Fawcett leaned towards Pilgrim: "Three plants?" Pilgrim looked thoughtful and said nothing.

Bruno said: "It may have occurred to some of you that I have accomplices among the audience. Well, you can't *all* be accomplices because then you wouldn't bother to come and see me, even if I could afford to pay you all, which I can't. But this should remove all doubt." He picked up a paper plane and said: "I'm going to throw this among you and although I can do lots of things I can't control the flight of a paper plane. Nobody ever could. Perhaps the person it touches would be good enough to come to the stage."

He threw the paper plane over the audience. It swooped and darted in the unpredictable fashion of all paper planes then, again in the fashion of all paper planes, ended its brief flight in an ignominious nose dive, striking the shoulder of a youth in his late teens.

Somewhat diffidently he left his seat and mounted the stage. Bruno gave him an encouraging smile and a sheet of paper and envelope similar to those he'd given the women.

"What I want you to do is simple. Just write down three figures and put the sheet inside the envelope. This the youth did, while Bruno stood with his back to him. When the paper was inside the envelope Bruno turned, but did not even look at the paper, far less touch it. He said: "Add the three numbers and tell me what the total is."

"Twenty."

"The numbers you wrote down were seven, seven and six."

The youth extracted the paper and held it up for the audience to see. Seven, seven and six it was.

Fawcett looked at Pilgrim, who had now adopted a very thoughtful expression indeed: clearly, if Bruno were not genuine then he was either a consummate magician or an extraordinarily devious character.

Then Bruno announced his most difficult feat of all—that of displaying that he was possessed of a photographic memory, that of identifying, given the location, of any word in a double-spread of any magazine, irrespective of language. Masters left nothing to chance or the impetuousness of any eager-beaver who might care to forestall him, for he was on stage before Bruno had finished his explanation. Bruno, slightly lifting amused eyebrows, took the opened magazine from him, glanced at it briefly, handed it back and looked interrogatively at Masters.

Masters said: "Left page, second column, let me see now, seven lines down, middle word." He looked at Bruno with a half-smile of triumphant expectation.

Bruno said: " 'Canada.' "

The half-smile vanished. Masters' nondescript features seemed to fall apart, then he shrugged his shoulders in genuine disbelief and turned away.

Outside, Fawcett said: "I hardly think that Bruno is likely to have the inside track on the CIA. Convinced?"

"Convinced. When does the performance start?"

"Half an hour."

"Let's go watch him on the high wire or whatever. If he's half as good out there—well, he's our man."

The exhibition hall that housed the three-ring circus was completely full. The air was alive with music, this time more than tolerable music from a very competent orchestra, an air that was charged with tension and excitement and anticipation, with thousands of young children transported into an enchanted fairyland—almost, indeed, to the extent their grandparents were. Everything glittered, but it was no cheap tinsel glitter, but a background that seemed the integral and inevitable part of everything a circus should be. Apart from the dun-coloured sand in the three rings, a dazzling rainbow of colours caught the eye even more than the music the ear. Circling the ring were beautiful and beautifully dressed girls on the most outrageously caparisoned elephants, and if there was any colour in the spectrum that the designer had omitted it wasn't apparent to the eye. In the rings themselves clowns and pierrots vied with each other in the ludicrousness of their antics and the ridiculousness of their costumes, while both of them vied with the tumblers and the stately procession of stilt-walkers. The audience watched it all in fascination—albeit with an element of impatience, for this spectacle, magnificent as it was, was only the warm-up, the prelude to the action to come. There is no atmosphere in the world quite like that in the charged atmosphere of the big top just before the performance begins.

Fawcett and Pilgrim sat together in excellent viewing seats, almost opposite the centre of the main ring. Fawcett said: "Which is Wrinfield?"

Without appearing to do so, Pilgrim indicated a man sitting only two seats away in the same row. Immaculately clad in a dark blue suit, matching tie, and white shirt, he had a lean, thoughtful, almost scholarly face, with neatly parted grey hair and pebble glasses.

"*That's* Wrinfield?" Pilgrim nodded. "Looks more like a college professor to me."

"I believe he was once. Economics. But bossing a modern circus is no longer a seat-of-the-pants job. It's big business and running it requires corresponding intelligence. Tesco Wrinfield is a highly intelligent man."

"Maybe too intelligent. With a name like that and on a job like this is going to be—"

"He's a fifth-generation American."

The last of the elephants left the arena and then, to the accompaniment of a blare of trumpets and the suddenly amplified effects of the orchestra, a golden chariot, drawn by two magnificently adorned black stallions, erupted into the arena at full gallop, followed by a dozen horsemen. From time to time these horsemen retained some form of contact with their horses, but for the most part performed a series of acrobatic feats as spectacular as clearly suicidal. The crowd yelled and cheered and applauded. The circus had begun.

The performance that followed more than bore out the circus's claim that it had no peer in the world. It was superbly arranged and superbly presented and, as was to be expected, it numbered among its acts some of the best in the world: Heinrich Neubauer, an all but incomparable trainer with an uncanny power over a dozen very unpleasant Nubian lions; his only equal, Malthius, who treated the same number of even more unpleasant Bengal tigers as if they were kittens; Carraciola, who had no trouble at all in making his chimpanzees look a great deal more intelligent than he was; Kan Dahn, billed as the strongest man in the world, which, on the basis of his extraordinary one-handed feats on the high wire and trapeze while seemingly unencumbered by the presence of several attractive young ladies who clung to him with a touching degree of devotion, he might well have been; Lennie Loran, a high-wire-walking comedian, who would have made any insurance agent in the country jump on his pen; Ron Roebuck, who could perform feats with a lasso that a rodeo cowboy wouldn't even dare dream about; Manuelo, knife-thrower, who could extinguish a lit cigarette at twenty feet—with his eyes bandaged; the Duryans, a Bulgarian teeter-board team who made people shake their heads in wonder; and a dozen other acts, ranging from aerial balletists to a group who climbed up tall ladders and balanced there entirely unsupported while they threw Indian clubs at each other.

After an hour or so of this Pilgrim said graciously: "Not bad. Not bad at all. And here, I take it, is our star turn."

The lights dimmed, the orchestra played suitably dramatic if somewhat funereal music, then the lights came on again. High up on the trapeze platform, with half a dozen coloured spotlights trained on them, stood three men clad in sparkling, sequinned leotards. In the middle was Bruno. Without his mandarin's gown he now looked singularly impressive, broad-shouldered and hard and heavy muscled, every inch the phenomenal athlete he was reputed to be. The other two men were fractionally slighter than he. All three were blindfolded. The music died away, and the crowd watched in eerie silence as the three men pulled hoods over their blindfolds.

Pilgrim said: "On balance, I think I would prefer to be down here."

"That's two of us. I don't think I want to look."

But look they did as The Blind Eagles went through their clearly impossible aerial routine—impossible because, apart from the occasional roll of a solitary drum in the orchestra, they had no means of knowing where each other was, of synchronising their sightless movements. But not once did a pair of hands fail to smack safely and securely into another and waiting pair, not once did an outstretched pair of hands appear even remotely liable to miss a silently swinging trapeze. The performance lasted for all of an interminable four minutes and at the end there was another hushed silence, the lights dimmed a second time and almost the entire audience was on its feet, clapping and shouting and whistling.

Pilgrim said: "Know anything about his two brothers?"

"Vladimir and Yoffe, I believe they're called. Nothing. I thought this was going to be a one-man job."

"It is. And Bruno has the motivation? The incentive?"

"If any man ever had. I was making enquiries when I was in Eastern Europe time before last. I couldn't find out much from our man there, but enough, I think. There were seven of the family in the circus act—dad or mum more or less retired—but only those three made it over the border when the secret police closed in. I don't even know *why* they closed in. That was six, maybe seven years ago. Bruno's wife is dead, that's for sure, there are witnesses who will testify to that—well, they would, if they didn't live in the part of the world they do. He'd been married two weeks. What happened to his youngest brother, his father and his mother, nobody knows. They just disappeared."

"Along with a million others. He's our man, all right. Mr. Wrinfield is willing to play. Will Bruno?"

"He'll play." Fawcett was confident, then looked thoughtful. "He'd better. After all those weeks of of trouble you've been to."

The lights brightened. The Blind Eagles were now on a wire platform some twenty feet above ground, the wire itself stretching to another platform on the far side of the centre ring. Both other rings were empty and there was no other performer in sight except one—and he was on the ground. There was no music and among the crowd the silence was absolute.

Bruno straddled a bicycle. Across his shoulders was strapped a wooden yoke, while one of his brothers held a twelve-foot steel pole. Bruno edged the bicycle forward until the front wheel was well clear of the platform, and waited until his brother had placed the pole in slots across the yoke. It was totally insecure. As Bruno moved off, bringing both feet on to the pedals, the brothers caught hold of the pole, leaned forward in perfect unison and swung themselves clear of the platform until, again in perfect unison, they hung suspended at the full length of their arms. The wire sagged noticeably, but Bruno didn't: slowly and steadily he pedalled away.

For the next few minutes, balanced partly by himself but mainly by the perfect timing of Vladimir and Yoffe, Bruno cycled backwards and forwards across the wire while the brothers went through a series of controlled but intricate acrobatics. On one occasion, while Bruno remained perfectly steady for seconds at a time, the brothers, necessarily moving with the same immaculate synchronisation, gradually increased their pendulum swings until they were doing hand-stands on the pole. The same extraordinary hush remained with the audience, a tribute that wasn't entirely due to the performance they were witnessing: directly below them as they performed were Neubauer and his twelve Nubian lions, the head of every one of which was turned yearningly upwards.

At the end of the performance the silence in the audience was replaced by a long and far from silent collective sigh of relief, then once again came the same standing ovation, as heartfelt and prolonged as the one that had gone before.

Pilgrim said: "I've had enough—besides, my nerves can't take any more. Wrinfield will follow me. If he brushes by you on the way back to his seat that means that Bruno is willing to talk and that you're to follow him at a discreet distance at the end of the show. Wrinfield, I mean."

Without making any signs or looking in any particular direction, Pilgrim rose leisurely and left. Almost at once Wrinfield did the same.

A few minutes later the two men were closeted in one of Wrinfield's offices, a superbly equipped secretary's dream, albeit somewhat compact. Wrinfield had a much larger if ramshackle office where most of his work was normally carried out just outside the arena itself; but that did not possess a cocktail bar as this one did. On the principle that he forbade anyone to have liquor on the circus site proper, Wrinfield accordingly denied himself the privilege also.

The office was but a tiny part of a complex and beautifully organised whole that constituted the mobile home of the circus. Every person in the circus, from Wrinfield downwards, slept aboard this train except for some independent die-hards who insisted on dragging their caravans across the vast spaces of the United States and Canada. On tour the train also accommodated every single performing animal in the circus: at the end, just before the brake-van, were four massive flat-cars that accommodated all the bulky equipment, ranging from tractors to cranes that were essential for the smooth operation of the circus. In all, it was a minor miracle in ingenuity, meticulous planning and the maximum utilisation of available space. The train itself was a monster, over half a mile in length.

Pilgrim accepted a drink and said: "Bruno's the man I want. You think he will accept? If not, we may as well cancel your European tour."

"He'll come, and for three reasons." Wrinfield's speech was like the man himself, neat, precise, the words chosen with care. "As you've seen, the man doesn't know what fear is. Like all newly naturalised Americans—all right, all right, he's been naturalised for over five years but that rates as yesterday—his patriotism towards his adopted country makes yours and mine look just that little shabby. Thirdly, he's got a very big score to settle with his former homeland."

"Now?"

"Now. And then we speak to you?"

"I'm the last person you speak to. For both our sakes you want to be seen with me as little as possible. And don't come within a mile of my office—we have a whole battalion of foreign agents who do nothing but sit in the sun and watch our front door all the time. Colonel Fawcett—he's the uniformed person who was sitting beside me and the chief of our East European Field Operations—knows a great deal more about it than I do."

"I didn't know that you carried uniformed personnel in your organisation, Mr. Pilgrim."

"We don't. That's his disguise. He wears it so often

that he's more readily recognisable in it than in civilian clothes, which is why nearly everyone calls him 'the Colonel.' But never underestimate him."

Fawcett waited until the end of the show, dutifully applauded, turned and left without glancing at Wrinfield: Wrinfield had already given him the signal. Fawcett left the circus and made his way through the darkness and the steadily increasing rain, moving slowly so that Wrinfield might not lose him. Eventually he came to the large, dark limousine in which he and Pilgrim had arrived, and climbed into the back seat. A dark figure was pushed up against the far corner, his face as deeply in shadow as possible.

Fawcett said: "Hello. My name's Fawcett. I hope that no one saw you arrive?"

The driver answered. "No one, sir. I was keeping a pretty close look-out." He looked out through the rain-spattered windows. "It's not much of a night for other people to be minding other people's business."

"It isn't." He turned to the shadowy figure. "A pleasure to meet you." He sighed. "I have to apologise for all this comic-opera cloak and dagger business, but I'm afraid it's too late now. Gets in our blood, you know. We're just waiting for a friend of yours—ah, here he comes now." He opened the door and Wrinfield got in beside him. What little could be seen of his face didn't display a great deal in the way of carefree rapture.

"Poynton Street, Barker," Fawcett said.

Barker nodded in silence and drove off. Nobody spoke. Wrinfield, more than a little unhappy, kept turning restlessly in his seat and finally said: "I think we're being followed."

Fawcett said: "We'd better be. If not the driver of that car would be out of a job tomorrow. That car's following us to make sure that no other car follows us. If you follow me, that is."

"I see." From the tone of his voice it was questionable whether Wrinfield did. He became increasingly unhappy as the car moved into what was very close to a slum area and unhappier still when it drew up in an ill-lit street outside a sleazy walk-up apartment block. He said, complainingly: "This isn't a very nice part of town. And *this*—this looks like a house of ill-fame."

"And a house of ill-fame it is. We own it. Very handy places, those bordellos. Who, for instance, could ever imagine that Tesco Wrinfield would enter one of those places? Come inside."

2

For such an unsalubrious place in such an unsalubrious area the sitting-room was surprisingly comfortable, although the person who had furnished it would appear to have had a fixation about the colour russet, for the sofa, armchairs, carpet and heavily discreet curtains were all of the same colour or very close to it. A smokeless coal fire—for this was a smokeless area—did its best to burn cheerfully in the hearth. Wrinfield and Bruno occupied an armchair apiece: Fawcett was presiding over a cocktail cabinet, one of the portable kind.

Bruno said carefully: "Tell me again, please. About this anti-matter or whatever you call it."

Fawcett sighed. "I was afraid you might ask me that. I know I got it right first time, because I'd memorised what I had to say and just repeated it parrot fashion. I had to because I don't really know what it's all about myself." Fawcett handed round drinks —a soda for Bruno—and rubbed his chin. "I'll try and simplify it this time round. Then maybe I'll be able to get some inklings of understanding myself.

"Matter, we know, is made up of atoms. There are lots of things that go to make up those atoms—scientists, it seems, are becoming increasingly baffled about the ever-increasing complexity of the atom—but all that concerns our simple minds are the two basic constituents of the atom, electrons and protons. On our earth—in the universe, for that matter—electrons are invariably negatively charged and protons positively charged. Unfortunately, life is becoming increasingly difficult for our scientists and astronomers—for instance, it has been discovered only this year that there are particles, made of God knows what, that travel at many times the speed of light, which is a very upsetting and distressing concept for all those of the scientific community—and that was one hundred per cent—who believe that nothing could travel faster than the speed of light. However, that's by the way.

"Some time ago a couple of astronomers—Dicke and Anderson were their names—made the inconvenient discovery, based on theoretical calculations, that there must exist positively charged electrons. Their existence is now universally accepted, and they are referred to today as positrons. Then, to complicate things still further, the existence of anti-protons was discovered—this was in Berkeley—again electrically opposite to our protons. A combination of positrons and anti-protons would give rise to what is now termed 'anti-matter.' That anti-matter does exist no serious scientists seriously dispute.

"Nor do they dispute that if an electron or positron or proton and anti-proton collided or both sets collided the results would be disastrous. They would annihilate each other, giving off lethal gamma rays and creating, in the process, a considerable local uproar and a blast of such intense heat that all life within tens or perhaps hundreds of square miles would be instantaneously wiped out. On this scientists are agreed. It is estimated that if only two grams of anti-matter struck our planet on the side outfacing the sun the result would be to send the earth, with all life immediately extinct, spinning into the gravitational orbit of the sun. Provided, of course, it didn't disintegrate immediately on contact."

"A delightful prospect," Wrinfield said. He did not have the look of a convert about him. "No offence, but it sounds like the most idle science-fiction speculation to me."

"Me, too. But I have to accept what I'm told. Anyway, I'm beginning to believe it."

"Look. We don't have any of this anti-matter stuff on earth?"

"Because of anti-matter's unpleasant propensity for annihilating all matter with which it comes into contact, that should be fairly obvious."

"Then where does the stuff come from?"

"How the hell should I know?" Fawcett hadn't intended to be irritable, he just disliked treading the murky waters of the unknown. "We think ours is the only universe. How do we know? Maybe there lies another universe beyond ours, maybe many. It seems, according to latest scientific thinking, that if there are such universes, there is no reason why one or more should not be made of anti-matter." Fawcett paused gloomily. "I suppose if any intelligent beings existed there they would consider our universe as being composed of anti-matter. Of course, it could have been some rogue material thrown off at the moment of creation of our own universe. Who's to say?"

Bruno said: "So the whole matter is speculation. It's just a hypothesis. Theoretical calculations, that's all. There is no proof, Colonel Fawcett."

"We think there is." He smiled. "Forgive the use of the 'we.' What could have been, in the terms of human lives, a disaster of the first magnitude occurred in a happily unpopulated area of Northern Siberia in 1908. When Russian scientists got around to investigating this—almost twenty years later—they discovered an area of over a hundred square miles where trees had been destroyed by heat: not by fire but by instantaneous incineration which, in many cases, led to the petrifaction of trees in the upright position. Had this extraordinary phenomenon occurred over, say, New York or London, they would have become blackened cities of the dead."

"Proof," Bruno said. "We were speaking of proof, Colonel."

"Proof. Every other known damage caused to the earth by the impact of bodies from outer space has, without exception, been caused by meteors. There was no trace of the meteor that might have caused this Siberian holocaust and no signs of any mark upon the ground where the meteor might have crashed into it: when meteors crashed into Arizona and South Africa they left enormous craters in the ground. The now accepted and indeed inevitable conclusion is that Siberia was struck by a particle of anti-matter with a mass of something of the order of one hundredth of a millionth of a gram."

There was a considerable silence, then Wrinfield said: "Well, we have already covered this. Second time round it's a bit clearer, but not much. So?"

"Some dozen years ago there was scientific speculation as to whether the Russians had discovered the secret of anti-matter, but this was dismissed out of hand because—well, because of anti-matter's unpleasant propensity of annihilating all matter with which it comes into contact, the creation, harnessing and storage of it was impossible.

"*Was* impossible. What if it were possible or about to become possible? The nation that held this secret could hold the world to ransom. Comparatively, nuclear weapons are inoffensive toys for the amusement of little toddlers."

For a long minute no one spoke, then Wrinfield said: "You would not be talking in this fashion unless you had reason to believe that such a weapon exists or could exist."

"I have reason so to believe. This possibility has obsessed the intelligence agencies of all the modern world for some years now."

"Obviously this secret is not in our hands, or you wouldn't be telling us all this."

"Obviously."

"And it wouldn't be in the hands of a country such as Britain?"

"That would give us no cause for anxiety."

"Because when the chips are down they would be allies with responsible hands?"

"I couldn't have put it better myself."

"Then this secret resides—if it does reside anywhere—in the hands of a country which, when the chips were down, would be neither friendly nor responsible?"

"Precisely." Pilgrim, Fawcett reflected, had warned him not to underrate Wrinfield's intelligence.

Wrinfield said slowly: "Pilgrim and I have already made some tentative arrangements, come to preliminary agreements. You will know that. But he never told me any of this."

"The time wasn't right."

"So now it is?"

"Now or not at all."

"Of course, you want this secret or formula or whatever?"

Fawcett began to revise his opinion of Wrinfield's intelligence. "What do you think?"

"What makes you think our hands are more responsible than those of a score of other nations?"

"I'm a paid employee of the United States Government. Mine is not to reason why."

"It will not have escaped you that that was precisely the reasoning adopted by the Gestapo and the SS in Germany during the Second World War or by Russia's KGB since?"

"It has not escaped me. But I don't think the analogy is very exact. The United States doesn't really want more power—armed power, that is. You don't have to have me tell you that we have already overkill capacity. Can you imagine what would happen if this secret fell into the hands of, say, the certifiable leaders of a couple of the new Central African republics? We simply think we have more responsible hands than most."

"We have to hope we have."

Fawcett tried to conceal his long, slow exhalation of relief. "That means you'll go along."

"I'll go. A moment ago you said the time was now right to tell me. Why?"

"I hope I was right in saying I was right."

Bruno stirred. "What do you want of me, Colonel?"

There were times, Fawcett was aware, when there was little point in beating about the bush. He said: "Get it for us."

Bruno rose and poured himself another soda. He drank it all down then said: "You mean, steal it?"

"Get it. Would you call taking a gun away from a maniac stealing?"

"But why me?"

"Because you have unique gifts. I can't discuss what type of use we would propose making of those gifts until I have some sort of answer. All I know is that we are pretty certain that there is only one formula in existence, only one man who has the formula and is capable of reproducing it. We know where both man and formula are."

"Where?"

Fawcett didn't hesitate. "Crau."

Bruno didn't react in at all the way Fawcett had expected. His voice, when he spoke, was as bereft of expression as his face. Tonelessly, he repeated the word: "Crau."

Bruno didn't reply immediately. He returned to his chair, sat in it for a full minute, then said: "If I do agree, how do I get there? Illegal frontier crossing? Parachutes?"

Fawcett made a heroic—and successful—effort to conceal his sense of exultation. Wrinfield and Bruno—he'd got them both in a matter of minutes. He said matter-of-factly: "Nothing so dramatic. You just go along with the circus."

This time Bruno seemed to be beyond words, so Wrinfield said: "It's quite true, Bruno. We—that is, I—have agreed to co-operate with the government on this issue. Not that I had any more idea, until this moment, what the precise issue involved was. We are going to make a short tour of Europe, mainly Eastern Europe. Negotiations are already well advanced. It's quite natural. They send circus acts, dancers, singers to us: we're just reciprocating."

"The *whole* circus?"

"No, naturally not. That would be impossible. Just the cream of the cream, shall we say." Wrinfield smiled faintly. "One would have imagined that to include you."

"And if I refuse?"

"We simply cancel the tour."

Bruno looked at Fawcett. "Mr. Wrinfield's lost profits. This could cost your government a million dollars."

"Our government. We'd pay a billion to get hold of this."

Bruno looked from Fawcett to Wrinfield then back to Fawcett again. He said abruptly: "I'll go."

"Splendid. My thanks. Your country's thanks. The details—"

"I do not need my country's thanks." The words were cryptical but without offence.

Fawcett was slightly taken aback, sought for the meaning behind the words then decided he'd better not. He said: "As you will. The details, as I was about to say, can wait until later. Mr. Wrinfield, did Mr. Pilgrim tell you that we'd be grateful if you would take along two additional people when you go abroad?"

"He did not." Wrinfield seemed somewhat miffed. "It would appear that there were quite a number of things that Mr. Pilgrim did not tell me."

"Mr. Pilgrim knows what he is doing." Now that he had them both, Fawcett took off the velvet gloves but still remained urbane and polite. "There was no point in burdening you with unnecessary details until we had secured the co-operation of both you gentlemen. The two people in question are a Dr. Harper and an equestrienne, Maria. Our people. Very important to our purpose. That, too, I'll explain later. There are some things I must first discuss urgently with Mr. Pilgrim. Tell me, Bruno, why have you agreed to do this? I must warn you that it might be extremely dangerous for you and if you're caught we'll have no option but to disown you. Why?"

Bruno shrugged. "Who's to say why? There can be many reasons that a man can't explain even to himself. Could be gratitude—America took me in when my own country threw me out. There are people there to whom I would like to perform as great a disservice as they did to me. I know there are dangerous and irresponsible men in my old country who would not hesitate to employ this weapon, if it exists. And then you say I am uniquely equipped for this task. In what ways I don't yet know, but if it is the case how could I let another go in my place? Not only might he fail in getting what you want but he could well be killed in the process. I wouldn't like to have either of those things on my conscience." He smiled faintly. "Just say it's a bit of a challenge."

"And your real reason?"

Bruno said simply: "Because I hate war."

"Mmm. Not the answer I expected, but fair enough." He stood up. "Thank you, gentlemen, for your time, your patience and above all your co-operation. I'll have the cars take you back."

Wrinfield said: "And yourself? How do you get to Mr. Pilgrim's office?"

"The madame here and I have an understanding of sorts. I'm sure she'll provide me with some form of transport."

Fawcett had keys in his hands when he approached Pilgrim's apartment—Pilgrim both worked and slept in the same premises—but he put them away. Pilgrim, most uncharacteristically, had not even locked his door, he hadn't even closed it properly. Fawcett pushed the door and went inside. The first partly irrational thought that occurred to him was that he could have been just that little bit optimistic when he had assured Wrinfield that Pilgrim knew what he was doing.

Pilgrim was lying on the carpet. Whoever had left

him lying there had clearly a sufficiency of ice-picks at home, for he hadn't even bothered to remove the one he'd left buried to the hilt in the back of Pilgrim's neck. Death must have been instantaneous, for there wasn't even a drop of blood to stain his Turnbull and Asser shirt. Fawcett knelt and looked at the face. It was as calmly expressionless as it had habitually been in life. Pilgrim had not only not known what hit him, he hadn't even known he'd been hit.

Fawcett straightened, crossed to the phone and lifted it.

"Dr. Harper, please. Ask him to come here immediately."

Dr. Harper wasn't exactly a caricature or a conceptualised prototype of the kindly healer, but it would have been difficult to visualise him in any other role. There was a certain medical inevitability about him. He was tall, lean, distinguished in appearance, becomingly grey at the temples and wore a pair of pebbled horn-rimmed glasses which lent his gaze a certain piercing quality which might have been illusory, intentional or just habitual. Horn-rimmed pebble glasses are a great help to doctors; the patient can never tell whether he is in robust health or has only weeks to live. His dress was as immaculate as that of the dead man he was thoughtfully examining. He had his black medical bag with him but wasn't bothering to use it. He said: "So that's all you know about tonight?"

"That's all."

"Wrinfield? After all, he was the only one who knew. Before tonight, I mean."

"He knew no details before tonight. No way. And he'd no opportunity. He was with me."

"There's such a thing as an accomplice."

"No chance. Wait until you see him. His record's immaculate—don't you think Pilgrim spent days checking. His patriotism is beyond question, it wouldn't surprise me if he's got a 'God Bless America' label sewn on to his undershirt. Besides, do you think he would have gone to the time and trouble of arranging to take his whole damn circus—well, most of it—to Europe if he had intended to do this? I know there's such a thing as erecting a façade, lying down a smoke screen, dragging red herrings—you name it—but, well, I ask you."

"It's not likely."

"But I think we should have him and Bruno up here. Just to let them see what they're up against. And we'll have to notify the Admiral immediately. Will you do that while I get hold of Barker and Masters?"

"That's the scrambler there?"

"That's the scrambler."

Dr. Harper was still on the phone when Barker and Masters arrived, Barker the driver and Masters the grey man who had confronted Bruno on the stage. Fawcett said: "Get Wrinfield and Bruno up here. Tell them it's desperately urgent but don't tell them anything about this. Bring them in by the rear tunnel. Be quick."

Fawcett closed but did not lock the door behind them as Dr. Harper hung up. Harper said: "We're to keep it under wraps. According to the Admiral, who is the one man who would know, he had no close relatives so he died of a heart attack. Me and my Hippocratic oath. He'll be right around."

Fawcett was gloomy. "I thought he might be. He's going to be very happy about this. Pilgrim was the apple of his eye, and it's no secret that he was next in line for the Admiral's chair. Well, let's have up a couple of the boys with their little cans of dusting powder and let them have a look around. Not, of course, that they'll find anything."

"You're so sure?"

"I'm sure. Anyone cool enough to walk away leaving the murder weapon *in situ,* as it were, is pretty confident in himself. And you notice the way he's lying, feet to the door, head pointing away?"

"So?"

"The fact that he's so close to the door is almost sure proof that Pilgrim opened it himself. Would he have turned his back on a murderer? Whoever the killer was, he was a man Pilgrim not only knew but trusted."

Fawcett had been right. The two experts who had come up with their little box of tricks had turned up nothing. The only places fingerprints might conceivably have been, on the ice-pick handle and doorknobs, were predictably clean. They were just leaving when a man entered without benefit of either permission or knocking.

The Admiral looked like everybody's favourite uncle or a successful farmer or, indeed, what he was, a Fleet Admiral, albeit retired. Burly, red-faced, with pepper-and-salt hair and radiating an oddly kind authority, he looked about ten years younger than his acknowledged if frequently questioned fifty-five. He gazed down at the dead man on the floor, and the more kindly aspect of his character vanished. He turned to Dr. Harper.

"Made out the death certificate yet? Coronary, of course." Dr. Harper shook his head. "Then do so at once and have Pilgrim removed to our private mortuary."

Fawcett said: "If we could leave that for a moment, sir. The mortuary bit, I mean. I have two people coming up here very shortly, the owner of the circus and our latest—ah—recruit. I'm convinced neither of them has anything to do with this—but it would be interesting to see their reactions. Also, to find out if they still want to go through with this."

"What guarantee can you offer that they won't leave here and head for the nearest telephone? There isn't a newspaper in the country that wouldn't give their assistant editor for this story."

"You think that had not occurred to me, sir?" A slightly less than cordial note had crept into Fawcett's tone. "There is no guarantee. There's only my judgement."

"There's that," the Admiral said pacifically. It was the nearest he could ever bring himself to an apology. "Very well." He paused and to recover his position said: "They are not, I trust, knocking and entering by the front door?"

"Barker and Masters are bringing them. By the rear tunnel."

As if on cue, Barker and Masters appeared in the doorway, then stepped aside to let Wrinfield and

Bruno in. The Admiral and Dr. Harper, Fawcett knew, were watching their faces as intently as he was. Understandably, neither Wrinfield nor Bruno was watching them: when you find a murdered man lying at your feet your ocular attention does not tend to stray. Predictably, Bruno's reactions were minimal, the narrowing of the eyes, the tightening of the mouth could have been as much imagined as real, but Wrinfield's reactions were all that anyone could have wished for: the colour drained from his face, leaving it a dirty grey, he put out a trembling hand against the lintel to steady himself and for a moment he looked as if he might even sway and fall.

Three minutes later, three minutes during which Fawcett had told him what little he knew, a seated Wrinfield, brandy glass in hand, was still shaking. Bruno had declined the offer of a restorative. The Admiral had taken the floor.

He said to Wrinfield: "Do you have any enemies in the circus?"

"Enemies? In the circus?" Wrinfield was clearly taken aback. "Good God, no. I know it must sound corny to you but we really are one big happy family."

"Any enemies anywhere?"

"Every successful man has. Of a kind, that is. Well, there's rivalry, competition, envy. But enemies?" He looked almost fearfully at Pilgrim and shuddered. "But not in this way." He was silent for a moment, then looked at the Admiral with an expression that approximated pretty closely to resentment and when he spoke again the tremor had gone from his voice. "And why do you ask me those questions? They didn't kill me. They killed Mr. Pilgrim."

"There's a connection. Fawcett?"

"There's a connection. I may speak freely, sir?"

"I beg your pardon?"

"Well, there are telephone boxes and sacrificial assistant editors—"

"Don't be a fool. I've already apologised for that."

"Yes, sir." Fawcett briefly searched his memory and found no apology there. It seemed pointless to mention this. "As you say, sir, there's a connection. There's also been a leak and it can only have come from within our own organisation. As I said, sir, and as I have explained to these gentlemen, it's clear that Pilgrim was killed by someone well known to him. There can't have been any specific leak—only you, Pilgrim, Dr. Harper and myself really knew what the intentions were. But any of up to a dozen people more —researchers, telephone operators, drivers—within the organisation knew that we had been in regular touch with Mr. Wrinfield. It would be unusual, if not unique, to find any intelligence or counter-intelligence agency in the world whose ranks have not been infiltrated by an enemy agent, one who eventually becomes so securely entrenched as to become above suspicion. It would be naïve of us to assume that we are the sole exception.

"It was hardly top secret that Mr. Wrinfield had been in the formative stages of planning a European tour—a primarily Eastern European tour—and it would have been comparatively simple to discover that Crau was on the list of towns to be visited. As far as the gentlemen in Crau are concerned—more precisely, the gentlemen responsible for the research taking place in Crau—coincidence could be coincidence but the obvious tie-up with the CIA would be that little bit too much."

"So why kill Pilgrim? As a warning?"

"In a way, sir, yes."

"You would care to be more specific, Mr. Fawcett?"

"Yes, sir. No question but that it was a warning. But to make Pilgrim's death both understandable and justifiable from their point of view—for we have to remember that though we are dealing with unreasonable men we are also dealing with reasoning men—it had to be something more than just a warning. His murder was also an amalgam of invitation and provocation. It is a warning they wished to be ignored. If they believe Mr. Wrinfield's forthcoming tour is sponsored by us, and if, in spite of Pilgrim's death—which they won't for a moment doubt that we'll be convinced has been engineered by them—we still go ahead and proceed with the tour, then we must have extraordinarily pressing needs to make it. Conclusive proof they would expect to find in Crau.

"And then we would be discredited internationally. Imagine, if you can, the sensational impact of the news of the internment of an entire circus. Imagine the tremendously powerful bargaining weapon it would give the East in any future negotiations. We'd become an international laughing-stock, all credibility throughout the world gone, an object of ridicule in both East and West. The Gary Powers U-2 plane episode would be a bagatelle compared to this."

"Indeed. Tell me, what's your opinion of locating this cuckoo in the CIA nest?"

"As of this moment? Zero."

"Dr. Harper?"

"I agree totally. No chance. It would mean putting a watcher on every one of your several hundred employees in this building, sir."

"And who's going to watch the watchers? Is that what you mean?"

"With respect, sir, you know very well what I mean."

"Alas." The Admiral reached into an inside pocket, brought out two cards, handed one to Wrinfield, the other to Bruno. "If you need me, call that number and ask for Charles. Any guesses you may have as to my identity—and you must be almost as stupid as we are if you haven't made some—you will please keep to yourselves." He sighed. "Alas again, I fear, Fawcett, that your reading of the matter is entirely correct. There is no alternative explanation, not, at least, a remotely viable one. Nevertheless, getting our hands on this document overrides all other considerations. We may have to think up some other means."

Fawcett said: "There are no other means."

Harper said: "There are no other means."

The Admiral nodded. "There are no other means. It's Bruno or nothing?"

Fawcett shook his head. "It's Bruno *and* the circus or nothing."

"Looks like." The Admiral gazed consideringly at Wrinfield. "Tell me, do you fancy the idea of being expendable?"

Wrinfield drained his glass. His hand was steady again and he was back on balance. "Frankly, I don't."

"Not even being interned?"

"No."

"I see your point. It could be bad for business. Am I to take it from that that you have changed your mind?"

"I don't know, I just don't know." Wrinfield shifted his gaze, at once both thoughtful and troubled. "Bruno?"

"I'll go." Bruno's voice was flat and without colour, certainly with no traces of drama or histrionics in it. "If I have to go, I'll go alone. I don't know—yet—how I'll get there and I don't know—yet—what I have to do when I arrive. But I'll go."

Wrinfield sighed. "That's it, then." He smiled faintly. "A man can only stand so much. No immigrant American is going to put a fifth-generation American to shame."

"Thank you, Mr. Wrinfield." The Admiral looked at Bruno with what might have been an expression of either curiosity or assessment on his face. "And thank you, too. Tell me, what makes you so determined to go?"

"I told Mr. Fawcett. I hate war."

The Admiral had gone. Dr. Harper had gone. Wrinfield and Bruno had gone and Pilgrim had been carried away: in three days' time he would be buried with all due solemnity and the cause of his death would never be known, a not unusual circumstance amongst those who plied the trades of espionage and counter-espionage and whose careers had come to an abrupt and unexpected end. Fawcett, his face as bleak and hard as the plumpness of his face would permit, was pacing up and down the dead man's apartment when the telephone rang. Fawcett picked it up immediately.

The voice in the receiver was hoarse and shaking. It said: "Fawcett? Fawcett? Is that you, Fawcett?"

"Yes. Who's that?"

"I can't tell you over the phone. You know damn well who it is. You got me into this." The voice was trembling so much as to be virtually unrecognisable. "For God's sake get down here, something terrible has happened."

"What?"

"Get down here." The voice was imploring. "And for God's sake come alone. I'll be in my office. The circus office."

The line went dead. Fawcett jiggled the receiver bar but dead the line remained. Fawcett hung up, left the room, locked the door behind him, took the lift to the underground garage and drove down to the circus through the darkness and the rain.

The external circus lights were out except for some scattered weak illumination—it was already late enough for all the circus members to have sought their night accommodation aboard the train. Fawcett left the car and hurried into the animals' quarters where Wrinfield had his shabby little portable office. The lighting here was fairly good. There were no signs of human life, which Fawcett, on first reaction, found rather surprising, for Wrinfield had a four-footed fortune in there: the second and almost immediate reaction was that it wasn't surprising at all, for nobody in his right mind was going to make off with an Indian elephant or Nubian lion. Not only were they difficult animals to control, but disposal might have presented a problem. Most of the animals were lying down, asleep, but the elephants, asleep or not and chained by one foreleg, were upright and constantly swaying from side to side, and in one large cage twelve Bengal tigers were prowling restlessly around, snarling occasionally for no apparent reason.

Fawcett made for Wrinfield's office then halted in puzzlement when he saw no light coming from its solitary window. He advanced and tested the door. It wasn't locked. He opened it and peered inside and then all the world went black for him.

3

Wrinfield hardly slept that night, which, considering the recent events and the worries they had brought in their wake, was hardly a matter for surprise. He finally rose about five o'clock, showered, shaved and dressed, left his luxurious quarters aboard the train and headed for the animal quarters, an instinctive practice of his whenever he was deeply troubled, for Wrinfield was in love with his circus and felt more at home there than anywhere else in the world: the degree of rapport that existed between him and his animals certainly exceeded that which had existed between him and the reluctant economics students whom —as he now regarded it—he had wasted the best years of his life teaching. Besides, he could always pass the time with Johnny the night watchman, who, despite the vast gulf in status that lay between them, was an old crony and confidant of his. Not that Wrinfield had any intention of confiding in anyone that night.

But Johnny wasn't there and Johnny wasn't the man ever to fall asleep on the job, undemanding though it was—his job was to report to the trainer concerned or the veterinary surgeon any animal that might appear off-colour. No more than slightly puzzled at first, then with increasing anxiety, Wrinfield carried out a systematic search and finally located him in a dark corner. Johnny, elderly, wizened and crippled—he'd taken one fall too many from the low wire—was securely bound and gagged but otherwise alive, apparently unharmed and furiously angry. Wrinfield loosened the gag, undid the bonds and helped the old man to his shaking legs. A lifetime in the circus had left Johnny with an extraordinary command of the unprintable and he didn't miss out a single epithet as he freely unburdened his feelings to Wrinfield.

Wrinfield said: "Who did this to you?"

"I don't know, boss. Mystery to me. I didn't see anything. Didn't hear nothing." Tenderly, Johnny rubbed the back of his neck. "Sand-bagged, it feels like."

Wrinfield examined the back of the scrawny neck. It was badly bruised and discoloured but the skin was unbroken. Wrinfield put an arm round the frail shoulders. "Sand-bagged you were. Come on. A seat in the office. I've got a little something there that'll set you up. Then we get the police."

They were halfway towards the office when

Johnny's shoulders stiffened under the supporting arm and he said in an oddly harsh and strained voice: "I reckon we've got something a bit more important than a sand-bagging to report to the cops, boss."

Wrinfield looked at him questioningly, then followed the direction of his staring eyes. In the cage of the Bengal tigers lay the savagely mauled remains of what had once been a man. Only by the few shreds of clothing left him and the pathetically heroic rows of medal ribbons did Wrinfield recognise that he was looking at all that remained of Colonel Fawcett.

Wrinfield gazed in horrified fascination at the still predawn scene—circus workers, artistes, policemen in uniform and plainclothes detectives all milling around the animal quarters, all of them busily engaged in eradicating forever any putative clues there may have been. Ambulance men were wrapping up the unidentifiable remains of Fawcett and placing them on a stretcher. In a small group remote from the others were Malthius, the tiger trainer, Neubauer, the lion tamer, and Bruno, the three men who had gone into the cage and taken Fawcett out. Wrinfield turned to the Admiral, whom he had first called and who, since his arrival, hadn't bothered to explain his presence or identity to anyone and it was markedly noticeable that no policeman had approached him to ask him to justify his presence there: clearly, some senior police officer had said: "Do not approach that man."

Wrinfield said: "Who in God's name could have done this terrible thing, sir?"

"I'm terribly sorry, Mr. Wrinfield." It was completely out of character for the Admiral to say that he was sorry about anything. "Sorry all around. Sorry for Fawcett, one of my ablest and most trusted deputies and a damned fine human being at that. And sorry for you, that I should have been responsible for involving you in this ghastly mess. This is the kind of publicity that any circus could do without."

"The hell with the publicity. Who, sir, who?"

"And I suppose I feel a bit sorry for myself, too." The Admiral shrugged his shoulders heavily. "Who? Obviously the same person or persons who killed Pilgrim. Your guess as to who they are is as good as mine. The one thing for sure is that they—whoever *they* are—knew he was coming down here or they wouldn't have silenced the guard in advance—he can count himself lucky that he wasn't found inside that cage with Fawcett. There was almost certainly a false phone call. We'll soon know. I have them checking on it."

"Checking on what?"

"Every call to our office, incoming or outgoing, except of course on the scrambler phones, is recorded. With luck, we'll have that recording within minutes. Meantime, I'd like to talk to those three men who took Fawcett out of the cage. Individually. I understand that one of those men is your tiger trainer. What's his name?"

"Malthius. But—but he's above suspicion."

"I don't doubt it." The Admiral was trying to be patient. "Do you think any murder mystery would ever be solved if we questioned only the suspects? Please have him brought."

Malthius, a dark-eyed Bulgarian with an open face,

was plainly deeply upset. The Admiral said, kindly for him: "You've no need to be so distressed."

"*My* tigers did this, sir."

"They would probably do it to anyone in the country except you. Or would they?"

"I don't know, sir. If a person were lying quietly, I really don't think so." He hesitated. "But, well, under certain circumstances they might." The Admiral waited patiently and Malthius went on: "If they were provoked. Or—"

"Yes?"

"If they smelled blood."

"You're sure of that?"

"Of course he's sure." The Admiral, who was quite unaware of Wrinfield's intense loyalty to his men, was surprised at the asperity in his voice. "What do you think, sir? We feed them on horse meat or beef and those are raw and smell of blood. The tigers can't wait to get at the meat and tear it to pieces with teeth and claws. Have you ever seen tigers at feeding time?"

The Admiral had a mental vision of how Fawcett must have died and shuddered involuntarily. "No, and I don't think I'll ever want to either." He turned back to Malthius. "So he could have been alive, conscious or not—blood doesn't flow when you're dead—stabbed and thrown into the cage?"

"That is possible, sir. But you won't find any trace of a stab wound now."

"I realise that. You found the door locked on the outside. Is it possible to do that from the inside?"

"No. You can bolt it from the inside. It wasn't bolted."

"Isn't that a rather curious arrangement?"

Malthius smiled for the first time, albeit faintly. "Not for a tiger trainer, sir. When I go into the cage I turn the key on the outside and leave it in position. Once I get inside I bolt the door—can't risk having the door swing open or being pulled open by one of the tigers and letting them loose among the crowd." He smiled a second time, again without mirth. "It could come in useful for me, too. If things get unpleasant for me, I just slide the bolt, get away from there and turn the key on the outside."

"Thank you. Would you ask that friend of yours—"

"Heinrich Neubauer, sir. The lion trainer."

"I'd like to see him." Malthius walked dejectedly away and the Admiral said: "He seems *very* unhappy to me."

"Wouldn't you be?" Again the unexpected asperity in Wrinfield's voice. "He not only feels personally responsible but his tigers have for the first time acquired a taste for human flesh. Malthius is human flesh too, you know."

"I hadn't thought of that."

The Admiral asked Neubauer a few desultory and inconsequential questions, then asked for Bruno. When he arrived the Admiral said: "You're the only one I really wanted to talk to. The other two men were only a cover—we're being watched both by circus people and the police. Some of the police, by the way, think I'm a very senior officer, others that I'm from the FBI, although why they should imagine that I can't imagine. A dreadful thing, Bruno, a quite dreadful thing. Well, it looks as if poor Fawcett was correct, we're being pushed to the limit to find out how really desperate we are to go to Crau. Well, I've been pushed far enough. Who knows who's going to be next? I have no right, no one has any right, to ask you to be involved in this ghastly business any more. There's a limit to patriotism—being patriotic did Pilgrim and Fawcett a great deal of good, didn't it? You are now released from any obligations, real or imagined, that you may have had."

"Speak for yourself." Wrinfield's tone had remained unchanged. Whatever touched Wrinfield's beloved circus touched his rawest nerve: this had become a personal matter. "Two good men have died. You want them to have died in vain? I'm going to Europe."

The Admiral blinked and turned to Bruno. "And you?"

Bruno looked at him in a silence that verged on the contemptuous.

"Well." The Admiral was momentarily nonplussed. "Off again, on again. If you're prepared to accept the risks, I'm prepared to accept your sacrifices. Utterly selfish, I know, but we desperately want those papers. I won't try to thank you, I honestly wouldn't know how to, but the least I can do is to arrange protection. I'll assign five of my best men to you—as a press corps, shall we say?—then once you are aboard the boat—"

Bruno spoke in a very quiet voice. "If you assign any of your men to us, then nobody's going anywhere, and that includes me. And from what I'm told, although I don't understand it yet, if I don't go then there's no point in anyone else going anyway. The exception, of course, is Dr. Harper, a dead man vouched for him and you can't get any better recommendation than that. As for the rest of your men—who do you think killed Pilgrim and Fawcett? Without their protection, we might have a chance." Bruno turned abruptly and walked away. The Admiral looked after him, with a slightly pained expression on his face, at a momentarily but highly unusual lack for words, but was saved the necessity of making comment by the arrival of a police sergeant carrying a small black box. That the uniform was not the property of the man inside it Wrinfield was quite certain. When it came to local colour Charles—it was the only way Wrinfield could think of him—was not a man who missed much.

The Admiral said: "The recording?" and when the sergeant nodded: "May we use your office, please, Mr. Wrinfield?"

"Of course." Wrinfield looked around him. "Not here. In the train. Too many people."

The office door closed behind them, the sergeant took the recorder from its casing and Wrinfield said: "What do you expect to hear?"

"You." Wrinfield looked his astonishment. "Or a very close approximation of your voice. Or Bruno's. Yours were the only two voices in the circus that Fawcett knew: he wouldn't have come for anyone else."

They heard the recording through. At the end Wrinfield said calmly: "That's meant to be me. Shall we hear it again?"

They heard it through a second time, then Wrinfield said positively: "That's not my voice. You know it isn't."

"My dear Wrinfield, I never dreamed it would be.

I know it isn't. *Now* I know it isn't. But I had to hear it a second time to make sure. When a man speaks in that hurried and distressed fashion, his voice takes on abnormal overtones. A piece of silk stretched across the mouthpiece is a great help. I don't blame poor Fawcett for being fooled, especially when he had only the one thing on his mind at the time. But it's a damned good imitation all the same." The Admiral paused, ruminated, then looked at Wrinfield consideringly. "To the best of my knowledge and belief, and to yours, you don't know and never have talked to any of my men. Right?" Wrinfield nodded. "So I put it to you that this call was made by someone who knew your voice intimately and had studied it."

"That's preposterous. If you're suggesting—"

"Precisely what I *am* suggesting, I'm afraid. Look, man, if our organisation can be infiltrated don't you think your damned circus can't be too? After all, you've got twenty-five nationalities working for you: I've got only one."

"You're the CIA. *Everyone* would want to infiltrate the CIA. Who'd want to infiltrate a harmless circus?"

"Nobody. But in the eyes of the ungodly you're not a harmless circus, you're an affiliate of the CIA and therefore ripe for infiltration. Don't let blind loyalty blind your intelligence. Let's hear that recording again. Only this time don't listen for your own voice, listen for someone else's, I should imagine you know the voice of every man in your employment. And to narrow the field, remember that most of your men speak with fairly heavy foreign accents. This is an Anglo-Saxon voice, probably American, although I can't be sure."

They played the recording through four more times and at the end Wrinfield shook his head. "It's no good. The distortion is far too heavy."

"Thank you, Officer, you may leave." The sergeant snapped the case shut and left. Briefly, the Admiral paced up and down the full length of the office—three steps in either direction—then shook his head in the reluctant acceptance of the inevitable. "What a charming thought. A link-up between my lot and yours."

"You're terribly certain."

"I'm terribly certain of one thing and that's this. There isn't one man in my lot who wouldn't give up his pension rather than open the door of a tiger's cage."

Wrinfield nodded with an equally reluctant acceptance. "I suppose it's my turn to say that I should have thought of that."

"That's unimportant. Point is, what are we going to do? You're under hostile surveillance, my career's on that." He paused in momentary gloom. "Whatever my career's going to be worth when all this is over."

"I thought we'd settled all that." The now accustomed touch of asperity was back in Wrinfield's voice. "You heard what I said back in the circus. You heard what Bruno said. We go."

The Admiral regarded him thoughtfully. "A marked change of attitude since last night. Or, more properly, a marked hardening in attitude."

"I don't think you quite understand, sir." Wrinfield was being patient. "This is my life, my whole life. Touch me, touch my circus. Or vice versa. We have one major card in the hole."

"I've missed it?"

"Bruno's still in the clear."

"I hadn't missed it and it's because I want him to stay that way that I'd like you to take this girl of ours into your employ. Her name is Maria Hopkins, and although I don't know her all that well Dr. Harper assures me she is a very bright operative and that her loyalty is beyond question. She's to fall in love with Bruno and he with her. Nothing more natural." The Admiral put on his sad smile. "If I were twenty years younger I'd say there was nothing easier. She's really rather beautiful. That way she can liase with Bruno, yourself, Dr. Harper—and, up to the time of your departure, with myself—without raising any eyebrows. As an equestrienne, perhaps? That was Fawcett's idea."

"No perhaps. She may think she's good, she may actually be good, but there's no place for amateurs in the circus. Besides, there's not a man or woman on my performing staff who wouldn't spot immediately that she's not a trained circus equestrienne: you couldn't devise a surer way of calling attention to her."

"Suggestions?"

"Yes. Fawcett mentioned this possibility in this dreadful bordello place he took us to and I've given the matter some thought. Didn't require much, really. My secretary is getting married in a few weeks to a very strange fellow who doesn't like circuses: so she's leaving. This is common knowledge. Let Maria be my new secretary. Every reason for her to be in constant contact with me, and through me your doctor and Bruno without any questions being asked."

"Couldn't be better. Now, I'd like you to put a

large box ad in the papers tomorrow for a doctor to accompany the circus to Europe. I know this isn't the way one normally recruits a medical man but we've no time to wait to use the more professional channels. This must be made clear in the ad. Besides it will make it perfectly clear that you are seeking a doctor with no one in mind and that your choice will essentially be a random one. You may have quite a few replies—it would make a nice holiday for someone who has just, say, completed his internship—but you will, of course, choose Dr. Harper.

"He hasn't practised medicine for years, although I dare say he'd find an aspirin if you twisted his arm. That's irrelevant. What matters is that he is an outstanding intelligence agent."

"So, I was led to believe, was Pilgrim. And Fawcett."

The Admiral made a quick gesture of irritation. "Things don't always happen in threes. Fortunes turn. Those two men knew the risks. So does Harper. Anyway, no suspicion attaches to him. There's no connection between him and the circus."

"Has it occurred to you that 'they' may check on his background?"

"Has it occurred to *you* that I might make a better owner and managing director of a circus than you are?"

"*Touché*. I asked for that."

"Yes, you did. Two things. There's no more reason why they should check on him than any of your hundreds of employees. His background is impeccable: he's a consultant at the Belvedere and this is his way of spending part of his sabbatical at someone else's expense. Much higher qualifications and much more experienced than any of the other applicants you'll have. A natural choice. You're lucky to have him."

"But he hasn't practised—"

"He has consulting rooms in the hospital. One of our branch offices."

"Is nothing sacred to you people?"

"Not much. How soon are you prepared to leave?"

"Leave?"

"For Europe."

"I have a number of alternative dates and places pencilled in for there. That's not the problem. Three more days here, then we have three more engagements on the East Coast."

"Cancel them."

"Cancel them? We never cancel—I mean, we have all arrangements made, theatres booked, saturation advertising, thousands of tickets sold in advance—"

"Compensation, Mr. Wrinfield, will be on a princely scale. Think of a suitable figure and it will be lodged in your bank tomorrow."

Wrinfield was not much given to wringing his hands, but he looked as if he would have liked to indulge in just a little right then. "We are an annual institution in those places. We have a tremendous amount of goodwill—"

"Double the figure you first thought of. Cancel. Your sea transport will be ready in New York in one week. When you sign up Dr. Harper, he'll organise vaccinations and inoculations. If you have any visa problems, we'll do a little leaning. Not that I expect any trouble from the East European embassies or consulates—their countries are just dying to have you. I will be around tonight for the evening performance. So will the ravishing Miss Hopkins—but not with me. Have someone show her around, but not you."

"I have a very bright nephew—"

"Fine. Tell him nothing. Have him give her a thorough guided tour, the new secretary getting acquainted with the physical background of her new job. Have her introduced to some of your top performers. Especially, of course, to Bruno. Let Bruno know the score in advance."

Henry Wrinfield looked a great deal more like Tesco Wrinfield's son than a nephew had any right to look, although he undoubtedly was his nephew. He had the same dark eyes, the same lean studious face, the same quick intelligence; and if he wasn't quite in the same cerebral league as his uncle, he was, as his uncle had said, a very bright young fellow indeed, or at least bright enough to find no hardship in the chore of escorting Maria Hopkins round the backstage of the circus. For an hour or so he completely forgot the blue-stocking Ivy Leaguer to whom he was engaged and was slightly surprised that, when he remembered her about an hour later—he rarely spent ten minutes without thinking about her—he experienced no twinges of conscience.

Few men would have found cause for complaint in the performance of such a task as had been entrusted to Henry, and those only misogynists in an irretrievably advanced state. She was a petit figure, although clearly not suffering from malnutrition, with long dark hair, rather splendid liquid dark eyes and an extraordinarily infectious smile and laugh. Her resemblance to the popular concept of an intelligence agent was nonexistent, which may have been one of the reasons why Dr. Harper reportedly held her in such high regard.

Henry, quite unnecessarily guiding her by the upper arm, showed her round the tethered and caged animals and introduced her to Malthius and Neubauer, who were putting the big cats through their last-minute paces. Malthius was charming and graceful and wished her a very pleasant stay: Neubauer, though civil enough, didn't know how to be charming and wished her nothing.

Henry then led her through to the raucous blare of the fairground. Kan Dahn was there, toying with an enormous bar-bell and looking more impressively powerful than ever: he took her small hand carefully in his own gigantic one, smiled widely, announced that she was the best recruit to arrive at the circus since he himself had joined it years ago and altogether gave her a welcome so courteous it bordered on the effusive. Kan Dahn was always in high humour, although nobody was quite sure whether it stemmed from an innate good nature or because he had discovered quite some time ago that it was unnecessary for him to be unpleasant to anyone. Manuelo, the Mexican genius with the knife, was standing behind the counter of a booth, benevolently watching considerable numbers of the young and not so young throwing rubber-tipped knives at moving targets. Occasionally he would come round to the front of his booth and, throwing double-handed, would knock down six targets in half that number of seconds, just to show his customers that there was really nothing to it. He welcomed Maria with a great deal of Latin enthusiasm, putting himself entirely at her service during her stay in the circus. A little further on Ron Roebuck, the lasso specialist, gave her a grave but friendly welcome: as she walked away from him she was astonished and then delighted to see a shimmering whirling circle of rope drop down over her, barely touch the ground, then effortlessly rise and disappear without once touching her clothes. She turned and gave Roebuck a wide smile and he no longer looked grave.

Bruno emerged from his little performing hall as Henry and Maria approached it. He was clad in the same mandarin robe as previously and, also as before, looked anything but impressive. Henry made the introductions and Bruno looked at her with a kind of inoffensive appraisal. As usual, it was almost impossible to tell what he was thinking, and then he smiled, a rare gesture for Bruno but one that transformed his face.

He said: "Welcome to the circus. I hope your stay is a long and happy one."

"Thank you." She smiled in turn. "This is an honour. You—you are the star of the circus?"

Bruno pointed skywards. "All the stars are up there, Miss Hopkins. Down here there are only performers. We all do what we can. Some of us are lucky in that we have acts more spectacular than others, that's all. Excuse me. I must hurry."

Maria, thoughtful, watched him go. Henry said in amusement: "Not quite what you expected?"

"Well, no."

"Disappointed?"

"A little, I suppose."

"You won't be tonight. Nobody ever is, not when they watch the impossible."

"Is it true that he and his brothers are completely blindfolded up there? They can't see at all?"

"No faking. They are in total darkness. But you'll notice that it's Bruno that conducts the orchestra. He's the co-ordinator and catcher. Maybe the three brothers share some telepathic gift. I don't know. Nobody else seems to know either. And, if Bruno and his brothers know, they're not saying."

"Maybe it's something else." She indicated the legend "The Great Mentalist." "A photographic memory, they say, and can read people's minds."

"I hope he did read yours tonight."

"Please. And he can read the contents of sealed envelopes. If he can see through paper why can't he see through a blindfold?"

He looked at her in genuine surprise. He said: "Miss Hopkins, you're not just a pretty face. Do you know, I'd never thought of that." He pondered for a moment, then gave up. "Let's go take our seats for the show. Like it, so far?"

"Very much."

"Anything special?"

"Yes. Everybody's so terribly nice and polite."

Henry smiled. "We're not all just down from the trees." He took her arm and guided her towards the arena. His blue-stocking fiancée wasn't even a cloud on his rose-coloured horizon.

There was someone in the circus at that moment who was not being terribly nice and polite, but then the Admiral was not a member of the circus and he certainly was not accustomed to having his will thwarted. Further, he'd had a long, tiring and very frustrating day and his normal amiability had deserted him.

"I don't think you heard me properly," the Admiral said with ominous restraint.

"You heard me, all right." Because the back-stage entrance to the circus was ill-lit, because it was very dark and still raining just outside and because his faded eyes no longer saw too well, Johnny, the night watchman, had failed to identify the Admiral. "The entrance for the public is further along there. Get going."

"You're under arrest," the Admiral said without preamble. He turned to a shadowy figure behind him. "Take this fellow to the nearest station. Have him charged with obstructing the course of justice."

"Easy, now, easy." Johnny's tone had undergone a marked change. "There's no need—" He leaned forward and peered up at the Admiral. "Aren't you the gentleman who was here when we had this bit of bother this morning?"

"If by a bit of bother you mean murder, yes. Take me to Mr. Wrinfield."

"Sorry, sir. I'm on duty here."

"Johnny, isn't it? You still want to be on duty tomorrow, Johnny?"

Johnny took the Admiral to Mr. Wrinfield.

The Admiral's interview with Wrinfield was brief.

He said: "You're clear for Europe. There'll be no trouble with visas."

"Twenty-five different nationalities? In one day?"

"I have a staff of four hundred amongst some of whom the eagle-eyed may detect some glimmerings of intelligence. Dr. Harper will be here at ten in the morning. Be here, please. He will begin immediately. Our personal investigations and police enquiries into the murders of Pilgrim and Fawcett have turned up nothing. I don't expect that they will. Future events may."

"What kind of events?"

"I don't know. Fairly drastic in nature, I should imagine. Next, I've just put a scare into Johnny, your night watchman. That was to ensure his co-operation. He's truculent and a bit dim but I suppose reliable."

"I'd trust him with my life."

"We all put different values on our lives. I'm putting six men on to patrol the sleeping quarters of the train at night. They're not from our organisation, so you need have no worries on that score. They will be here nightly until you leave—which, incidentally, will be in five days' time."

"Why the patrol? I'm not sure I like that."

"Frankly, it doesn't matter whether you like it or not." The Admiral smiled, albeit tiredly, to rob the words of offence. "From the moment you accepted this assignment, you're under government orders. It's for security. I want Johnny to act as guidedog."

"Whose security?"

"Bruno's, Maria's, Harper's—and yours."

"Mine? *I'm* in danger?"

"Quite candidly, I'm sure you're not, if for no other reason than if anything happened to you the trip would be cancelled—which wouldn't suit our friends at all. But I'm not taking the ghost of a chance."

"And you think this patrol will help?"

"Yes. In a closed community like this their presence will be common knowledge within the hour. Put it about that the police have received threats against unspecified members of your staff. If you have any bogey-men among your crew members, this news will make them lie very low indeed."

"As you say, you don't take many chances, do you?"

The Admiral said drily: "I think the shadows of Pilgrim and Fawcett would entirely approve. Have Bruno and Maria met yet?" Wrinfield nodded. "Reactions?"

"Bruno hasn't got any. If he has, he never shows them. As for Maria, well, Henry said she didn't exactly fall over."

"Unimpressed, one might say?"

"One might."

"She's watching the show?"

"Yes. With Henry."

"I wonder if she's still unimpressed."

"Still unimpressed?" Henry asked. He clearly wasn't, but then he couldn't keep his eyes off her.

Maria didn't answer immediately. She was staring, as if hypnotised—as ten thousand other people were doing—as The Blind Eagles went through their unbelievable and seemingly suicidal aerial routine. At the end of the performance she released her breath in a long soundless sigh.

"I don't believe it." Her voice was almost a whisper. "I just don't believe what I've seen."

"I can hardly believe it myself—and I've seen it a hundred times. First impressions can be wrong, no?"

"Just how wrong?"

Half an hour later she was with Henry just outside the dressing-room area when Bruno emerged, dressed in street clothes. He was back to his old, relatively unimpressive self. He stopped, smiled at her, and said: "I saw you at the show."

"Blindfolded?"

"On the low wire. On the bicycle."

She looked at him in astonishment. "Doing that impossible act? You have time to look around the audience?"

"I have to have something to occupy my attention," he said with mock bravado. "Enjoy it all?" She nodded and he smiled again. "Even The Blind Eagles? I'm only searching for compliments, of course."

Maria looked at him without smiling, pointed upwards and said: "A star has fallen from the sky." She turned and walked away. From the slight corrugation of Bruno's brow it was impossible to tell whether he was puzzled or amused.

Dr. Harper, looking every inch the high-powered consultant that he wasn't, arrived precisely at ten o'clock the following morning, but had to wait over half an hour while Wrinfield went through the motions of interviewing several other would-be circus doctors who had turned up quite some time before ten o'clock.

Wrinfield was alone in his office when Harper knocked and entered. Harper said: "Good morning. I'm Dr. Harper."

Wrinfield looked at him in considerable astonishment and had just opened his mouth to speak, doubtless to inform Harper that he was not likely to have forgotten him due to the fact that they had made their first acquaintance over the dead body of Pilgrim, when Harper handed him a hand-written note. It read: "This office may be bugged. Interview me as you would any other candidate."

"Good morning." Wrinfield hadn't even blinked. "I'm Wrinfield, the owner." He launched smoothly into the interview: Harper, both while listening and answering, sat down and scribbled another note. He handed it across. It read: "End the interview and give me the job. Ask me my immediate plans then invite me outside for a look around."

Wrinfield said: "Well, that's it. I'm too busy a man to spend a lifetime on making decisions. The job's yours. Frankly, when I have the choice between an experienced consultant and the young interns I've been seeing—well, I don't have much of a choice. I'm not so naïve as to imagine that you're making this a full-time career. A sabbatical—or part of it?"

"Twelve years in the Belvedere is a long time."

"How soon could you be free, Doctor?"

"Now."

"Splendid. And what would your immediate plans be?"

"Depends on how soon you want to leave on this foreign tour."

"Let's work towards four or five days from now."

"Little enough time. First, Mr. Wrinfield, I'd like your authorisation for medical supplies. Then a collection of all the passports until I see what's required in the way of vaccinations and inoculations—I understand your circus has never toured abroad before. I'm afraid that some of your high-wire and trapeze artists will have to curtail their acts quite a bit in the next few days."

"All that I can arrange immediately. First of all, though, I suggest you have a look around. When you see what you've taken on you might want to change your mind."

The two men left the office and Wrinfield led the way to the centre ring of the circus itself, a spot which, insofar as potential eavesdroppers were concerned, was probably more secluded than any place for a mile around. Nonetheless, Wrinfield scuffed the sand with the toe of his shoe and looked casually around before speaking.

He said: "And what was all that for?"

"Sorry about all that cloak-and-dagger stuff. We don't usually go in for it—spoils our image. Incidentally, congratulations—you'd make a splendid recruit to our organisation. Anyway, I was speaking to Charles just before I came here, and we both came up with the same very nasty suspicion at the same time."

"That my office was bugged?"

"If it were, it could explain a great deal."

"But why all the paper notes you handed me? Why didn't you just phone and warn me?" Harper half-smiled at him and Wrinfield tapped his own head. "That wasn't very bright. The phone could have been bugged too."

"Indeed. In a few minutes' time you can expect another applicant for my job. His name is Dr. Morley and he will be carrying the regulation black medical bag. But he's no doctor, he's an electronics expert and his bag is packed with extremely advanced equipment for locating bugging devices. Ten minutes alone in your office and he'll find out whether it's clean or not."

Fifteen minutes later, as Wrinfield and Harper approached the office, a tall dark man with a black bag descended the steps from it. For the benefit of any watchers or listeners Wrinfield introduced them and suggested a cup of coffee in the canteen. They sat at a remote corner table.

Morley said: "Two bugs. Miniaturised radio transmitters. One in the ceiling light, the other in the phone."

"So I can breathe again," Wrinfield said. Neither of the other two made any immediate reply so he went on rather uncertainly: "I mean, those devices have been removed or deactivated?"

"Most certainly not," Harper said: "The bugs are still there and there they will remain, probably until we return from Europe. Do you think we want the ungodly to know that we know? Think of all the amount of false and confusing and misleading information we can feed them." One could see that, mentally, Harper was positively rubbing his hands. "From now on you will conduct only routine circus business in that office." He smiled almost dreamily. "Unless, of course, I give instructions to the contrary."

In the days that followed, four subjects increasingly and exclusively dominated conversation in the circus.

The first of those, inevitably, emanated from the mounting excitement over the forthcoming trip to Europe, a euphoric state that was not, understandably, shared by the unfortunates who were not making the foreign tour but would be returning to the winter headquarters in Florida: for purely logistical reasons, only just two-thirds of the personnel would be able to make it. But for the two-thirds who were going the European visit, especially as it included a two-way ocean voyage, was regarded as nothing less than a holiday. An extremely arduous holiday it promised to be from the moment of disembarkation, but nonetheless a holiday. About half the crew were American, few of whom had ever been abroad before, partly from financial considerations, partly because the circus season was so long that they had only three weeks free in the year and this at the wrong time of the year—in the dead of winter: for them, this could be a once-in-a-lifetime experience. The remainder were predominantly European, mainly from the other side of the Iron Curtain, and this was, possibly, also a once-in-a-lifetime experience—that of seeing their native countries and families again.

The second subject concerned the much-maligned activities of Dr. Harper and his two temporarily employed trained nurses. Their degree of unpopularity was high. Harper was rigorous to the point of ruthlessness, and when it came to vaccinations and inoculations no one passed through the meshes of the wide net he cast, and when any to-be-or-not-to-be questions arose he never gave anyone the benefit of the doubt. Circus people are undoubtedly tougher and fitter than the average run of mankind, but when it came to a profound aversion to injections, scratches and consequent sore arms they were no different from anyone else. But nobody could possibly doubt that they had a genuine and dedicated doctor in their midst.

The third concerned two sets of mysterious activities. The first was the patrol that so closely guarded the sleeping quarters on the train during the night. No one seriously believed that threats to lives had been made by parties unknown but, then, they didn't know what else to believe. Then there was the baffling incident of two alleged electrical engineers who had come to examine the wiring of the train. They had almost finished their task before their authenticity had been questioned and the police called. Unknown to anyone in the circus except Harper, they had been detained in custody for precisely five minutes, which was all the time it took for one of them to phone the Admiral and reassure him that none of the sleeping quarters on the train had been bugged.

The last, but unquestionably the most engrossing topic of the lot, concerned Bruno and Maria. To the vexation of Henry, who was engaged in a battle with his conscience, they were not only seen increasingly in each other's company, but were seen actively and with no attempt at concealment to seek out each other's company. The reactions to this particular development were predictably mixed. Some were amused to see Bruno's hitherto inviolate defences being breached. Others were envious—the men because Bruno had undoubtedly and apparently without effort attached the affections of a girl who politely but pointedly ignored any other approaches made to her, the women because Bruno, by far the most eligible bachelor in the circus, politely but pointedly ignored any approaches made to him. Many more were happy for Bruno, and this despite the fact that apart from Kan Dahn, Manuelo and Roebuck he had no real friends in the circus, because it was common knowledge that since the death of his wife he had been a sad, lonely and withdrawn man who never looked at women. But the majority regarded it as only natural and inevitable that the undisputed star of the circus should come together with a girl who was arguably the most lovely young lady among a plethora of lovely young ladies.

It was not until the last performance of their last night in town that Bruno rather diffidently asked her along to see his quarters aboard the train. Maria showed no diffidence in accepting the offer. He guided her stumbling footsteps along the rutted siding track, then helped her up the steep steps at the end of a coach.

Bruno had rather splendid and completely enclosed quarters, consisting of a sitting-room, kitchen-cum-dinette, bathroom—with, of all things, a sunken bath—and bedroom. Maria looked almost dazed as he led her back to the sitting-room.

He said: "I'm told I mix what the Americans call a

rather mean martini. Only time I ever drink is after I've finished a series in a town. Alcohol and the trapeze don't mix. Will you join me?"

"Please. I must say you do live in style. You should have a wife to share all this."

Bruno fetched ice. "Is that a proposal?"

"No, it's not. But all this—just for one man."

"Mr. Wrinfield is very kind to me."

She said drily: "I don't think Mr. Wrinfield is losing out on the deal. Does anyone else have accommodations like these?"

"I haven't gone around examining—"

"Bruno!"

"No."

"Certainly not me. I have a place like a horizontal telephone box. Ah, well, I suppose there's a vast gap in status between a trainee secretary and you."

"That's so."

"Men! Modesty! I just don't know!"

"Come with me on the high trapeze. Blindfolded. Then you'll know."

She shuddered, not altogether affectedly. "I can't even stand on a chair without getting vertigo. Truly. You're welcome to your palace. Well, I suppose I can always come along and visit the palace."

He handed her a drink. "I'll have a special welcome mat made out for you."

"Thank you." She lifted her glass. "To our first time alone. We're supposed to be falling in love. Any idea how the others think we are doing?"

"I can't speak for the others. I think I'm doing very well." He glanced at the compressing lips and said hastily: "I think *we're* doing very well. I suppose, as of this moment, that must be the general idea. By this time at least a hundred people must know that you're here with me. Aren't you supposed to blush or something?"

"No."

"It's a lost art. Well, I don't suppose you came along just for my dark eyes. You have something to tell me?"

"Not really. You asked me, remember?" She smiled. "Why?"

"Just polishing up our act." She stopped smiling and put down her glass. He reached forward quickly and touched the back of her hand. "Don't be a silly goose, Maria." She looked at him uncertainly, smiled a token smile, and picked up her glass again. "Tell me. What am I supposed to do when we get to Crau—and how am I supposed to do it?"

"Only Dr. Harper knows, and he's not ready to talk yet. I should imagine that he'll tell you—us—either on the way across or when we get to Europe. But two things he did tell me this morning—"

"I knew you had something to tell me."

"Yes. I was just trying to be a tease. It didn't work, did it? Remember those two so-called electrical engineers that the police escorted to the train? They were our people, electronic experts searching for listening devices—bugs. They concentrated on your apartment."

"Bugs? In my apartment. Come on, Maria, that *is* a bit melodramatic."

"Is it? The second item of news is that a few days ago they found two bugs in Mr. Wrinfield's office—one for the room, one for the telephone. I suppose that's melodramatic, too?" When Bruno made no reply she went on: "They haven't removed the bugs. Mr. Wrinfield, on Dr. Harper's suggestion, is on the phone to Charles several times a day, dropping vague hints and making veiled suggestions about certain members of the circus who might be of interest to him. Nothing about us, of course. In fact he's made so many suggestions that if they—whoever 'they' may be—are keeping tabs on the suggested suspects they won't have time to look at far less think about anyone else. Which, of course, includes us."

"I think they're nuts," Bruno said candidly. "And by 'they,' this time, I don't mean 'they,' I mean Wrinfield and Harper. Playing little kiddies' games."

"The murders of Pilgrim and Fawcett. That was a game?"

"Preserve me from feminine logic. I wasn't talking about them."

"Dr. Harper has twenty years' experience behind him."

"Or one year's twenty times over. Okay, so I leave myself in the safe arms of the experts. Meantime, I suppose there's nothing for the sacrificial calf to do?"

"No. Well, yes. You can tell me how to get in touch with you."

"Knock twice and ask for Bruno."

"You have a sealed-off suite here. I won't be able to see you when the train is in motion."

"Well, well." Bruno smiled widely, a rare thing for him: it was the first time she had seen his smile touch his eyes. "I make progress. You think you'll be wanting to see me?"

"Don't be silly. I may *have* to see you."

Bruno nodded forwards. "It's illegal to seal off any part of a coach in motion. There's a door in the corner of my bedroom that leads to the passage beyond. But it's only got one handle and that's on my side."

"If I knock tat-tat, tat-tat, you'll know it's me."

"Tat-tat, tat-tat," he said solemnly. "I love those kiddies' games."

He escorted her back to her compartment. At the foot of the steps he said: "Well, good night. Thanks for the visit." He bent forward and kissed her lightly.

She didn't object, just said mildly: "Isn't that carrying realism a bit too far?"

"Not at all. Orders are orders. We are supposed to be creating a certain impression, and the chance was too good to pass up. There are at least a dozen people watching us."

She made a face, turned and went up the steps.

4

Most of the following day was given up to dismantling the bewildering variety and daunting amount of equipment inside the arena, the back-stage and the fair-ground and loading up the half-mile-long train. To transfer this, the animal cages, the prefabricated offices, the fair-ground booths and Bruno's ramshackle mentalist theatre, not to mention the animals and circus members to the coaches and flat-cars, was a massive undertaking that to the layman would have appeared well-nigh impossible: the circus, with its generations of experience behind it, performed the task with an almost ludicrous ease, a smooth efficiency that reduced a seemingly hopeless confusion to a near-miracle of precision and order. Even the loading up of provisions for the hundreds of animals and humans would have seemed a most formidable task: in the event the last of the provision trucks departed less than an hour after the first had arrived. The whole operation could have been likened to an exercise in military logistics with the sole proviso that any unbiassed and expert observer would have conceded that the circus had unquestionably the edge in efficiency.

The circus train was due to pull out at ten o'clock that night. At nine o'clock, Dr. Harper was still closeted with the Admiral, studying two very complicated diagrams.

The Admiral had a pipe in one hand, a brandy in the other. He looked relaxed, calm and unconcerned. It was possible that he might just have been relaxed and calm but, as the sole instigator of the forthcoming operation, the man who had conceived and planned it all down to the last and most intimate detail possible, it was impossible that he should not be concerned. He said: "You have it all? Guards, entry, interior layout, exit and escape route to the Baltic?"

"I have it all. I just hope that damned ship is there for rendezvous." Harper folded the diagrams and pushed them deeply into the inside pocket of his coat.

"You break in on a Tuesday night. They'll be cruising offshore from the Friday to the following Friday. A whole week's grace."

"Won't the East Germans or the Poles or the Russians be suspicious, sir?"

"Inevitably. Wouldn't you?"

"Won't they object?"

"How can they? Since when has the Baltic been

anyone's private pond? Of course they're going to tie up the presence of the ship—or ships—with the presence of the circus in Crau. Inevitable, and nothing we can do about it. The circus, the circus." The Admiral sighed. "You'd better deliver the goods, Harper, or I'm going to be on welfare before the year is out."

Harper smiled. "I wouldn't like that, sir. And you know better than anyone that the ultimate responsibility for the delivery of the goods doesn't lie in my hands."

"I know. Have you formed any personal impression of our latest recruit yet?"

"Nothing more than is obvious to anyone else, sir. He's intelligent, tough, strong and appears to have been born without a nervous system. He's a very close person. Maria Hopkins says that it's impossible to get next to him."

"What?" The Admiral quirked a bushy eyebrow. "That delightful young child? I'm sure if she really tried—"

"I didn't quite mean it that way, sir."

"Peace, Harper, peace. I do not endeavour to be facetious. There are times that are sent to try men's souls. Although I know we have no option it is not easy to have to rely in the final analysis on an unknown. Apart from the fact that if he fails—well, there's only one way he can fail and then he'll be on my conscience for the remainder of my days. And don't you add to that burden."

"Sir?"

"Mind your back is what I mean. Those papers you've just stuck—securely, I trust—in your inside pocket. You are aware, of course, what will happen if you are caught with those in your possession?"

Harper sighed. "I am aware. I'll have my throat cut and end up, suitably weighted, in some canal or river. Doubtless you can always find a replacement."

"Doubtless. But the way things are going I'm going to be running out of replacements quite soon, so I'd rather not be put to the trouble. You are quite sure you have the times of transmission and the code totally memorised?"

Harper said gloomily: "You don't have much faith in your subordinates, sir."

"The way things have been going recently, I don't have much faith in myself, either."

Harper touched the bottom of his medical bag. "This postage stamp transceiver. You sure you can pick me up?"

"We're using NASA equipment. We could pick you up on the moon."

"I somehow wish I was going there."

Some six hours after departure the circus train drew into a shunting yard. Arc-lamps apart, the darkness was total and the rain very heavy. There, after an interminable period of advancing, reversing, bumping, clanking and screeching of wheels on points—the combination of all of which effectively succeeded in waking up everyone aboard—a considerable number of preselected coaches were detached, subsequently to be hauled south to their winter quarters in Florida. The main body of the train continued on its way to New York.

Nothing untoward had happened en route. Bruno,

who invariably cooked for himself, had not left his quarters once. He had been visited twice by his brothers, once by Wrinfield and once by Harper but by no one else: known to everybody as a loner, he was invariably treated as such.

Not until the train had arrived on the quay alongside the container-passenger ship that was to take them to Genoa—selected not so much for its strategical geographical position as the fact that it was one of the few Mediterranean ports with the facilities to off-load the crane-breaking coaches and flat-cars—did Bruno leave his quarters. It was still raining. One of the first persons he encountered was Maria. She was dressed in navy slacks, a voluminous yellow oilskin and looked thoroughly miserable. She gave him the nearest she would ever be able to come to a scowl and came to the point with what he had now come to regard as her customary straightforwardness.

"Not very sociable, are you?"

"I'm sorry. But you did know where I was."

"I had nothing to tell you." Then, inconsequentially: "You knew where *I* was."

"I find telephone boxes cramping."

"You could have invited me. While I know we're supposed to be striking up some special relationship I don't go openly chasing after men."

"You don't have to." He smiled to rob the next words of offence. "Or do you prefer to do it discreetly?"

"Very amusing. Very clever. You have no shame?"

"For what?"

"Your shameful neglect."

"Lots."

"Then take me to dinner tonight."

"Telepathy, Maria. Sheer telepathy."

She gave him a look of disbelief and left to change.

They switched taxis three times on the way to the pleasant Italian restaurant Maria had chosen. When they were seated Bruno said: "Was all that necessary? The taxis, I mean?"

"I don't know. I follow orders."

"Why are we here? You miss me so much?"

"I have instructions for you."

"Not my dark eyes?" She smiled and shook her head and he sighed. "You can't win them all. What instructions?"

"I suppose you're going to say that I could easily have whispered them to you in some dark corner on the quayside?"

"A prospect not without its attractions. But not tonight."

"Why?"

"It's raining."

"What is it like to be a romantic at heart?"

"And I like it here. Very pleasant restaurant." He looked at her consideringly, at the blue velvet dress, the fur cape that was far too expensive for a secretary, the sheen of rain on her shining dark hair. "Besides, in the dark I wouldn't be able to see you. Here I can. You're really very beautiful. What instructions?"

"What?" She was momentarily flustered, unbalanced by the sudden switch, then compressed her lips in mock ferociousness. "We sail at eleven o'clock tomorrow morning. Please be in your cabin at six o'clock in the evening. At that hour the purser will arrive to discuss seating arrangements, or some such, with you. He's a genuine purser but he's also something else. He will make absolutely certain that there are no listening devices in your cabin." Bruno remained silent. "I notice you're not talking about melodrama this time."

Bruno said with some weariness: "Because it hardly seems worth talking about. Why on earth should anyone plant bugs in my cabin? I'm not under any suspicion. But I will be if you and Harper keep on behaving in this idiotic cloak-and-dagger fashion. Why the bugging of Wrinfield's office? Why were two men sent to look for bugs in my place aboard the train? Why this character now? Too many people seeing that I'm debugged, too many people knowing that I can't possibly be all that I claim to be or that the circus claims that I am. Too many people having their attention called to me. I don't like it one little bit."

"Please. There's no need to be like that—"

"Isn't there? Your opinion. And don't be soothing to me."

"Look, Bruno, I'm just a messenger. Directly, there's no reason on earth why you should be under suspicion. But we are—or we're going to be up against an extremely efficient and suspicious secret police who certainly won't overlook the slightest possibility. After all, the information we want is in Crau. We're going to Crau. You were born in Crau. And they will know that you have the strongest possible motivation—revenge. They killed your wife—"

"Be quiet!" Maria recoiled, appalled by the quiet ferocity of his voice. "Nobody has spoken of her to me in six and a half years. Mention my dead wife again and I'll pull out, wreck the whole operation and leave you to explain to your precious chief why it was your gaucherie, your ill manners, your total lack of feeling, your incredible insensitivity that ruined everything. You understand?"

"I understand." She was very pale, shocked almost, tried to understand the enormity of her blunder and failed. She ran a slow tongue across her lips. "I'm sorry, I'm terribly sorry. That was a very bad mistake." She still wasn't sure what the mistake was about. "But never again, I promise."

He said nothing.

"Dr. Harper says please be outside your cabin at 6:30 P.M., sitting on the floor—sorry, deck—at the foot of the companionway. You have fallen down and damaged your ankle. You will be found and helped to your cabin. Dr. Harper will, of course, be there almost immediately. He wishes to give you a full briefing on the nature of the operation."

"Has he told you?" There was still a singular lack of warmth in Bruno's voice.

"He told me nothing. If I know Dr. Harper he'll probably tell you to tell me nothing either."

"I will do what you ask. Now that you've completed your business, we may as well get back. Three taxis for you, of course, rules are rules. I'll take one straight back to the ship. It's quicker and cheaper and the hell with the CIA."

She reached out a tentative hand and touched his arm.

"I have apologised. Sincerely. How long must I

keep on doing it?" When he made no answer she smiled at him and the smile was as her hand had been, tentative and uncertain. "You'd think a person who earns as much money as you do could afford to buy a meal for a working girl like myself. Or do we go Dutch? Please don't leave. I don't want to go back. Not yet."

"Why?"

"I don't know. It's—it's just one of those obscure —I don't know. I just want to make things right."

"*I* was right. First time out. You *are* a goose." He sighed, reached out for the menu and handed it to her. He gave her an odd look. "Funny. I thought your eyes were dark. They've gone all brown. Dark, flecked brown, mind you, but still brown. How do you do it? Have you a switch or something?"

She looked at him solemnly. "No switch."

"Must be my eyes then. Tell me, why couldn't Dr. Harper have come and told me all this himself?"

"It would have created a very odd impression if you two were seen leaving together. You never speak to each other. What's he to you or you to him?"

"Ah!"

"With us it's different. Or had you forgotten? The most natural thing in the world. I'm in love with you and you're in love with me."

"He's still in love with his dead wife." Maria's voice was flat, neutral. Elbows on the guard-rail, she was standing on the passenger deck of the M.C. *Carpentaria,* apparently oblivious of the chill night wind, watching in apparent fascination but without really registering what she was seeing as the giant dockside cranes, with their blazing attached arc-lamps, swung the coaches inboard.

She started as a hand laid itself on her arm and a teasing voice said: "Who's in love with whose wife, then?"

She turned and looked at Henry Wrinfield. The thin intelligent face, chalk-white in the glare of the arc-lamps, was smiling.

"You might have coughed or something," she said reproachfully. "You did give me a fright, you know."

"Sorry. But I could have been wearing hobnailed boots and you wouldn't have heard me above the racket of those damned cranes. Well, come out with it, who's in love with who?"

"What *are* you talking about?"

"Love," Henry said patiently. "You were declaiming something about it when I came up."

"Was I?" Her voice was vague. "I wouldn't be surprised. My sister says I talk non-stop in my sleep. Maybe I was asleep on my feet. Did you hear any other Freudian slips or whatever?"

"Alas, no. My loss, I'm sure. What on earth are you doing out here? It's cold and starting to rain." He had lost interest in the remark he'd overheard.

She shivered. "Day-dreaming. I must have been. It's cold."

"Come inside. They have a beautiful old-fashioned bar aboard. And warm. A brandy will make you warmer."

"Bed would make me warmer still. Time I was there."

"You spurn a night-cap with the last of the Wrinfields?"

"Never!" She laughed and took his arm. "Show me the way."

The lounge—it could hardly have been called a bar—had deep green leather armchairs, brass tables, a very attentive steward and excellent brandy. Maria had one of those, Henry had three and at the end of the third Henry, who clearly had no head for alcohol, had developed a distinct, if gentlemanly, yearning look about the eyes. He took one of her hands in his and yearned some more. Maria looked at his hand.

"It's unfair," she said. "Custom dictates that a lady wears an engagement ring when she is engaged, a wedding ring when she is married. No such devolves upon a man. I think it's wrong."

"So do I." If she'd said he ought to wear a cowbell around his neck he'd have agreed to that too.

"Then where's yours?"

"My what?"

"Your engagement ring. Cecily wears one. Your fiancée. Remember? The green-eyed one at Bryn Mawr. Surely you can't have forgotten?"

The fumes evaporated from Henry's head. "You've been asking questions about me?"

"Never a one and no need to ask either. You forget I spend a couple of hours a day with your uncle. No children of his own, so his nieces and nephews have become his pride and joy." She gathered her handbag and rose. "Thank you for the night-cap. Good night and sweet dreams. Be sure to dream about the right person."

Henry watched her go with a moody eye.

Maria had been in bed no more than five minutes when a knock came at her cabin door. She called: "Come in. It's not locked."

Bruno entered and closed the door behind him.

"It should be locked. What with characters like myself and Henry prowling around—"

"Henry?"

"Last seen calling for a double brandy. Looks like a Romeo who's just found out that he's been serenading the wrong balcony. Nice cabin."

"You've come to discuss décor at this time of night?"

"You allocated this room?"

"Funny question. As a matter of fact, no. There were seven or eight cabins to choose from; the steward, a very nice old boy, offered me my pick. I took this one."

"Liked the décor, eh?"

"Why did you come, Bruno?"

"To say good night, I guess." He sat beside her, put an arm around her shoulders and held her close. "And to apologise for snapping at you in the restaurant. I'll explain to you later—when we're on our way home." He rose as abruptly as he had sat down, opened the door, said: "Lock it," and closed the door behind him. Maria stared at the door in total astonishment.

The *Carpentaria* was big—close on thirty thousand tons—and had been built primarily as a bulk ore ship capable of immediate conversion into a container vessel. She was also capable of carrying nearly two hundred passengers, though hardly in transatlantic passenger line style. Her front two holds were at the moment taken up by twenty circus train coaches, animal and crew member coaches mainly, while the contents of a dozen others had been unloaded on the quay and carefully stowed away in the holds. The flat-cars were securely clamped on the reinforced fore-deck. In Italy, they were to be met by a sufficiency of empty coaches and a locomotive powerful enough to haul them across the mountains of Central Europe.

At six o'clock on the following evening the *Carpentaria,* in driving rain and a heavy swell—she was stabilised to reduce roll to a minimum—was seven hours out from New York. Bruno was stretched out on a settee in his cabin—one of the very few rather sumptuous staterooms available on the vessel—when a knock came to the door and a uniformed purser entered. To Bruno's total lack of surprise he was carrying a thick black brief-case.

He said: "Good evening, sir. Were you expecting me?"

"I was expecting someone. I suppose that's you."

"Thank you, sir. May I?" He locked the door behind him, turned to Bruno and tapped his case. "The paper work for a modern purser," he said sadly, "is endless."

He opened the brief-case, extracted a flat, rectangular metal box, liberally covered with dials and controls, extended an antenna from it, clamped on a pair of earphones and began, slowly, to traverse first the stateroom and then the bathroom, assiduously twirling his controls as he went. He looked like a cross between a mine detector and a water diviner. After about ten minutes he divested himself of his equipment and stowed it away in his brief-case.

"Clear," he said. "No guarantee, mind you—but as sure as I can be."

Bruno indicated the brief-case. "I know nothing about those things but I thought they were foolproof."

"So they are. On dry land. But on a ship you have so much iron, the hull being used as a conductor, magnetic fields from all the heavy power cables—well, anyone can be fooled. I can. So can my electronic friend here." He put out a hand to a bulkhead to steady himself as the *Carpentaria,* apparently forgetting all about its stabilisers, gave an unexpected lurch. "Looks like a nasty night coming up. Shouldn't be surprised if we have a few sprains and bruises this evening. First night out, you know—people haven't had time to find their sea-legs." Bruno wondered if he had seen a wink or not; it could have been imagination and he had no means of knowing how much the purser was in Harper's confidence. He made a non-committal remark to the purser, who thanked him politely, unlocked the door and left.

Precisely at six-thirty Bruno stepped out into the passageway. It was, fortunately, quite deserted. The foot of the companionway was only six feet away. Half seated, half lying, he seated himself as comfortably as possible in the most suitably uncomfortable-looking position on the deck and awaited developments. Five minutes passed, and he was beginning to develop an acute cramp in his right knee, when a couple of stewards appeared and rescued him from his misery. To the accompaniment of much tongue-clacking they assisted him sympathetically to his stateroom and lowered him tenderly to his settee.

"Just you hang on a minute, guv'nor," one of them said. He had a powerful Cockney accent. "I'll have Dr. Berenson here in a jiffy."

It hadn't occurred to Bruno—as it apparently hadn't occurred to Harper—that the *Carpentaria* would be carrying its own doctor, which was an elementary oversight on both their parts: over and above a certain passenger capacity international law made the carrying of a ship's doctor mandatory. He said quickly: "Could I have our own doctor, please—the circus doctor? His name is Dr. Harper."

"I know his cabin, next deck down. At once, sir."

Harper must have been waiting in his cabin, medical bags in hand, for he arrived in Bruno's cabin, tongue clucking and looking suitably concerned, inside thirty seconds. He locked the stateroom door after the stewards' departure, then set to work on Bruno's ankle with some extremely pungent salve and about a yard of elasticised bandage.

He said: "Mr. Carter was on schedule?"

"If Mr. Carter is the purser—he didn't introduce himself—yes."

Harper paused in his ministrations and looked around. "Clean?"

"Did you expect anything else?"

"Not really." Harper inspected his completed handiwork: both the visual and olfactory aspects were suitably impressive.

Harper brought over a low table, reached into an inside pocket, brought out and smoothed two detailed plans and set some photographs down beside them. He tapped one of the plans.

"This one first. The plan outline of the Lubylan Advanced Research Centre. Know it?"

Bruno eyed Harper without enthusiasm. "I hope that's the last stupidly unnecessary question you ask this evening." Harper assumed the look of a man trying not to look hurt. "Before the CIA recruited me for this job—"

"How do you know it's the CIA?"

Bruno rolled his eyes upwards then clearly opted for restraint. "Before the Boy Scouts recruited me for this job they'd have checked every step I've taken from the cradle. To your certain knowledge you know I spent the first twenty-four years of my life in Crau. How should I not know Lubylan?"

"Yes. Well. Oddly enough, they do carry out advanced research in Lubylan, most of it, regrettably, associated with chemical warfare, nerve gases and the like."

"Regrettably? The United States doesn't engage in similar research?"

Harper looked pained. "That's not my province."

Bruno said patiently: "Look, Doctor, if you can't trust me how can you expect me to repose implicit trust in you? It is your province and you damned well know it. Remember the Armed Forces courier centre at Orly Airport? All the top-secret classified communications between the Pentagon and the American Army in Europe were channelled through there. Remember?"

"I remember."

"Remember a certain Sergeant Johnson? Fellow

with the splendidly patriotic Christian names of Robert Lee? Russia's most successful planted spy in a generation, passed every U.S.-Europe top military secret to the KGB for God knows how long. Remember?"

Harper nodded unhappily. "I remember." Bruno's briefing was not going exactly as he'd planned it.

"Then you won't have forgotten that the Russians published photo copies of one of the top-secret directives that Johnson had stolen. It was the ultimate U.S. contingency plan if the Soviet Union should overrun Western Europe. It suggested that in that event the United States intended to devastate the continent by waging bacteriological, chemical and nuclear warfare: the fact that the entire civilian population would be virtually wiped out was taken for granted. This caused a tremendous furor in Europe at the time and cost the Americans the odd European friend, about two hundred million of them: I doubt whether it even made the back page of the Washington *Post*."

"You're very well informed."

"Not being a member of the CIA doesn't mean you have to be illiterate. I can read. German is my second language—my mother was a Berliner. Two German magazines carried the story at the same time."

Harper was resigned. "*Der Spiegel* and *Stern*, September 1969. Does it give you any particular pleasure in putting me on a hook and watching me wriggle?"

"That wasn't my intention. I just want to point up two things. If you don't level with me all the time and on every subject you can expect no co-operation from me. Then I want you to know why I've really gone along with this. I have no idea whether the Americans really would go ahead with this holocaust. I can't believe it but what I believe doesn't matter: it's what the East believes and if they believe that America would not hesitate to implement this threat, then they might be sorely tempted to carry out a pre-emptive strike. From what I understand from Colonel Fawcett a millionth of a gram of this anti-matter would settle America's hash once and for all. I don't think anyone should have this weapon, but, for me, it's the lesser of two evils: I'm European by birth but American by adoption. I'll stick to my adopted parents. And now, could we get on with it. Lay it all on the line. Let's say I've never heard of or seen Crau and go on from there."

Harper looked at him without enthusiasm. He said sourly: "If it was your intention to introduce a subtle change in our relationship you have succeeded beyond any expectation you might have had. Only, I wouldn't call it very subtle. Well. Lubylan. Conveniently enough, it's situated only a quarter of a mile from the auditorium where the circus will be held: both buildings, though in the town, are, as one would expect, on the outskirts. Lubylan, as you can see, faces on to a main street."

"There are two buildings shown on that diagram."

"I'm coming to that. Those two buildings, incidentally, are connected by two high walls which are not shown in the plan." Harper quickly sketched them in. "At the back of Lubylan is only wasteland. The nearest building in that direction is an oil-fired electric power station.

"This building that abuts on the main street—let's

call it the West building—is where the actual research is carried out. In the East building, the one abutting the wasteland at the back, research is also carried out, but research of a different kind and almost certainly much nastier than that carried out in the West building. In the East building they carry out a series of highly unpleasant experiments—on human beings. It's run entirely by the secret police and is the maximum security detention centre for the enemies of the State, who may range from a would-be assassin of the Premier to a weak-minded dissident poet. The mortality rate, I understand, is rather higher than normal."

"I suppose it's my turn to say that you are very well informed."

"We don't send a man in blindfolded and with his hands tied behind his back. This, crossing the courtyard here, is an elevated fifth-floor corridor connecting the two buildings. It is glass-sided and glass-topped and kept brightly illuminated from dusk to dawn. It is impossible for anyone to use it without being seen.

"Every window in both buildings is heavily barred. All are nevertheless fitted with burglar alarms. There are only two entrances, one for each building, both time-locked and heavily guarded. The buildings are both nine stories high and the connecting walls are the same height. The whole upper perimeter of the walls is lined with closely spaced, outward curving metal spikes, the whole with two thousand volts running through them. There's a watch-tower at every corner. The guards there have machine-guns, searchlights and klaxons. The courtyard between the two buildings, like the elevated glass corridor, is brightly lit at night—not that that matters so much: killer Doberman pinschers roam the place all the time."

Bruno said: "You have a great gift for encouraging people."

"You'd rather not know those things? There are only two ways of escaping from this place—death by torture or death by suicide. No one has ever escaped." Dr. Harper indicated the other diagram. "This is the plan layout of the ninth floor of the West building. This is why the government is mounting a multimillion-dollar operation—to get you in here. This is where Van Diemen works, eats, sleeps and has his being."

"Should I know the name?"

"Most unlikely. He's almost totally unknown to the public. In the Western world fellow-scientists speak of him with awe. An acknowledged genius—*the* only indisputable genius—in particle research. The discoverer of anti-matter—the only man in the world who has the secret of making, storing and harnessing this fearful weapon."

"He's Dutch?"

"Despite his name, no. He's a renegade West German, a defector. God only knows why he defected. Here you can see his laboratories and office. Here is the guards' room—the place, understandably, is guarded like Fort Knox twenty-four hours a day. And this is his living quarters—just a small bedroom, an even smaller bathroom and a tiny kitchenette."

"You mean he hasn't got a home? It would make things a damn sight easier if he had."

"He's got a home, all right, a splendid lake-forest mansion given him by the government. He's never even been there. He lives for nothing but his work and he never leaves here. One suspects the government is just as happy that he continues to do so: it makes their security problem comparatively simple."

"Yes. To come back to another simple problem. You say that no one has ever escaped from Lubylan. Then how the hell do you expect me to get in there?"

"Well, now." Harper cleared his throat; he was putting his first foot on very delicate ground. "We'd given the matter some thought, of course, before we approached you. Which is why we approached you and only you. The place, as I've said, is ringed with a two-thousand-volt fence of steel. The power has to come from someplace: it comes from the electric power station at the back of the East building. Like most high-power transmissions it comes by overhead cable. It comes by a single loop, three hundred yards long, from a pylon in the power station to the top of the East building."

"You're way out of your mind. You must be. If you're so crazy as to suggest—"

Harper prepared to be diplomatic, persuasive and reasonable all at once. "Let's look at it this way. Let's think of it as just another high wire. As long as you are in contact with this cable, with either hands or feet, and don't earth yourself to anything such as the anchor wire for a pylon insulator, then—"

"Let's think of it as just another high wire," Bruno mimicked. "Two thousand volts—that's what they use, or used to use, in the electric chair, isn't it?"

Harper nodded unhappily.

"In the circus you step from a platform on to the wire, and step off on to another platform at the other end. If I step off from the pylon on to the wire or from the wire on to the prison wall, I'll have one foot on the cable and the other to earth. I'll be frizzled in a second flat. And three hundred yards long—have you *any* kind of idea what kind of sag that entails? Can you imagine what the effects of that sag combined with whatever wind may be blowing would be like? Has it occurred to you that, at this time of year, there might be both ice and snow on that wire? God's sake, Dr. Harper, don't you know that our lives depend on the friction coefficient between the soles of our feet and the wire—the cable, in this case. Believe me, Doctor, you may know a lot about counter-espionage but you know damn all about the high wire."

Harper looked even more unhappy.

"And should I ever live to cross that cable how do I ever live to cross that courtyard—that *illuminated* courtyard patrolled by Dobermans—or cross over that transparent aerial corridor, assuming I could ever get to it in the first place? And if I do get to the West building, how am I going to get past the guards?"

Harper was now looking acutely unhappy.

"And if I do manage that—I'm not a gambler but I'll lay you a thousand to one I never make it—how am I going to locate the place where those papers are kept? I mean, I don't suppose they'd just be lying around on a table. They'll be locked away—Van Diemen may just even sleep with them under his pillow."

Harper studiously avoided Bruno's eye. He was

distinctly and understandably uncomfortable. He said: "Locked filing cabinets or safes are no problems—I can give you keys that should open any commercial office lock."

"And if it's a combination?"

"Looks as if you're going to need a little luck all the way."

Bruno gazed at the deckhead, considered the enormity of this understatement, pushed the papers away and relapsed into speechlessness. After quite some time he stirred, looked at Harper, sighed and said: "I'm afraid I'm going to need a gun. A silenced gun. With plenty of ammunition."

Harper went through his own speechless act then said: "You mean you're going to try?" If he were experiencing any feelings of hope or relief he didn't show them: there was only a dull disbelief in his voice.

"Once a nut, always a nut. Not a gun that fires bullets. A gas gun or one that fires anaesthetic darts. Possible?"

"That's what diplomatic bags are for," Harper said, almost absently. "Look, I don't think I'd properly appreciated the difficulties myself. If you think it's outright impossible—"

"You're mad. I'm mad. We're all mad. But you've got the whole damned circus at sea now—as far as I'm concerned we're at sea in more ways than one—and if nothing else we owe it to your murdered colleagues. The gun."

Harper, clearly, was searching for suitable words and failed. He said: "You will keep those diagrams and pictures in a place of absolute safety?"

"Yes." Bruno rose, picked up papers and photographs, tore them into little pieces, took them to the bathroom and flushed them down the toilet. He returned and said: "They're safe now."

"It would be difficult for anyone to get their hands on them now. A remarkable gift. I'd be grateful if you didn't fall down the stairs—genuinely, this time—land on your head and give yourself amnesia. Any idea how you're going to set about this?"

"Look, I'm a mentalist, not Merlin the wizard. How long have you known about this?"

"Not long. A few weeks."

"Not long. A few weeks." Bruno made it sound like a few years. "And have *you* worked out any solution yet?"

"No."

"And you expect me to do it in a few minutes?"

Harper shook his head and rose. "I suppose Wrinfield will be along to see you in a short time—he's bound to hear of your accident any moment and he doesn't know it was rigged, although you can tell him that. How much do you propose telling him?"

"Nothing. If I told him this suicidal scheme you have in mind for me he'd have this ship turned round in less time than it could take him to wash his hands of you."

The days passed uneventfully enough, if somewhat unsteady: the *Carpentaria*'s stabilisers didn't seem quite to understand what was expected of them. For the circus crew there was little enough to do other than feed the animals and keep their quarters clean. Those performers who could practise their esoteric arts practised them: those who couldn't possessed their souls in patience.

Bruno spent sufficient time with Maria to lend credence to the now almost universal belief among the circus people that here indeed was a romance that was steadily blossoming: what was even more intriguing that there seemed to be a distinct possibility that there might be two romances getting under way, for whenever Bruno was not with her Henry Wrinfield was solicitously unsparing in the attentions he paid her. And, as Bruno spent most of his time with Kan Dahn, Roebuck and Manuelo, Henry lacked neither the time nor the opportunity; he made the most of both.

The lounge bar, a large room that seated well over a hundred people, was invariably well patronised before dinner. On the third night out Henry sat at a remote corner table, talking earnestly to Maria. On the far side of the lounge Bruno sat playing cards with his three friends. Before the game, Roebuck and Manuelo spent their ritual ten minutes bemoaning the fact that they had no opportunity to practise their arts with lasso and knives respectively. Kan Dahn was in no way concerned about himself: clearly he was of the belief that his massive strength wasn't going to drain away from him in a matter of days: it was a belief that was widely shared.

Poker was their game. They played for low stakes and Bruno almost invariably won. The others claimed that this was because he could see through their cards, a claim that Bruno stoutly denied, although the fact that on the previous night, wearing a blindfold, he had won four consecutive hands put a query mark to his assertion. Not that he was ever in pocket at the end of a game: the winner paid for the drinks, and although he, Roebuck and Manuelo consumed very little, the capacity of Kan Dahn's three hundred pound frame for beer was awesome.

Kan Dahn drained another uncounted pint,

glanced across the room and tapped Bruno on the arm. "You'd best look at your defences, my lad. Your lady-love is under siege."

Bruno glanced across and said mildly: "She's not my lady-love. Even if she were I don't think Henry is the type to snatch her and run. Not that he could run very far in the middle of the Atlantic."

"Far enough," Roebuck said darkly.

"His fair-haired dear one is back in the States," Manuelo said severely. "Our little Maria is here. It makes a difference."

"Somebody," Roebuck said, "should tell her about Cecily."

"Our little Maria knows all about Cecily. She told me so herself. Even knows the kind of engagement ring she wears." Bruno glanced at the couple again, then returned to his cards. "I do not think that they are discussing affairs of the heart."

Maria and Henry were not, indeed, discussing affairs of the heart. Henry was being very very earnest, very intense and very genuinely concerned. He suddenly broke off, looked across to the bar, then back to Maria again.

"That proves it!" Henry's voice held a mixture of triumph and apprehension.

Maria said patiently: "What proves what, Henry?"

"The fellow I told you about. The fellow who's been following you. That steward that just entered and went behind the bar. The chap with the weasel face. He's no right to be here. He doesn't work here."

"Oh, come on now, Henry. He hasn't got a weasel face, just thin, that's all."

"He's English," Henry said inconsequentially.

"I've met some Englishmen who weren't criminals. And you haven't overlooked the fact that this is a British ship?"

Henry was persistent. "I've seen him follow you half a dozen times. I know, because I've followed the two of you." She looked at him in surprise, but this time without smiling. "He also follows my uncle."

"Ah!" She looked thoughtful. "His name's Wherry. He's a cabin steward."

"I told you he shouldn't be here. Keeping tabs on you, that's what." He checked himself. "A cabin steward. How do you know? Your cabin steward?"

"Your uncle's. That's where I saw him first. In your uncle's cabin." Her thoughtful expression deepened. "Now that you mention it, I have seen him around rather a lot. *And*, two or three times when I've been walking about, I turned around and found him close behind."

"You bet you did."

"And what's that meant to mean, Henry?"

"I don't know," he admitted. "But I'm making no mistake."

"Why should anyone follow me? Do you think he's a detective in disguise and I'm a wanted criminal? Or do I look like a counter-spy or a secret agent or Mata Hari fifty years on?"

Henry considered. "No, you don't look the part. Besides, Mata Hari was ugly. You're beautiful." He adjusted his glasses the better to confirm his judgment. "Really beautiful."

"Henry! Remember this morning? We had agreed to confine our discussions to intellectual matters."

"The hell with intellectual matters." Henry thought and weighed his words with care. "I really believe I'm falling in love with you." He thought some more.

"Fallen."

"I don't think Cecily would—"

"The hell with her, too—no, I didn't mean that. Sorry. Although I did mean what I said about you." He half turned in his seat. "Look, Wherry's leaving."

They watched him go, a small thin dark man with a small thin dark moustache. At his nearest approach to their table, which was about ten feet away, he flickered a glance at them then as quickly looked away again. Henry leaned back in his seat and gave her his "I told you so" look.

"A criminal. Written all over him. You saw that?"

"Yes." She was troubled. "But why, Henry, why?"

He shrugged. "Do you have any valuables? Any jewellery?"

"I don't wear jewellery."

Henry nodded his approval. "Jewellery is for women who need it. But when a person is as lovely as you are—"

"Henry, it's getting so I just can't talk to you. This morning I said it was a lovely day and you put on your soulful expression and made disparaging remarks about the day. When I commend my peach Melba you say it's not half so sweet as I am. And when we looked at the beautiful colourings of the sunset tonight—"

"I have a poetic soul. Ask Cecily. No, on second

thoughts, don't ask Cecily. I can see that I'm going to have to keep a very, very close eye on you."

"I should say that you are making a pretty good start already."

"Ah." An unrepentant Henry, eyes slightly glazed but not from alcohol, made no attempt to switch his adoring gaze to pastures less green. He said wistfully: "You know, I've always wanted to be someone's Sir Galahad."

"I wouldn't, if I were you, Henry. There's no place in the world today for Sir Galahads. Chivalry is dead, Henry. The lances and the bright swords and the days of knightly combat are gone: this is the era of the knife in the back."

Alas for Henry, all his senses, except that of sight, were temporarily in abeyance. Her words fell on deaf ears.

On the fourth night out Dr. Harper joined Bruno in his stateroom. He was accompanied by Carter, the purser, who had been so busy with the debugging equipment on the first night out. Carter extended his customary courteous good evening, wordlessly repeated the search performance, shook his head and left.

Harper nodded to the cocktail cabinet, poured himself a drink, savoured it and said with some satisfaction: "We will pick up your guns in Vienna."

"Guns?"

"Indeed."

"You have been in touch with the States? Doesn't the radio operator raise an eyebrow?"

It was Harper's night to indulge himself to a moderate degree. He smiled. He said: "I am my own radio operator. I have a very high-frequency radio transceiver, no bigger than the average book, which can't possibly interfere with normal ship's frequencies. As Charles says, it could reach the moon. Anyway, I transmit in code. Show you the thing sometime—in fact, I'll have to show it to you and explain its operation in case you have to use it. In case something should go wrong with me."

"What should go wrong with you?"

"What should have gone wrong with Pilgrim and Fawcett? Now, we'll be picking up two guns for you, not one, and that for a reason. The anaesthetic dart gun—the missiles are more like needles, actually—is the more effective, but the word is that Van Diemen has a long-standing heart condition. So, if you should have to quieten him, the use of a dart gun is, as they say, contra-indicated. For him, the gas gun. Have you figured out a way to get inside yet?"

"A battery-powered helicopter would be splendid, only there are no such things. No, I haven't figured out a way into the damned place yet."

"Early days and fingers crossed. You know you're slated to dine with me at the captain's table tonight?"

"No."

"Passengers are rotated for the privilege. A normal courtesy. See you then."

They had just seated themselves at the table when a steward approached, bent and whispered something discreetly into the captain's ear. The captain rose, excused himself and followed the steward from the dining saloon. He was back inside two or three minutes, looking more than vaguely perturbed.

"Odd," he said. "Very odd. Carter—you've met him, he's chief purser—claims that he has just been assaulted by some thug. 'Mugged,' I believe, is the American term for it. You know, caught round the neck from behind and choked. No marks on him, but he does seem a trifle upset."

Harper said: "Couldn't he just have taken a turn?"

"If he did, then his wallet left his inside pocket of its own volition."

"In which case he's been attacked and his wallet—minus the contents, of course—is now probably at the bottom of the Atlantic. Shall I have a look at him?"

"It might be wise. Berenson is holding hands with some silly old trout who thinks she's having a heart attack. Thank you, Doctor. I'll get a steward to take you."

Harper left. Bruno said: "That pleasant courteous man. Who would rob a person like that?"

"I don't think Carter's character would come into it. Just someone who was short of money and reasoned that if any person would be liable to be carrying money it would be the ship's purser. An unpleasant thing to have happen on one's ship—in fact I've never known or heard of an instance before. I'll have my chief officer and some men investigate."

Bruno smiled. "I hope we circus people don't automatically come under suspicion. Among some otherwise reasonable citizens our reputation is not what it could be. But I don't know more honest people."

"I don't know who is responsible, and the question, I'm afraid, is of academic importance anyway. I don't think my chief has a hope in hell of finding him."

Bruno leaned over the taffrail of the *Carpentaria,* gazing contemplatively at the slight phosphorescence of the ship's wake. He stirred and turned as someone came up beside him. He said: "Anyone in the vicinity?"

"No one," Manuelo said.

"No bother?"

"No bother." The startlingly white teeth gleamed in the darkness. "You were quite right. The unfortunate Mr. Carter does indeed take a regular—what do you call it—?"

"Constitutional."

"Right. Takes his constitutional at that time of evening on the boat deck. Lots of shadows on the boat deck. Kan Dahn kind of leaned on him a little bit, Roebuck took the purser's cabin keys, brought them down to me and kept watch in the passageway while I went inside. It didn't take long. There was a funny electrical gadget inside a brief-case—"

"I think I know about that. Looked like a small radio except there were no wave-bands on it?"

"Yes. What is it?"

"A device for locating listening devices. They're a very suspicious lot aboard this boat."

"With us around you're surprised?"

"What else?"

"There was fifteen hundred dollars, in tens, at the bottom of a trunk—"

"I didn't know about *that*. Used?"

"No. New. And in sequence."

"How careless."

"Looks like." He handed a piece of paper to Bruno. "I wrote down the serial numbers of the first and last numbers."

"Good, good. You're quite sure they were genuine notes?"

"My life on it. I wasn't in all that hurry and I passed one out to Roebuck. He agrees."

"That was all?"

"There were some letters addressed to him. Not to any particular address but to Poste Restante in a few cities, mostly London and New York."

"What language? English?"

"No. I didn't recognise it. The postmark said Gdynia. That would make it Polish, wouldn't it?"

"It would indeed. Then everything was left as found, door locked and the keys returned to the sleeping Mr. Carter."

Manuelo nodded. Bruno thanked him, left, returned to his stateroom, glanced briefly at the serial numbers on the piece of paper that Manuelo had given him, then flushed it down the toilet.

To no one's surprise, Carter's assailant was never found.

On the evening before their arrival in Genoa, Dr. Harper came to Bruno's stateroom. He helped himself to a scotch from Bruno's virtually untouched liquor cabinet.

He said: "How goes the thinking on this entry

business? Mine, I'm afraid, has bogged down to a halt."

Bruno said gloomily: "Maybe it would have been better, especially for the sake of my health, if mine had bogged down too."

Harper sat up in his armchair and pursed his lips. "You have an idea?"

"I don't know. A glimmering, perhaps. I was wondering—have you any further information for me? Anything at all? About the interior layout of the West building and how to gain access to the ninth floor. Take the roof. Is there any access by way of ventilator shafts, trap-doors or suchlike?"

"I honestly don't know."

"I think we can forget the ventilator shafts. In a maximum security place like this the air circulation probably vents through the side walls and would have impossibly narrow exit apertures. Trapdoors, I would have thought, they must have. How else could the guards get up to their towers or the electricians service the electric fence when the need arises. I can hardly see them climbing up ninety-feet-high vertical steel ladders bolted to an inside wall. Do you know whether the Lubylan runs to lifts?"

"That I do know. There's a stairs shaft runs from top to bottom in each building with two lifts on either side of the shafts."

"Presumably it services the ninth floor as well as the rest. That means that the lift-head—you know, where they have the pulley mechanism for the cables—must protrude above the roof. That could provide a way in."

"It would also provide an excellent way of having yourself crushed to death if you were descending the shaft as the lift came up. It's happened before, you know, and not seldom either, with service men working on top of a lift."

"That's a risk. Walking a frozen two-thousand-volt cable in a high wind—we have to assume the worst—isn't a risk? What's on the eighth floor? More laboratories?"

"Oddly, no. That belongs to the East building—the detention centre. The senior prison officers and the prison office staff sleep there—maybe they can't stand the sound of the screams, maybe they don't want to be around in the detention centre if the enemies of the State do manage to break loose—I don't know. All the prison offices and records offices are kept there. Apart from the guards' sleeping quarters and dining quarters, all of the detention centre is given over to cells. Apart, that is, from a few charming places in the basement which are euphemistically referred to as interrogation centres."

Bruno looked at him consideringly. "Would it be out of order for me to enquire where you get all this detailed information from? I thought that no stranger would ever be allowed inside and that no guard would ever dare talk."

"Not at all. We have, as they say, our man in Crau. Not an American, a native. He was imprisoned some fifteen years ago for some trifling political offence, became what we would call a trusty after a few years and had the complete run of the building. His privileged position did not affect in the slightest the complete and total hatred he nourishes for the regime in general and Lubylan and all those who work inside it in particular. He fell into our hands like an overripe apple from a tree. He still drinks with the guards and warders from the Lubylan and one way or another manages to keep us reasonably up to date with what's going on. It's over four years since he's been discharged but the guards still regard him as a trusty and talk freely, especially when he plies them with vodka. We provide the money for the vodka."

"It's a messy business."

"All espionage and counter-espionage is. The glamour quotient is zero."

"The problem still remains. There may just be a solution. I don't know. Have you mentioned any of this to Maria yet?"

"No. Plenty of time. The fewer people who know—"

"I'd like to talk to her tonight. May I?"

Harper smiled. "Three minds are better than two? That's hardly a compliment to me."

"If you only knew it, it is. I can't afford to have you too closely involved with anything I'm doing. You're the co-ordinator and the only person who really knows what is going on—I still don't believe that you have told me everything I might know, but it doesn't seem all that important any more. Besides, I have courted the young lady assiduously—although it was under instructions I haven't found the task too disagreeable—and people are accustomed to seeing us together now."

Harper smiled without malice. "They're also accustomed to seeing young Henry squiring her around too."

"I shall challenge him to a duel when we get to some suitably Central European background—the atmosphere has to be right. I don't need Maria's ideas. All I want from her is her co-operation. No point in discussing it with you until I have it."

"No harm. When?"

"After dinner."

"Where? Here?"

"Not here. It's perfectly proper for my doctor to come and see me—anxiously caring for one of the circus's prime properties. But, as you say—or as you infer from Carter's antics with his bug-detector—it's just possible that someone might be keeping a wary eye on me. I don't want them keeping a wary eye on her, too."

"Then I suggest her cabin."

Bruno thought. "I'll do that."

Before dinner, Bruno went into the lounge bar, located Maria sitting by herself at a small corner table, sat beside her and ordered a soft drink. He said: "This is intolerable. Incredible. Maria Hopkins sitting alone."

She said with some asperity: "And whose fault is that?"

"Never mine, surely?"

"I'm treated like a pariah, an outcast. There are lots of very nice men here who would love to buy me a drink and talk to me. But no, I'm the plague. The great Bruno might come in at any moment." She brooded a bit. "Or Henry. He's as bad. Not only is he the light and the joy of his uncle's heart—and it would be well to remember that his uncle is the big white chief—he's also developing a very intimidating line in scowls. The only person who doesn't give a damn is that enormous friend of yours. Do you know that he calls me your lady-love?"

"And are you? That's what's usually referred to as a keen, probing question."

She treated his remark with silent disdain.

"Ah, well. And where is the rival for my lady-love's hand tonight? I've just been talking about it with Dr. Harper. Henry and I are going to fight a duel when we get to the Carpathians. You should come and watch. After all, it's over you."

"Oh, do be quiet." She looked at him for a long moment, smiled widely in spite of herself and put her hand on his. "What's the masculine equivalent of 'lady-love'?"

"There isn't one or if there is I don't think I'd like to hear it. Where is Henry?"

"He's gone sleuthing." Subconsciously, she lowered her voice. "I think he's watching someone or shadowing someone. Henry has spent a great deal of time these past two days following someone he swears is following me."

Surprisingly, Bruno was not amused. He said: "Why didn't you tell me before?"

"I didn't think it important. I didn't take it seriously."

"Didn't? And now?"

"I'm just not sure."

"Why should anyone be following you?"

"If I knew I'd tell you, wouldn't I?"

"Would you?"

"Please."

"Have you told Dr. Harper?"

"No. That's the point. There's nothing to tell. I don't like being laughed at. I think Dr. Harper's got his reservations about me, anyway. I don't want him to think that I'm a bigger ninny than he already probably thinks I am."

"This mystery shadower. He has a name?"

"Yes. Wherry. A cabin steward. Small man, narrow face, very pale, narrow eyes, small black moustache."

"I've seen him. Your steward?"

"Mr. Wrinfield's."

Bruno was momentarily thoughtful, then appeared to lose interest. He raised his glass. "I'd like to see you after dinner. Your cabin, if you please."

She raised her glass and smiled. "And your good health, too."

Dinner over, Bruno and Maria made no secret of the fact that they were leaving together. This was commonplace, now, and no longer called for the raised eyebrow. Some twenty seconds after their departure Henry rose and sauntered from the dining saloon, leaving by the opposite door. Once outside he quickened his pace, crossed over to the other side, moved aft, descended a companionway and reached the passenger accommodations. Bruno and Maria were about fifty feet ahead of him. Henry moved in behind the companionway and stood in shadow.

Almost at once a figure emerged, or partially emerged from a side passage about twenty feet away on the left. He peered along the main passageway, saw Bruno and Maria and quickly withdrew into cover again but not so quickly that Henry couldn't recognise him. It was, unmistakably, Wherry. Henry experienced a very considerable degree of self-satisfaction.

Wherry ventured another look. Bruno and Maria were just disappearing round a corner to their left. Wherry moved out and followed them. Henry waited until he, too, had disappeared from sight, then moved out in stealthy pursuit. He reached the left-hand corner on soundless tiptoes, glanced round with one eye then immediately moved back into cover again. Wherry was less than six paces away, looking down a right-hand corridor. Henry didn't have to be told what Wherry was looking at—Maria's cabin was the fourth door down. When he looked again Wherry had vanished. Henry moved, took up the position Wherry had so recently occupied and did some more head-poking. Wherry was engaged in the undignified occupation of pressing his right ear hard against a cabin door. Maria's cabin. Henry drew back and waited. He was in no hurry.

Henry let thirty seconds pass then risked another look. The passageway was empty. Without haste Henry walked along the corridor, passed Maria's cabin—he could hear the soft murmur of voices—reached the end and dropped down another companionway. He hadn't spent two days so zealously—and, as he imagined, so unobtrusively—trailing Wherry without discovering where Wherry's quarters were. That that was where he had gone Henry did not for a moment doubt.

Henry was right. Wherry had indeed gone to his cabin and was apparently so confident of himself that he had even left the door ajar. That there may have been some other reason for this apparent carelessness did not occur to Henry. Wherry was sitting with his back three-quarters turned to him, a pair of earphones, the lead of which led to a radio, clamped over his head. There was nothing unusual in this; Wherry, as did all stewards, doubled up with one of his mates, and as they were frequently on different shifts and slept at different times, the earphones insured that one could listen to the radio without disturbing the other's sleep: it was standard practice on this and most passenger ships.

Maria sat on her cabin bed and stared at Bruno in shocked disbelief. Her face was drained of colour, leaving the eyes preternaturally huge. She said in a voice that was barely more than a whisper: "This is mad! It's crazy! It's suicidal!"

"It's all of that and a good deal else besides. But you have to appreciate that Dr. Harper is in an impossible spot. As ideas go, it was an ingenious one, a desperate ingenuity, mind you, but there were no other options open to him, at least none that he could see."

"Bruno!" She slipped off the bed and was on her knees beside his armchair, his left hand in both of hers: there was fear in her face and Bruno was uncomfortably aware that it wasn't fear for herself. "You'll be killed, you know you'll be killed. Don't. Please, please don't! No, Bruno. Nothing's worth your life, nothing! Oh, God, there isn't even a chance."

He looked at her in mild surprise. "And all the time I thought you were a tough young CIA agent."

"Well, I'm not. Tough, I mean." There was a sheen of tears in her eyes.

Almost absently, he stroked her hair. Her face was averted. "There might be another way, Maria."

"There can't be another way."

"Look." With his free hand he swiftly sketched a diagram. "Let's forget entrance via the power cable. The fact that those windows are barred may yet be the saving of us—well, me, anyway. I propose to go to this lane to the south of the research building. I'll take with me a length of rope with a padded hook at one end. A couple of casts and I should catch a bar on a first-floor window. I haul myself up to the first floor, unhook the rope, repeat the process and reach the second floor. And so on until I get to the top."

"Yes?" The scepticism now in her face hadn't replaced the fear, merely redoubled it. "And then?"

"I'll find some way of silencing the guard or guards in the corner tower."

"What is it, Bruno? What drives you? You are a driven man, don't you know that? You don't work for the CIA and this damnable anti-matter can't mean all the world to you. Yet I know—I don't think—I *know* you're willing to die to get inside that damnable prison. Why, Bruno, why?"

"I don't know." She couldn't see his face but for a moment it was disturbed, almost wary. "Perhaps you'd best go and ask the shades of Pilgrim and Fawcett."

"What are they to you? You hardly knew them." He made no reply. She went on wearily: "So you're going to silence the guards. How are you going to find a way of silencing two thousand volts of steel fencing?"

"I'll find a way, not by putting it out of action—that's impossible—but by by-passing it. But I'm going to need your co-operation and you might end up in prison."

"What kind of co-operation?" Her voice was toneless. "And what's prison if you're dead?"

Henry heard those words. Wherry had taken off his earphones to find some cigarettes and the conversation from Maria's cabin, faint and tinny and distorted though it was, was understandable and unmistakable. Henry craned his head a bit more and saw that the radio was not the only piece of electrical equipment in the cabin. There was a small tape recorder on the deck with both spools slowly turning.

Wherry found his cigarettes, lit one, resumed his seat, picked up the phones and was about to replace them on his head when Henry pushed the door wide and stepped inside. Wherry swung round, his eyes wide.

Henry said: "I'd like to have that recorder if you don't mind, Wherry."

"Mr. Wrinfield!"

"Yes, Mr. Wrinfield. Surprised? The recorder, Wherry." Involuntarily, as it seemed, Wherry switched his glance to a spot above Henry's left shoulder and Henry laughed. "Sorry, Wherry, but that's been done before."

Henry heard the last sound he was ever to hear, an almost soundless swish in the air behind him. His ears registered it for the fleeting fraction of a second but his body had no time to react. His legs crumpled and Wherry caught him just as he struck the deck.

"Didn't you hear me?" Maria's voice was still colourless, without expression. "What's prison, what's anything, if you're dead? Can't you think of me? All right, all right, so I'm being selfish, but can't you think of me?"

"Stop it! Stop it! Stop it!" He'd intended his voice to be harsh or at least cold but it sounded neither harsh nor cold to him. "We arrive in Crau on a Thursday and leave on the following Wednesday—it's the longest stop-over of the tour. We have shows Friday, Saturday, Monday and Tuesday. Sunday is free. So on Sunday we hire a car and have ourselves a little excursion into the country. I don't know how far we'll be allowed to go, I believe restrictions have been relaxed, but it doesn't matter. We can always travel around in ever-narrowing circles. What does matter—and this will have to be after dusk—is that on the way back we reconnoitre Lubylan and see if they have guards patrolling outside. If there are, I'll need your help."

"*Please* give up this crazy idea, Bruno. Please."

"When I'm climbing up the south side of the research building you'll be standing at the corner of the south lane and the main west street. This, I didn't mention, will be after the last show on the Tuesday night. The hired car, which I trust will be comprehensively insured, will be parked a few feet away in the main street. The windows will be open and you'll have a small can of gasoline ready on the front seat.

If you see a guard approaching, reach for the can, pour some fuel, not too much, on the front and rear upholstery, throw in a lighted match and stand smartly back. This will not only distract all attention but the blaze will cast such a heavy shadow round the corner that I should be able to climb in almost complete darkness. I'm afraid you could be caught and questioned, but the combination of Mr. Wrinfield and Dr. Harper should secure your release." He considered this for a moment. "On the other hand, it may not."

"You're quite mad. Quite."

"Too late to change my spots." He stood up and she with him. "Must get in touch with Dr. Harper now."

She reached up and locked her fingers round the back of his neck. Her voice reflected the misery in her face.

"Please. Please, Bruno. Just for me. Please."

He put his hands on her forearms but not to pull the fingers apart. He said: "Look, my lady-love, we're only *supposed* to be falling in love." His voice was gentle. "This way there's a chance."

She said dully: "Either way you're a dead man."

Halfway to his stateroom Bruno found a phone and called Dr. Harper. Harper was eventually located in the dining saloon. Bruno said. "My ankle's acting up again."

"Ten minutes and I'll be across."

And in ten minutes' time Harper was in the stateroom as promised. He made free of Bruno's liquor cabinet, made himself at armchair ease and heard out

Bruno's account of his conversation with Maria. At the end, and after due thought, he said: "I'd say it gives you at least a fighting chance. Better than mine, I must admit. When do you propose to carry this into effect?"

"The final decision is, of course, yours. I'd thought of making the reconnaissance on Sunday and making the entry on Tuesday night. Late Tuesday night. That seems like the best plan, the best time, for we will be leaving the following day and that will give the police less time for questioning if questioning there will be."

"Agreed."

"If we have to make a break for it—you have escape plans?"

"We have. But they're not finished yet. I'll let you know when they are."

"Coming via your little transceiver? Remember you promised to show me that some time."

"I shall. I've got to—I told you. I'll do three things at one time—show you the transceiver, give you the guns and give you the escape plans. I'll let you know when. What does Maria think of your idea?"

"A marked lack of enthusiasm. But then she was hardly over the moon about yours either. But, however unwillingly, she'll co-operate." Bruno stopped and looked around him in some puzzlement.

Harper said: "Something's wrong?"

"Not necessarily wrong. But the ship's slowing down. Can't you hear it? Can't you feel it? The engine revolutions have dropped right away. Why should a ship stop—well, anyway, slow down—in the middle of the Mediterranean? Well, I suppose we'll find out in good enough time."

They found out immediately. The door was unceremoniously thrown open, with a force sufficient to send it juddering on its hinges. Tesco Wrinfield almost ran into the room.

His face was grey, his breathing heavy and short at the same time. He said: "Henry's missing. He's missing! We can't find him anywhere."

Bruno said: "Is that why the *Carpentaria* is slowing down?"

"We've been searching everywhere." He gulped down the glass of brandy which Harper had handed to him. "The crew has searched, is still searching everywhere. There's just no trace of him. Vanished, just vanished."

Harper was soothing. He glanced at his watch. "Come on, now, Mr. Wrinfield, that couldn't have been more than fifteen minutes ago. And this is a very big ship."

"With a very big crew," Bruno said. "They have a standardised routine for this sort of thing—searching for a missing passenger, that is. From the lifeboats to the holds they can cover every conceivable area in less time than you would believe possible." He turned to the distraught Wrinfield. "Sorry I can't offer you any comfort, sir—but is the captain slowing down so as not to get too far away from the place where your nephew *may* have fallen overboard?"

"I think so." Wrinfield listened. "We're picking up speed, aren't we?"

"And turning," Bruno said. "I'm afraid that means, sir, that the captain is pretty sure that Henry is not aboard. He'll be taking the *Carpentaria* through a hundred eighty degrees and tracking back the way we came. If Henry *is* overboard he may well be swimming or afloat. This sort of thing has happened before: there's always a chance, Mr. Wrinfield."

Wrinfield looked at him with distraught disbelief on his face and Bruno did not blame him: he didn't believe it himself either.

They went on deck. The *Carpentaria,* retracing the course it had come, was making perhaps ten knots, no more. A motorised lifeboat, already manned, was swung out on its davits. Two powerful searchlights, one on either wing of the bridge, shone straight ahead. In the bows two seamen directed the beams of their portable searchlights almost vertically downwards. A little further aft two seamen on either side waited with rope-attached and illuminated life-belts. Beyond them still, rope-ladders, picked out in the beams of torches, hung over the side.

Twenty minutes of steadily mounting tension and dwindling hope passed. Wrinfield abruptly left his two companions and made his way to the bridge. He found the master on the starboard wing, binoculars to his eyes. He lowered them as Wrinfield came by his side and shook his head slowly.

He said: "Your nephew is not on the ship, Mr. Wrinfield. That is for certain." The captain looked at his watch. "It is now thirty-eight minutes since your nephew was last seen. We are now at the precise spot where we were thirty-eight minutes ago. If he is alive—I'm sorry to be so blunt, sir—he cannot be beyond this point."

"We could have missed him?"

"Most unlikely. Calm sea, windless night, no currents hereabouts worth speaking of and the Mediterranean, as you know, is virtually tideless. He would have been on the line we have taken." He spoke to an officer by his side: the man disappeared inside the bridge.

Wrinfield said: "And what now?"

"We'll take her round in a tight circle. Then in widening concentric circles, three, maybe four. Then, if we turn up nothing, we go back at the same speed to the spot where we turned."

"And that will be it?"

"That, I'm afraid, will be it."

"You are not very hopeful, Captain."

"I am not hopeful."

It took the *Carpentaria* forty minutes to complete the search pattern and return to the position where she had turned round. Maria, standing with Bruno in the shadow of a lifeboat, shivered as the throb of the engines deepened and the *Carpentaria* began to pick up speed.

She said: "That's it, then, isn't it?"

"The searchlights have gone out."

"And it's my fault. It's all my fault." Her voice was husky.

"Don't be silly." He put his arm round her. "There's no way this could have been prevented."

"It could! It could! I didn't take him seriously enough. I—well, I didn't quite laugh at him—but, well, I didn't listen to him either. I should have told you two days ago." She was openly weeping now. "Or Dr. Harper. He was *such* a nice person."

Bruno heard the word "was" and knew she had finally accepted what he himself had accepted an hour ago. He said gently: "It would be nice if you spoke to Mr. Wrinfield."

"Yes. Yes, of course. But—well, I don't want to see people. Couldn't we—I don't like asking, but if he could come here—if you could bring him and—"

"Not on your sweet life, Maria. You're not staying here alone."

He sensed her staring at him in the darkness. She whispered: "Do you think that someone—"

"I don't know what to think because I don't know how or why Henry died. All I'm certain of is it was no accident: he died because he found out that someone was too interested in you and because he must have made the mistake of finding out too much. I've been asking one or two questions. Apparently he left the dining saloon just after we did. He left by another door but I suppose he wanted to avoid any obvious connections. I'm sure he wasn't directly following us —he may have taken a dim view of my association with you, but he was straight, honest and the last Peeping Tom one could imagine. I think he was acting in his self-appointed guardian role. I think he was checking to see if anyone was following or watching us—Henry had a romantic streak and this sort of thing would have appealed to him. I can only assume that he did indeed find some such person, and that that person—or another person, God only knows how many unpleasant characters there may be aboard —found Henry in a highly compromising situation. Compromising to the villains, I mean. But that doesn't alter the fact that the primary object of attention was you. Just bear in mind that you can't swim very far if the back of your head has been knocked in in advance." He produced a handkerchief and carried out running repairs to the tear-stained face. "You come along with me."

As they walked along the boat-deck they passed and greeted Roebuck. Bruno made an unobtrusive follow-me gesture with his hand. Roebuck stopped, turned and sauntered along about ten paces behind them.

Wrinfield was finally located in the radio office, arranging for the dispatch of cablegrams to Henry's parents and relatives. Now that the initial shock was over Wrinfield was calm and self-composed and in the event he had to spend considerably more time in comforting Maria than she him. They left him there and found Roebuck waiting outside.

Bruno said: "Where's Kan Dahn?"

"In the lounge. You'd think there's a seven-year famine of beer just round the corner."

"Would you take this young lady down to her cabin, please?"

"Why?" Maria wasn't annoyed, just puzzled. "Am I not capable—"

Roebuck took a firm grip on her arm. "Mutineers walk the plank, young lady."

Bruno said: "And lock your door. How long will it take you to get to bed?"

"Ten minutes."

"I'll be along in fifteen."

Maria unlocked the door at the sound of Bruno's voice. He entered, followed by Kan Dahn, who was carrying a couple of blankets under his arm. Kan Dahn smiled genially at her, then wedged his massive bulk into the armchair and carefully arranged the blankets over his knees.

Bruno said: "Kan Dahn finds his own quarters a bit cramped. He thought he'd take a rest down here."

Maria looked at them, first in protest, then in perplexity, then shook her head helplessly, smiled and said nothing. Bruno said his good night and left.

Kan Dahn reached out, turned down the rheostat on the flexible bedside light and angled the remaining dim glow so that it was away from the girl's face and leaving him in deep shadow. He took her hand in his massive paw.

"Sleep well, my little one. I don't want to make a thing out of this but Kan Dahn is here."

"You can't sleep in that awful chair?"

"Not can't. Won't. I'll sleep tomorrow."

"You haven't locked the door."

"No," he said happily. "I haven't, have I?"

She was asleep in minutes and no one, most fortunately for the state of his continued good health, came calling on her that night.

6

The arrival, unloading and disembarkation at Genoa were smooth and uneventful and took place in a remarkably short space of time. Wrinfield was his usual calm, efficient and all-overseeing self and to look at him as he went about his business it would have been impossible to guess that his favourite nephew, who had been much more like a son to him, had died the previous night. Wrinfield was a showman first, last and all the way between: in the hackneyed parlance the show had to go on, and as long as Wrinfield was there that it would most certainly do.

The train, with the help of a small shunting engine, was assembled and hauled to a shunting yard about a mile away where some empty coaches and provisions for animals and humans were already waiting. By late afternoon the last of the preparations were complete, the small diesel shunter disengaged itself and was replaced by the giant Italian freight locomotive that was to haul them over the many mountains that lay in their way. In the gathering dusk they pulled out for Milan.

The swing through Europe, which was to cover ten countries—three in Western Europe, seven in Eastern Europe—turned out to be something more than a resounding success. It resembled a triumphal progress, and as the circus's fame travelled before it the welcome, the enthusiasm, the adulation became positively embarrassing until the stage was reached that there were half a dozen applications for each seat available at any performance—and some of the auditoriums were huge, some bigger than any in the United States. At dingy sidings in big cities they were greeted and seen off by crowds bigger than those paying homage to the latest fabulous group of singers—or cup-winning football teams—at international airports.

Tesco Wrinfield, determinedly and with a conscious effort of will, had put the past behind him. Here he was in his element. He revelled in solution of the complexities of the vast logistical problems involved. He knew Europe, especially Eastern Europe, where he had recruited most of his outstanding acts, as well as any European on the train and certainly far better than any of his executives or American-born artistes and workers. He knew that those audiences were more sophisticated about and more appreciative of the finer arts of the circus than American and Canadian audiences, and when those peoples' papers increasingly referred to his pride and joy as the greatest circus of all time it was undiluted balm to his showman's heart: even more heady, were that possible, were the increasing references to himself as the greatest showman on earth. Nor was he displeased with the pragmatic side of it all: the packed houses and the very high profits made ledger books a positive pleasure to peruse: one cannot be a great showman without being a great businessman as well. It came to the stage that he began calculating that, even without the United States Government backing he could still, America to America, have made a handsome profit on the tour. Not, of course, that the United States Government would be apprised of this.

At least as happy were those of his artistes—over half of them—who came from Eastern Europe. For them, especially for the Hungarians, Bulgarians, and Romanians, whose circus training schools were the best in Europe and probably in the world, this was the long-promised home-coming. In front of their own people they excelled themselves, reaching heights of professional brilliance never attained before. The morale in a top circus is always high: even so, Wrinfield had never seen those people so happy and contented.

They swung through Northern Italy, Yugoslavia, Bulgaria, Romania and Hungary, then across the Curtain back into Austria. It was after the final show of their first day in Vienna, the finale of which had been greeted with the now standard rapturous ovation, that Harper—who had kept their contacts on the Continent to the barest minimum—approached

Bruno. He said: "Come to my compartment when you are ready."

When Bruno arrived, Harper said without preamble: "I promised you I'd show you three things in one night. Here they are." He unclipped the bottom of his medical bag and drew out a metal container smaller even than a box of Kleenex tissues. "A little transistorised beauty. Earphones and mike. This switch is for power. This button is for a combination of preselected wavelength and call-up—the receiver in Washington is manned twenty-four hours a day. This spring-loaded lever is for speak-transmit. Simple."

"You said something about a code."

"I won't burden you with that. I know if I wrote it out you could commit it to memory in nothing flat, but the CIA has a thing about committing codes to paper, however temporarily. Anyway, if you do have to use this machine—which would mean, unfortunately for me, that I would no longer be around—you wouldn't want to bother with code anyway. You just shout 'Help!' in plain English.

"It's on this machine that I received confirmation of our escape route instructions today—this evening, in fact. There's a NATO exercise taking place in the Baltic in about ten days' time. An unspecified naval vessel—they're a very cagey lot in Washington; I assume it's American but I don't even know what type of craft it is—will be standing by or cruising off the coast from the Friday night until the following Friday. It carries an Air-Sea Rescue helicopter. It will land at a place I'll show you when we get there—I don't consider it wise to carry maps on me and, besides, I can't properly locate it until we get there. The ship is tuned to the same wave-length as Washington. We press this top button on the transceiver here—just as simple as that—and the helicopter comes a-running."

"All seems perfectly straightforward. You do seem to have this organised. You know, I'm beginning to think that the government regards Van Diemen's pieces of paper as very valuable indeed."

"One gathers that impression. By the way, I'm curious. How long does your memory span last?"

"As long as I want."

"So you'll be able to memorise the contents of those papers and reproduce them, say, a year later?"

"I should think so."

"Let's hope that's the way it's going to be—that you're going to be given the chance to reproduce them, I mean. Let's hope nobody ever finds out that you got in there, did your mentalist bit and left unseen. Let's hope, in other words, that you don't have to use those." From the breast pocket of his jacket Harper unclipped a couple of pens, one black, one red. They were of the heavy felt-Biro type with the release button at the top. "I picked these up in town today. I don't have to tell you where I picked them up."

Bruno looked at the pens then at Harper. "What on earth would I want to use those things for?"

"Whatever the faults of our science and research departments, it's not lack of imagination. They positively dote on dreaming up these little toys. You don't think I'm going to let you cross two Eastern frontiers with a couple of Peacemaker colts strapped to your waist? These are guns. Yes, guns. The red one is the nasty one, the one with the anaesthetic-tipped needles which are not so healthy for those with heart conditions: the other one is the gas gun."

"So small?"

"With the micro-miniaturisation techniques available today, those are positively bulky. The needle gun has an effective range of forty feet, the gas gun of not more than four. Operation is simplicity itself. Depress the button at the top and the gun is armed: press the pocket clip and the gun is fired. Stick them in your outside pocket. Let people get used to the sight of them. Now listen carefully while I outline the plans for Crau."

"But I thought you had already agreed to the plan—my plan."

"I did and I do. This is merely a refinement of the original part of that plan. You may have wondered why the CIA elected to send with you a medical person. When I have finished you will understand."

Some four hundred and fifty miles to the north, three uniformed men sat in a brightly lit, windowless and very austere room, the furniture of which consisted mainly of metal filing cabinets, a metal table and some metal-framed chairs. All three were dressed in uniform. From the insignia they wore, one was a colonel, the second a captain, the third a sergeant. The first was Colonel Serge Sergius, a thin, hawk-faced man with seemingly lidless eyes and a gash where his mouth should have been: his looks perfectly befitted his occupation, which was that of a very important functionary in the secret police. The second, Captain Kodes, was his assistant, a well-built athletic man in his early thirties, with a smiling face and cold blue eyes. The third, Sergeant Angelo, was remarkable for one thing only, but that one thing was remarkable enough. At six feet three, Angelo was considerably too broad for his height, a massively muscular man who could not have weighed less than two hundred and fifty pounds. Angelo had one function and one only in life—he was Sergius's personal bodyguard. No one could have accused Sergius of choosing without due care and attention.

On the table a tape recorder was running. A voice said: "and that is all we have for the moment." Kodes leaned forward and switched off the recorder.

Sergius said: "And quite enough. All the information we want. Four different voices. I assume, my dear Kodes, that if you were to meet the owners of those four voices you could identify them immediately?"

"Without the shadow of a doubt, sir."

"And you, Angelo?"

"No question, sir." Angelo's gravelly booming voice appeared to originate from the soles of his enormous boots.

"Then please go ahead, Captain, for the reservation of our usual rooms in the capital—the three of us and the cameraman. Have you chosen him yet, Kodes?"

"I thought young Nicolas, sir. Extraordinarily able."

"Your choice." Colonel Sergius's lipless mouth parted about a quarter of an inch, which meant that he was smiling. "Haven't been to the circus for thirty years—circuses had ceased to exist during the war—but I must say I'm looking forward with almost childish enthusiasm to this one. Especially one which is as highly spoken of as this one is. Incidentally, Angelo, there is a performer in this circus whom I'm sure you will be most interested to see, if not to meet."

"I do not care to see or meet anyone from an American circus, sir."

"Come, come, Angelo, one must not be so chauvinistic."

"Chauvinistic, Colonel?"

Sergius made to explain then decided against the effort. Angelo was possessed of many attributes but a razor-sharp intelligence was not among them.

"There are no nationalities in a circus, Angelo, only artistes, performers: the audience does not care whether the man on the trapeze comes from Russia or the Sudan. The man I refer to is called Kan Dahn and they say that he is even bigger than you. He is billed as the strongest man in the world."

Angelo made no reply, merely inflated his enormous chest to its maximum fifty-two inches and contented himself with a smile of wolfish disbelief.

The three-day stay in Vienna was by now the inevitable enormous success. From there the circus moved north and, after only one stop-over, arrived in the city where Sergius and his subordinates had moved to meet them.

At the evening performance, those four had taken the best seats, about six rows back facing the centre of the centre ring. All four were in civilian clothes and all four were unmistakably soldiers in civilian clothes. One of them, immediately after the beginning of the performance, produced a very expensive-looking camera with a telephoto lens, and the sight of this produced a senior uniformed police officer in very short order indeed. The taking of photographs was officially discouraged, while with Westerners the illegal possession of an undeclared camera, if discovered, was a guarantee of arrest and trial: every camera aboard the circus train had been impounded on entering the country and would not be returned until the exit frontier had been crossed.

The policeman said: "The camera please: and your papers."

"Officer." The policeman turned towards Sergius and gave him the benefit of his cold insolent policeman's stare, a stare that lasted for almost a full second before he swallowed what was obviously a painful lump in his throat. He moved in front of Sergius and spoke softly.

"Your pardon, Colonel. I was not notified."

"Your headquarters were informed. Find the incompetent and punish him."

"Sir. My apologies for—"

"You're blocking my view."

And, indeed, the view was something not to be blocked. No doubt inspired by the fact they were being watched by connoisseurs, and wildly enthusiastic connoisseurs at that, the company had in recent weeks gone from strength to strength, honing and refining and polishing their acts, continually inventing more difficult and daring feats until they had arrived at a now almost impossible level of perfection. Even Sergius, who was normally possessed of a mind like a refrigerated computer, gave himself up entirely to the fairyland that was the circus. Only Nicolas, the young—and very presentable—photographer, had his mind on other things, taking an almost non-stop series of photographs of all the main artistes in the circus. But even he forgot his camera and his assignment as he stared—as did his companions—in total disbelief as The Blind Eagles went through their suicidal aerial routine.

It was shortly after their performance that a nondescript individual approached Sergius and murmured: "Two rows back, sir, ten seats to your left." A brief nod was Sergius's only acknowledgment.

Towards the very end of the performance Kan Dahn, who appeared to grow fitter with the passing of every day, went through his paces. Kan Dahn spurned the use of props such as iron bars and bar-bells: a five-year-old could tie an iron bar in knots and lift a massive four-hundred-pound bar-bell, provided they were made of the right material, which could be anything except iron. He invariably worked with human beings: creatures who ran, jumped and turned cartwheels could not very well be made of feather-weight plastic.

As a finale, Kan Dahn paraded around the centre ring, with a heavy wooden pole resting in a yoke on his shoulders. On either side of the yoke sat five circus girls. If Kan Dahn was aware of the presence of their weight he showed no signs of it. Occasionally, he stopped to scratch the back of his left calf with his right instep. Sergius leaned across Kodes and spoke to Angelo, who was watching the spectacle with an air of determined indifference.

"Big, isn't he, Angelo?"

"All show muscle. Puffy. I once saw an old man in

Athens, seventy-five if he was a day, and not a kilo, I swear, over fifty, carrying a grand piano the length of a street. Friends must have put it on his back—he could never have straightened his legs under the load —and if he didn't keep them straight he would have collapsed."

Even as he spoke, Kan Dahn started climbing a massive stepladder in the centre of the ring. The platform on top was about three feet square. Kan Dahn reached this without any apparent difficulty, stepped on to an inset turntable, and by progressive twisting of his tree-trunk legs set the turntable in circular motion, slowly speeding up until the girls on the outer ends of the pole were no more than coloured kaleidoscopic blurs. Gradually he slowed, came to a stop, descended the ladder, knelt, then bowed his shoulders until the feet of the circus girls touched the sawdust. Sergius leaned across again.

"Could your old friend in Athens have done that with his piano?" Angelo made no reply. "Do you know that they say that he can do that with fourteen girls but the management won't allow him because they say nobody will believe it?" Angelo remained silent.

The performance ended and the rapturous applause, a standing ovation, lasted several minutes. When the audience started filing out, Sergius looked for and located Wrinfield and by judging his pace contrived to meet him at the exit gangway. He said: "Mr. Wrinfield?"

"Yes. I'm sorry, should I know you?"

"We haven't met." Sergius pointed to the picture on the front of the souvenir programme he carried.

"The likeness, you will agree, is unmistakable. My name is Colonel Sergius." They shook hands formally. "Stupendous, Mr. Wrinfield. Impossible. Had anyone told me that such a show existed I would have called him a liar to his face." Wrinfield beamed. Beethoven's Ninth left him cold—this was the music that reached his heart. "I've been a devotee of the circus ever since I was a young boy"—Sergius was as fluent a liar as the next man and a great deal more so than most—"but never in my life have I seen anything like this."

Wrinfield beamed some more. "You are too kind, Colonel."

Sergius shook his head sadly. "I wish I had the gift with words the way you have with those marvellous performers of yours. But that is not the sole reason for introducing myself. Your next stop, I know, is Crau." He produced a card. "I am the Chief of Police there." Sergius carried a considerable variety of cards with him. "Whatever I can do, I am at your service. Ask and it's done and I shall consider it a privilege. Not that I shall ever be very far from your side. It is my intention to attend every single performance, for I know I shall never see the like again. For the duration of your stay, crime in Crau can reign unchecked."

"Again, you are too kind. Colonel Sergius, you shall be my personal—and, I hope, permanent—guest at the circus. I would be honoured—" He broke off and looked at the three men who showed no intention of moving on. "They are with you, Colonel?"

"How thoughtless of me. I'm afraid I quite got carried away." Sergius performed the introductions while Wrinfield introduced Harper, who had been seated next to him.

Wrinfield went on: "As I was about to say, Colonel, I would be honoured if you and your men would join us in my office for a glass of your national drink." Sergius said that the honour would be entirely theirs. It was all very cordial.

In the office, one glass became two and then three. Nicolas, permission given, clicked his camera constantly, not forgetting to take at least a dozen of a smilingly protesting Maria, who had been seated behind her desk when they had entered.

Wrinfield said: "I wonder, Colonel, if you would like to meet some of our performers?"

"You're a mind-reader, Mr. Wrinfield! I must confess that I did have that very thought in mind but I didn't dare presume—I mean, I have sufficiently trespassed upon your hospitality—"

"Maria." Wrinfield rattled off a list of names. "Go to the dressing-rooms and ask them if they would be kind enough to come and visit our distinguished guest." Wrinfield, in recent weeks, had fallen victim to a certain Mid-European floweriness of speech.

And so they came to see the distinguished guest—Bruno and his brothers, Neubauer, Kan Dahn, Ron Roebuck, Manuelo, Malthius and half a dozen others. Apart from a certain reserve in Angelo's attitude when he greeted Kan Dahn, everything was very pleasant indeed, fulsome congratulations offered and as modestly received. Sergius did not overstay his welcome and left almost immediately after the last handshake, he and Wrinfield exchanging mutual expressions of goodwill and cordial anticipation of their next meeting.

Sergius had a large black limousine waiting outside, with a uniformed police chauffeur and a dark man in dark clothes beside him. After about a quarter of a mile, Sergius stopped the car and issued certain instructions to the plainclothes man, whom he addressed as Alex. Alex nodded and left the car.

Back in the hotel suite, Sergius said to Kodes and Angelo: "You had no trouble in matching the voices with the tapes?" Both men shook their heads. "Good. Nicolas, how long will it take you to develop those photographs?"

"To develop? Within the hour, sir. Printing will take considerably longer."

"Just print those of Mr. Wrinfield, Dr. Harper, the girl—Maria, isn't it?—and the leading circus performers." Nicolas left and Sergius said: "You may leave too, Angelo. I'll call you."

Kodes said: "Is one permitted to ask the object of this exercise?"

"One is permitted. I was about to tell you, which is why I asked Angelo to leave. A loyal soul, but one does not wish to overburden his mind with complexities."

Bruno and Maria, for the first time walking arm in arm, made their way along the ill-lit street, talking with apparent animation. Some thirty yards behind them Alex followed with the unobtrusive casualness of one who has had long practice in following people without calling attention to himself. He slowed his pace as the couple ahead turned through a doorway with an incomprehensible neon sign above.

The café was ill-lit and smoke-filled from an evil-smelling brown coal fire—the outside temperature hovered near the freezing point—but cosy and comfortable enough if one had a gas-mask ready to hand. It was half full. Seated in a wall booth were Manuelo and Kan Dahn, the former with a coffee, Kan Dahn with two litres of beer. Kan Dahn's legendary consumption of beer was excused—by Kan Dahn—on the grounds that he required it to keep his strength up: it certainly never affected his performance. Bruno spoke briefly to them and asked to be excused for not joining them. Kan Dahn smirked and said that that was perfectly all right by them: Bruno led Maria to a corner table. Only a few seconds later Roebuck sauntered in, acknowledged their presence with a wave of his hand and sat down with his two companions. The three of them talked desultorily, then started, casually at first, then with increasing urgency, to search through their pockets: from where Bruno sat it would appear that a certain degree of acrimony, not to say downright recrimination, had crept into their conversation. Finally Roebuck scowled, made a dismissive gesture, rose and crossed to Bruno's table.

He said sadly: "Roebuck, begging for alms. Not one of us bothered to check if the others were carrying money. As it turns out, we don't have a cent. Rather, we do have thousands of cents, but we doubt whether they'll accept dollars here and Kan Dahn appears to be against washing up in the kitchen. Now, if I had comrades in distress—"

Bruno smiled, brought out a wallet, handed some

notes to Roebuck, who thanked him and left. Bruno and Maria ordered an omelette apiece.

Alex, shivering in the cold on the pavement, waited until the food had been served, crossed the street and went into a phone booth. He fed in money, dialled a number and said: "Alex."

"Yes?"

"I followed the man and girl to the Black Swan. They're beginning to eat, so it looks as if they'll be there for some time yet. They spoke to two other people, at another table, after their arrival, before going to their own place."

"You sure you have the right ones?"

"I have their photographs, Colonel. A third man came in shortly after the man and girl had sat down at their own table. He sat with the other two men for some time then went across to this man Bruno. He seemed to be borrowing money, at least I saw notes change hands."

Sergius said: "Do you know any of those three men?"

"No, sir. But one of them I'd recognise if I didn't see him again for twenty years. A giant, the biggest man I've ever seen, bigger even than Angelo."

"I won't award myself any prizes for guessing who that is. Come back here. No, wait. Stay out of sight so that no one inside the café can see you. I'll send Vladimir and Josef down to relieve you. I'll give them their instructions. You just have to point those people out to them. A car will be there in a few minutes."

Inside the café, Maria said: "What's wrong, Bruno?"

"What should be wrong?"

"You look troubled."

"I am troubled. D-day approaches with uncommon haste. Just about a week now. Wouldn't you be troubled if you had to get inside that damned Lubylan?"

"It's not just that. You've become remote from me. Cool. Distant. I've done something you don't like? Said something wrong?"

"Don't be silly."

She put a hand on his arm. "Please."

"Is this affection? Or something more? Or something else?"

"Why do you hurt me so?"

"I don't want to." His voice lacked the ring of conviction. "Have you ever been an actress?"

She took her hand away. There was bafflement in her face, and pain. She said: "I can't think what I've done wrong, I can't think what I've said wrong—and you *do* want to hurt me. Suddenly you want to hurt me. Why don't you slap me, then? Right here in public? That way you can hurt both me and my pride. I don't understand you, I just don't understand you." She pushed back her chair. "I can find the way."

It was Bruno's turn to take her hand. Whether this was affection, appeal or just an attempt to restrain her it was difficult to say. He said: "I wish I could."

"Could what?"

"Find the way." He looked at her, his brow slightly corrugated. "You've been how long with the CIA?"

"Nearly four years." The bafflement was back in her face.

"Who appointed you to this particular job?"

"Dr. Harper. Why?"

"I thought it was this man called Charles."

"He appointed me. Dr. Harper made the suggestion. He was very insistent that I should be the one who should come along on this trip."

"I'll bet he was."

"What's that supposed to mean?"

"Merely congratulations. To Dr. Harper. On his impeccable good taste. Who's Charles?"

"Just Charles."

"He's not Charles. He has another name."

"Why didn't you ask him?"

"He wouldn't have told me. I'd hoped you might."

"You know that we can't divulge things such as that."

"Well, I like that. I'm going to risk my damned life for the CIA and they can't even trust me with a straightforward piece of information like that. I thought that at least by this time I could trust you or you could trust me. It seems I was wrong—on the second count, anyway. You're willing that I should die but you're not even willing to tell me that. Trust and faith and loyalty—those are great things, aren't they? Or used to be. There doesn't seem to be too much of it around nowadays."

"His name is Admiral George C. Jamieson."

Bruno looked at her for a long moment then his face slowly broke into a wide smile that transformed his whole expression. She snatched her hand away and looked at him furiously. At their table Kan Dahn nudged Roebuck and Manuelo in turn: all three watched the scene with interest.

"You horrid man! You deceitful, devious, conniving human being—if I can call you that! And you had the audacity to ask me if I had ever been an actress. I never have been but even if I had I could never hold a candle to you as an actor. Why did you do it? I don't deserve that."

Roebuck said: "She's getting madder by the minute."

"How little you know of human nature," Kan Dahn said. "She'll be proposing to him inside thirty seconds."

Bruno said: "I apologise. But I had to."

"Had to find out if I would trust you?"

"It's terribly important to me. Please forgive me." He took her unresisting hand again and examined its ringless state with care. He said: "It looks pretty bare to me."

"What does?"

"You know that we're only supposed to be in love?"

"Yes." It was Maria's turn to be silent. "Or do you think we should stop supposing?" Her voice was hesitant, unsure.

"I don't think. I know. Do you love me, Maria?"

The voice was a whisper but the answer immediate. "Yes." She looked at her left hand and smiled. "It does look a little bare, doesn't it?"

Kan Dahn leant back against the booth in an expansive fashion. "What did your Uncle Kan Dahn tell you? Somebody buy me a drink."

Bruno said: "Sure?"

"Even the most intelligent man can ask the most stupid questions. Can't you see it?"

"I think I can. At least, I hope I can."

"I've been in love with you for weeks." She had stopped smiling now. "In the early days I used to watch you blindfolded on that trapeze. Then after a while I had to leave the auditorium and go outside and be sick. Now I don't dare go inside at all and I'm still sick. A fraction of a second too early or too late . . ." She broke off and her eyes were wet. "But I can still hear the music, *your* music, and when it begins I die inside."

"Will you marry me?"

"Of course I will, you lunkhead." She was crying openly now.

"There's no need for such language. And I'd like to point out that Kan Dahn, Manuelo and Ron are taking the greatest interest in the proceedings. I have a feeling they're taking bets on us. I've also got the feeling that I'm going to suffer when they get me alone."

"I can't see them." Bruno passed his handkerchief and she mopped her eyes. "Yes, they are looking a bit this way, aren't they?" Unconsciously crumpling the handkerchief in her hand, she turned her gaze back to Bruno. "I love you, I want to marry you—isn't that old-fashioned—I'd marry you tomorrow—but I can't love and marry the greatest aerialist in the world. I know I can't. I think you know I can't. Do you want me to be sick all my life?"

"That wouldn't be nice for either of us. Well, it's all living and learning—I thought blackmail normally started *after* one married."

"You live in a strange world, Bruno, if you think honesty and blackmail are the same thing."

Bruno appeared to ponder. "You could always marry the greatest ex-aerialist."

"Ex?"

"No problem." Bruno made a throwaway gesture

with his right hand. "I'll burn my trapeze or whatever the phrase is."

She stared at him. "Just like—just like that? But it's your life, Bruno."

"I have other interests."

"What?"

"When your name is Mrs. Wildermann, I'll let you know."

"This year, next year, sometime, never." Matrimony was obviously closer to her heart than alternative occupations for a future husband.

"Could be the day after tomorrow."

She got back to staring at him. "Do you mean here? In this country?"

"Heaven forbid. No. In the States. Special licence. We could get the first plane out tomorrow. Nobody's going to stop us. I've plenty of money."

She took some time to assimilate this then said with conviction: "You don't know what you're saying."

Bruno said agreeably: "Lots of times that's true. This time, no. I know what I'm saying because—and it's no exaggeration—I know we're in deadly danger. I know they're on to me. I'm pretty sure they're on to you. We were followed here tonight. I don't want—"

"Followed? How do you know?"

"I know. Later. Meantime, I don't want you to die." For a moment Bruno rubbed his chin with a pensive hand. "Come to that, I don't particularly want to die myself."

"You'd let your brothers down? You'd let Mr. Wrinfield and the circus down? You'd abandon this entire mission?"

"I'd abandon anything in the world for you."

"You're running scared, Bruno?"

"Possibly. Let's go to the American Embassy now and get things fixed up. It's hardly office hours, but they wouldn't turn away a couple of nationals in distress."

She looked at him in total disbelief. Then the disbelief faded to be replaced with something very close to contempt. Then that look faded in turn to be replaced by a very thoughtful expression indeed. A faint smile touched her face, widened, and then suddenly she began to laugh. Bruno looked at her speculatively, the three men at the adjacent table in perplexity. She said: "You're impossible. It's not enough for you to test me once, you have to do it all over again."

It was as if she hadn't spoken. He said: "You heard me? I'd give up the world for you. Can't you do the same for me?"

"Willingly. The whole world. But not the whole world and Bruno. If we went to the embassy, do you know what would happen? I'd be on that plane tomorrow. But you wouldn't. Oh no, you'd stay here. Don't deny it. It's in your face. You think you're the inscrutable Bruno Wildermann. Everyone thinks so. Well, almost everyone. Three months and you won't have a secret left from me."

Bruno said: "I'm afraid of that. Okay, okay, so I tried and failed. Nothing new for me. Please don't tell Dr. Harper any of this. He'll not only think me a fool but he'll take a dim view of my mingling, shall we say, business and pleasure." He put money on the table. "Let's leave. When we get to the door I'm going to turn back on some pretext and have a word with Roebuck. While I do that, have a look around, see if there is any person who might be taking—or about to take—an interest in us."

At the doorway, Bruno, as if recalling something, turned back. He approached Roebuck and said: "What was he like?"

"Medium height. Black hair. Black moustache. Black coat. He followed you all the way from the circus."

"Your compartments may be bugged. I doubt it, but no chances. See you."

Arm in arm he walked along the street with Maria. She said curiously: "What are those three to you?"

"Very old friends. No more. You don't put friends' heads on the chopping block. Fellow all in black, black hair, black coat. See him?"

"Saw two, but none like that. One had that horrible marcelled blond hair, the other was as bald as a coot."

"Which means that Junior has returned to hand in his report to his boss."

"His boss?"

"Colonel Sergius."

"The Crau police chief?"

"He is not the Crau police chief. He's the head of the national secret police."

She stopped and looked at him. "How do you know? How *can* you know?"

"I know. I know him although he doesn't know me. You forget this is my country. But I know Sergius and I'll never forget him. Would you forget the man who killed your wife?"

"The man who—oh, Bruno!" She paused. "But he must know now."

"He knows."

"But then he must know why you're here!"

"I imagine so."

"I'll go with you tomorrow. I swear it." There was a note of hysteria in her voice. "That plane, Bruno, that plane. Don't you know you'll never leave this country alive?"

"I have things to do. And kindly modulate your voice. There's a character with horrible marcelled blond hair close behind."

"I'm scared. I'm scared."

"It's catching. Come along and I'll give you some real coffee."

"Where?"

"In this accommodation of mine you envy so much."

They walked some way in silence, then she said: "Have you thought that if they're on to you that they may have bugged your place?"

"Who says we've got to discuss affairs of state?"

Sergius was deeply engaged in discussing affairs of state. He said to Alex: "That's all that happened? Bruno and the girl went into this café, spoke briefly to the two men already seated, took the girl to a separate table and ordered a meal. Then a third man appeared, joined the other two men, went to Bruno's table, borrowed some money from him and returned to his seat?" Alex nodded. "And you said you didn't know the names of any of those men, had never seen them before, but that one of them was a giant, as big as Angelo here?"

Alex looked at Angelo. "Bigger," he said with some

satisfaction. Angelo was sadly lacking in Kan Dahn's genial good nature and did not make the most lovable of characters.

Angelo scowled blackly but no one paid him any attention, possibly because it was very difficult to differentiate between his black scowl and his normal expression.

Sergius said: "Well, we know who that is. Would you recognise the three men from their photographs?"

"Of course." Alex looked hurt.

"Angelo. Go tell Nicolas to bring whatever prints he has ready."

Angelo returned with Nicolas and about twenty prints. Silently, Sergius handed them to Alex, who leafed rapidly through them. He put one on the table. "That's the girl," he announced.

Sergius said with restraint, "We know that's the girl."

"Your pardon, Colonel." Alex selected three more. "Those."

Sergius took them and handed them to Kodes, who glanced at them briefly and said: Kan Dahn, Manuelo the knife-thrower and Roebuck, the expert with the cowboy rope."

"Precisely." Sergius smiled his mordant smile. "Have them shadowed at all times."

Kodes showed his surprise. "The presence of those three men could have been just coincidence. After all, they are among the outstanding artistes in the circus and it is natural that they should be friends. Besides, the Black Swan is, after all, the nearest café to the circus."

Sergius sighed. "Alas, it was ever thus. I am left

to fight on virtually alone. All the decisions have to be made, all the thinking has to be done by a senior officer, which is no doubt why I am a senior officer." A false modesty was not one of Sergius's besetting sins. "Our Bruno Wildermann is clever, he may also be dangerous. He suspected, only he knows how, that he was under surveillance and put his suspicions to the test. He had this man Roebuck standing by to follow whoever might follow him. This would make Roebuck—and, by implication, the other two—something just a little bit more than friends. Roebuck followed Alex. He didn't go to borrow money, he went to inform Bruno that he, Bruno, had been followed by a man with a black coat, black moustache, very stupid." He bestowed a pitying glance on the crest-fallen shadower. "I don't suppose it ever occurred to you, Alex, to look over your shoulder? Just once?"

"I'm sorry, Colonel."

Sergius gave him a look more commonly associated with a starving crocodile which has just spotted lunch.

7

The circus left for Crau on the Wednesday night. Before its departure Bruno had gone to Dr. Harper's rail compartment. For a man with so much on his mind, facing up to what was unquestionably the crucial moment of his professional career, Harper was remarkably calm and relaxed. It was more than could be said of Wrinfield, who sat there with a drink in his hand and a most dispirited expression on his face. Wrinfield had screwed his courage to the sticking point but now that the moment was at hand he had about him the air of a man who suspects that something is about to become unstuck. Crau was a huge black cloud on his horizon.

"Evening, Bruno. A seat. What will you drink?"

"Thank you. Nothing. I've only one week and I'm reserving that for later."

"With the fair Miss Hopkins, one would suppose?"

"One would suppose correctly."

"Why don't you marry the girl?" Wrinfield said sourly. "She's getting so she's almost useless to me now, either moping or dreaming the whole day long."

"I'm going to. Maybe she's worried and nervous. Like yourself, Mr. Wrinfield."

"Going to what?" Harper said.

"Marry her."

"Good God!"

Bruno took no offence. "Marriage is a common enough institution."

Wrinfield said suspiciously: "Does she know about this?" Wrinfield had become genuinely fond of her and had come to treat her as the daughter he'd never had, more especially since Henry's death.

"Yes." Bruno smiled. "So would you, if you kept your eyes open, sir. She sat next to you at table tonight."

Wrinfield clapped his palm against his forehead. "She was wearing a ring tonight. She's never worn a ring before. Fourth finger, left hand." He paused and came up with a triumphant solution. "An engagement ring."

"You've had a lot on your mind, sir. Like Maria. I bought it this afternoon."

"Well, congratulations. When we move off, we must come and toast the happy couple." Bruno winced but said nothing. "Eh, Dr. Harper?"

"Indeed. I couldn't be more pleased."

"Thank you. I didn't come to talk about the ring, though, just the company I had when I bought it. I'm afraid someone is on to me. A couple of nights ago I went with Maria to a café. It so happened Roebuck came along very soon after. He said he'd been intrigued by the behaviour of a character who emerged from the shadows of an alley near the circus when we'd passed by. Apparently he followed us all the way to the café, stopped when we stopped then took up a position across the road where he could watch us. It could have been coincidence or Roebuck's lively imagination. Last night I was pretty certain that Maria and I were being followed again but I wasn't sure. Today I was because it was in daylight. Not one shadow but two, taking the job in turns, one with artificially waved blond hair, the other completely bald. We wandered aimlessly, like a couple of tourists, wherever the fancy took us: they followed everywhere."

"I don't like this," Harper said.

"Thank you for not questioning my word. I don't much like it either. And I don't understand it. I've done nothing, absolutely nothing to attract any attention to myself. Maybe it's just because my name is Wildermann and Crau's my home town. It's anybody's guess. Maybe a dozen other circus people are under surveillance too. Who's to say?"

"Most disturbing," Wrinfield said. "Most disturbing. What are you going to do, Bruno?"

"What can I do? Just keep going, that's all. Play it as it comes. One thing's for sure, they won't be shadowing me on the night."

"The night?"

"Hasn't Dr. Harper told you?"

"Ah. Tuesday. I wonder where we'll all be then." With much clanking and shuddering the train began slowly to get under way.

"I know where I'll be. See you shortly." Bruno turned to go then stopped short at the sight of the miniature transceiver on Harper's desk. "Tell me. I've often wondered. How is it that the customs in various countries remove just about the fillings from our teeth while you manage to sail through with that transceiver?"

"Transceiver? What transceiver?" Harper clamped the earphones to his head, touched the microphone to Bruno's chest, switched on the power and moved the transmit switch backwards instead of forwards. The machine hummed and a narrow strip of paper emerged from an all but invisible slit at the side. After about ten seconds Harper switched off, tore the protruding few inches of paper away and showed it to Bruno. It had a long wavy line along the middle. "A cardiograph machine, my dear Bruno. Every travelling doctor needs one. You can't imagine the fun I've had taking the cardiographs of customs official after customs official."

"Whatever will they think of next." Bruno left, walked along the corridors of the now swaying train, picked up Maria from her compartment, took her along to his own, unlocked the handleless door and ushered her inside.

Bruno said: "Shall we have some music? Romantic, to fit the occasion? Then one of my incomparable dry martinis to celebrate—if that is the word—my descent into human bondage. And—it is just a thought—a few sweet nothings in your ear."

She smiled. "That all sounds very pleasant. Especially the sweet nothings."

He turned on the record player, keeping the volume low, mixed the martinis, set them on the table, sat on the settee beside her and pressed his face against the dark hair in the approximate area of where her ear could be presumed to be. From the expressions on Maria's face, first of startlement then of sheer incredulity, it was clear that Bruno had a line in sweet nothings that she had not previously encountered.

Crau lay just under two hundred miles distant so that even for a necessarily slow freight train it was no more than a brief overnight haul there, with two intermediate stops. They left in darkness, they arrived in darkness, and it was still dark when they disembarked. It was also extremely cold. The first overwhelming impression of Crau was one of bleak inhospitality, but then railway sidings, especially in cold and darkness, are not the most welcoming of places anywhere. The siding in which they had just drawn up was an inconvenient three quarters of a mile from the circus auditorium, but the organisational genius of Wrinfield and his executive staff had been functioning with its usual smooth efficiency and a fleet of trucks, buses and private cars were already waiting alongside.

Bruno walked beside the track towards a group of circus performers and hands who stood huddled under the harsh glare of an overhead arc-lamp. After exchanging the routine good mornings he looked around for his two brothers but failed to see them. He spoke to the man nearest him, Malthius, the tiger trainer.

"Seen my wandering brothers around? They're a very hungry couple who never fail to join me for breakfast but I haven't had the pleasure this morning."

"No." Malthius called out: "Anyone seen Vladimir and Yoffe this morning?" When it soon became apparent that no one had, Malthius turned to one of his assistant trainers. "Go and give them a shake, will you?"

The man left. Dr. Harper and Wrinfield, both with fur hats and collars upturned against the gently falling snow, came up and said their good mornings. Wrinfield said to Bruno: "Like to come with me and see what kind of exhibition hall they have for us here? For some odd reason it's called the Winter Palace, although I can't see it having any possible resemblance to that place in Leningrad." He shivered violently. "Even more important, however, is the fact that I am told that the central heating is superb."

"I'd like to. If you could just wait a moment. Two-thirds of The Blind Eagles seem to have slept in this morning. Ah! Here's Johann."

Urgency in his voice, Malthius's assistant said: "I think you'd better come, Bruno. Quickly." Bruno said nothing, just jumped quickly aboard the train. Dr. Harper and Wrinfield, after an uncomprehending glance at each other, followed closely behind him.

Vladimir and Yoffe had shared a double-bedded compartment, nothing like the princely quarters of their elder brother but comfortable enough for all that. They had become renowned and teased at for their almost compulsive tidiness: unquestionably, they would have been distressed to see its present state.

It was a shambles and looked as if a small but determined tornado had recently passed through it. Bedding lay scattered over the floor, two chairs were broken, glasses were smashed, a small hand-basin had been splintered and even a window—of heavy plate—had been cracked and starred without, however, shattering. Most ominously of all, there were bloodstains on the torn sheets and on the cream-panelled walls.

Bruno went to move inside but Harper put a restraining hand on his shoulder. "Don't. The police wouldn't like it."

The police, when they arrived, didn't like it at all. They were shocked that such a monstrous thing, the kidnapping of two famous American artistes—if they knew that Vladimir and Yoffe had been born less than half a mile from where they stood they were keeping the information to themselves—should happen upon their soil. The most immediate, the most rigorously thorough investigation would be held immediately. To begin with, said the inspector who had arrived to take charge, the area had to be completely cleared and cordoned off by his men, which was a lot less impressive than it sounded, for the cordoning-off consisted merely of stationing two of them in the corridor. The occupants of the coach in which the brothers had slept were to remain available for questioning. Wrinfield suggested the dining-room—the temperature outside was below freezing point—and the Inspector agreed. As they moved off, plainclothes detectives and fingerprint experts arrived on the scene. Wrinfield elected to join them in the dining-car, after directing his immediate deputies to proceed with the unloading of the train and the setting up of the circus and the cages in the arena immediately outside.

The air in the dining-wagon was almost unbearably warm—the giant locomotive was still hooked up and would remain so throughout the day to provide the necessary heat for the animals who would remain there until they were moved up to the circus in the evening.

Bruno stood apart with Wrinfield and Harper. Briefly, they discussed what could possibly have happened to the brothers and why, but as there was clearly no answer to either question they soon fell silent and remained that way until no less a person than Colonel Sergius himself made his entrance. His face was set in hard, bitter lines and he gave the impression that his anger was barely under control.

"Dastardly!" he said. "Unbelievable! Humiliating! That this should happen to guests in my country. I promise you, you shall have the full criminal investigating weight of our country behind this. What a welcome and what a black day for Crau!"

Harper said mildly: "This can hardly be laid at the door of any citizen of Crau. They were missing when we arrived here. We had two intermediate stops on the way up. It must have happened at one of those."

"True, true, Crau is exonerated. Does that make it any easier for us to bear, do you think? What hurts our country hurts us all." He paused and then his voice took on a deeper timbre. "It needn't have happened at either of those two stops." He looked at Bruno. "I'm sorry to have to suggest this but they might have been *thrown* off the train while in motion."

Bruno didn't stare at him, his feelings and emotions were always too tightly under control for that, but he came close to it. "Why should anyone do that? Why should anyone even lay hands on them? I know my brothers better than anyone in the world—they never did anyone any harm."

Sergius looked at him pityingly. "Don't you know that it is always the innocent who suffer? If you want to commit a burglary you don't go to the home of a notorious gangster to do it." He turned to an aide. "Get the radio telephone in here and get the Minister of Transport on the line for me. No, do it yourself. If he complains about still being in bed tell him I'll come and talk to him personally. Tell him I want every inch of track between the capital and here searched for two missing people. Tell him it's urgent. Tell him they may be badly hurt and that the temperature is below freezing. Tell him I want a report within two hours. Then call the Air Force. Tell them the same thing but only to use helicopters. I want their report within the hour." The aide left.

Wrinfield said: "You think there's a serious possibility—"

"I think nothing. A policeman's job is to overlook nothing. We'll know inside the hour. I have no faith in that old fuddy-duddy transport minister, but the Air Force is a different matter altogether. Pilots flying at ten metres, a trained observer for either side." He looked at Bruno with what he probably intended to be a sympathetic expression. "I commiserate with you, Mr. Wildermann. I also commiserate with you, Mr. Wrinfield."

Wrinfield said: "With me? Admittedly, two of my very best artistes are gone. True, I held them in the highest regard. But so did a score of others. So, for that matter, did everyone else in the circus."

"The others won't have to pay the ransom. I merely advance a possibility. If such a possibility existed you would pay a great deal of money to get them back, would you not?"

"What are you talking about?"

"Alas, even in our glorious country, we have our villains. We even have kidnappers—and their favourite method of seizing a victim is from a train. And they are very desperate men—kidnapping is a capital offence in our country. This is but supposition, but a fairly strong one." He looked again at Bruno and the gash that substituted for his mouth parted fractionally. Sergius was smiling. "And we commiserate with ourselves. It looks as if we shall not be seeing The Blind Eagles in Crau."

"You'll be seeing one of them."

Sergius looked at him. A score of people looked at him. Maria slowly passed a tongue across her lips. Sergius said: "Am I to understand—"

"I used to be a solo act before my brothers were old enough to join me. A few hours' practice and I can do it again."

Sergius looked at him for a considering moment. "We all know you are a man totally without nerves. Are you also a man totally without feelings?"

Bruno turned away without reply.

Sergius looked after him thoughtfully then turned away also. He said: "All the occupants of that coach here?"

"All present, Colonel," Wrinfield said. "But you voiced the opinion that kidnappers were—"

"Might. And you heard what I said—a policeman's job is to overlook nothing. Anybody here heard any noise, any unusual sound, during the night?" From the loud silence it was apparent that no one had heard anything. "Very well. The brothers slept in the end compartment in the coach. Who slept next to them?"

Kan Dahn moved his massive bulk forward. "I did."

"Surely you heard something?"

"I already haven't answered your question. That means no. I'm a very heavy sleeper."

Sergius looked thoughtful. "You're big enough to do it singlehanded."

Kan Dahn's tone was mild. "Are you accusing me?"

"I'm making an observation."

"Vladimir and Yoffe were good friends of mine, very good friends. Everyone knows this for years. Why should I wait until now and then do something crazy like this? Besides, if I did it there would have been no sign of a struggle. An arm round each and I would have just carried them away."

Sergius was sceptical. "Indeed?"

"Perhaps the Colonel would like a demonstration?"

"It should be interesting."

Kan Dahn indicated two burly uniformed policemen standing together. He said: "They are bigger, much bigger, and stronger than the two brothers?"

"I should have thought so."

For the giant that he was Kan Dahn moved with the speed of a cat. Before the two policemen had time to assume defensive postures Kan Dahn was upon them, a gorilla arm round each of them, pinning their own arms to their sides. A moment later both men were off their feet, struggling furiously to free themselves from what, judging by the expressions on their faces, was a far from affectionate embrace.

Kan Dahn, his voice still mild, said: "Stop struggling or I shall have to squeeze."

Doubtless under the impression that Kan Dahn could squeeze no more, the men intensified their efforts to escape. Kan Dahn squeezed some more. One man cried out, the other grunted, both expressions of agony. Kan Dahn tightened the inexorable pressure. Both men stopped struggling. Carefully, gently, Kan Dahn set them on their feet and stood back and watched sorrowfully as the two men collapsed to the floor.

Sergius regarded the tableau thoughtfully. "Angelo should be here this morning. You, Kan Dahn, are exonerated." The tone was totally humourless. He turned as Captain Kodes hurried in. "Well?"

"All we have are fingerprints, Colonel. There are many sets of two different fingerprints. Those must belong to the brothers. But we also found two other sets in rather unusual positions—against the walls, on the window, on the inside of the door—places where men might have braced themselves in the course of a violent fight."

"So." Sergius thought briefly, absently watching the painful efforts of the two policemen to struggle to their feet. Their sufferings obviously left him completely unmoved. He turned to Wrinfield. "Every man in this circus will have to be fingerprinted this morning. In the exhibition hall, where your circus is being held."

"Is it really necessary—"

Sergius affected weariness. "I have a job to do. And, for the third time, a policeman's job is to overlook nothing."

Although Crau lay roughly to the north of the capital, the main railway station did not, as one might have expected, lie to the south of the town: because of unfavourable terrain the railway line curved round the city and entered from the north. Consequently, when the black limousine of uncertain vintage set out for the Winter Palace, it drove due south along what, downtown, developed into the main thoroughfare of the city. This north-south street was, confusingly enough, called West Street.

Bruno sat in the back seat and beside him was Dr. Harper. Wrinfield, whose gloomy expression was indication enough that his dark forebodings about Crau were in the process of being confirmed, sat silently beside the driver. The weather was hardly calculated to lend a certain buoyancy to the spirits: it was just after dawn, a bleak and bitter dawn with snow swirling down from the darkly lowering clouds.

Some hundred yards from the siding Harper, who was sitting in the right-hand corner, rubbed the steamy window, peered out and up, then touched Bruno on the arm.

"Never seen anything like it. What on earth is that?"

"I can't see from here."

"On top of those buildings. Bushes, shrubs—good heavens, they've even got trees growing up there."

"Roof gardens. Very common in Central Europe. Living in a flat doesn't have to mean that you can't have your own little plot of land. Lots of them even have lawns." Bruno rubbed his own window. The building to his left was as grim, bleak and forbidding as any he had ever seen. He counted the stories: there were nine of them. He saw the windows, each one heavily barred. He observed the curving menace of the steel spikes that surrounded the roof, the watch-towers at the north and south corners: from that angle it was impossible to see what might be on the roofs of those towers but Bruno knew there would be searchlights and klaxons mounted there. He looked at Harper and lifted an eyebrow: the driver had smilingly shrugged when addressed in English, but the chances were high that he was one of Sergius's men and Sergius would not have picked a non-English speaker for the job. Harper caught his glance and nodded, although the confirmation was really superfluous: the reality of Lubylan all too dismayingly matched Harper's description of it. The prospect of trying to effect any entry into the fortress was as chilling as the dawn.

Some quarter of a mile further on they passed by a row of stationary black cars lining the right-hand pavement. At the front was a wreath-covered hearse: the hour was not early but the day was: the cortège, Bruno reflected, must have quite some way to go. Across the pavement from the hearse was an establishment with draped black velvet curtains in the windows, those being the framing for what the proprietor obviously regarded as being his choicest selection of wreaths, artificial bouquets under glass domes and unengraved marble tombstones, all in black. The adjacent door was also of the same cheerful colour, relieved only by a white cross. Bruno caught a glimpse of the door opening and the foot of a coffin on the shoulders of the two leading bearers.

"How very convenient," Bruno murmured.

Dr. Harper appeared not to have heard him.

The Winter Palace was the pride of Crau, and deservedly so. Deliberately baroque in construction, both inside and out, it was in fact only three years old. It was a reinforced steel and concrete structure, cladded both inside and out with white marble veneer from which, presumably, the name of the building arose. The building itself consisted of a very large, elliptical covered forecourt which gave on to the much greater elliptical stadium beyond it. The interior could not have been in greater contrast to the spires, minarets and gargoyles which so liberally befestooned the exterior: here all the latest ideas in spectacle presentation had been incorporated, so that everything was modern, almost excruciatingly so, functional and above all adaptable. The permutations of staging and seating, always to the best advantage of performers and audience, were practically limitless. It could be and was used for opera, theatre, cinema and music-hall: it was also used for the presentation of sporting spectacles ranging from ice-hockey to covered court tennis: as the setting for a circus amphitheatre it was nothing short of superb. In the last capacity, the sharply tiered seats, each one upholstered and with its own armrests, could accommodate no fewer than eighteen thousand spectators.

It was, Wrinfield declared, the finest auditorium he had ever seen, no mean compliment coming from a man who had seen the best in North America and Europe, especially when it was borne in mind that the population of Crau totalled just under a quarter million.

The mass fingerprinting of the entire circus staff took place during the course of the forenoon in one of the many restaurants and bars—empty at that time of day—that lined the inner side of the forecourt. Resentment and indignation at what was pretty well regarded as cavalier and unnecessary treatment ran high, and it required much of Wrinfield's considerable tact and powers of persuasion to ensure co-operation. Sergius, supervising by remote control from the comparative comfort of Wrinfield's prefabricated office and armoured in his seemingly pachydermatous hide, remained totally unmoved by the sullenness of the circus employees, the numerous, far from affectionate glances that were cast in his direction. Towards the end of the fingerprinting he received a telephone message, but as he spoke in his own language neither Wrinfield nor Maria, who were present with him, could understand the burden of the conversation.

Sergius drained his glass of vodka—he had the same osmotic affinity for his national drink as parched sand has for water—and said: "Where is Bruno Wildermann?"

"He's in the stadium. But—but you're not seriously thinking of fingerprinting him? His own brothers—"

"Please. I look so foolish? Come. It concerns you too."

As the two men approached, Bruno turned away from the supervision of the rigging of a low wire across the centre ring. He looked without expression at Sergius and said: "You have word, Colonel?"

"Yes. Both from the railways and the Air Force. But I'm afraid both reports are negative. No trace of any person lying alongside the railway tracks."

"So that has to make it kidnapping?"

"There would appear to be no other obvious solution."

Late that afternoon, when Bruno was rehearsing his solo act on the newly slung high trapeze, he was summoned to Wrinfield's office. He slid to the ground, put on his mentalist's mandarin cloak and went to the office, which, as seemed inevitable, was only feet from the as yet empty tigers' cage. Wrinfield was at his desk, Maria at hers. Sergius and Kodes were standing. The atmosphere was halfway between the tense and the funereal.

Sergius took a piece of paper that Wrinfield was studying and handed it to Bruno. It held a printed message, in English, which said: "The Wildermann brothers will be returned alive on the receipt of 50,000 dollars. Used bills. Any denomination. Instructions for transfer on Sunday, delivery Monday. Failure to deliver will result in delivery of two left little fingers Monday. Same fingers delivered if notes received but found to be treated for identification by infra-red, ultra-violet or X-ray. Two fingers on Tuesday. On Thursday, two one-handed trapeze artists."

Bruno handed the note back to Sergius.

"Your suspicions were correct."

"I was right. No nerves. No feelings. Yes, it would appear so."

"They seem ruthless."

"They are."

"And professionals?"

"Yes."

"Do they keep their promises?"

Sergius sighed. "Are you so naïve as to try to trap me into something? You are about to say that I seem to know a lot about them. If they are who I think they are—and this has all the hallmarks of previous ransom demands—then they are an extremely able and efficient gang of kidnappers who have carried out a number of such kidnappings in the past few years."

"You know the members of this gang?"

"We think we know one or two."

"Then why are they still at large?"

"Suspicion, my dear Wildermann, is not proof. One cannot ask for the death penalty on suspicion."

"I did ask an earlier question. About their promises. Will they carry out their mutilation threats? If the ransom is paid, will they return my brothers alive?"

"I can offer no guarantee. But, judging by past experiences, the chances are high. It's only logical and good business for them, as specialists in kidnapping operations, to do so. Sounds ridiculous in this context, but it builds up good faith and goodwill. If a kidnappee is returned promptly and unharmed after th payment of the ransom, then the parents and relatives of the next victim will meet the demands at once, knowing the chances are good that the victim will be returned. But if kidnappers were to accept the ransom and then kill the victim, then the relatives of the next victim might conclude that the paying of a ransom was a waste of time."

"What are the chances of tracing them before Monday?"

"Four days? Very little, I'm afraid."

"Then we'd better have the money ready, hadn't we?" Sergius nodded and Bruno turned to Wrinfield. "It would take me a year to pay you back, sir."

Wrinfield smiled, a not very happy smile. "I'd do it for the boys themselves without any hope of return. And—I'm being purely selfish, of course—there is not and never will be another group like The Blind Eagles."

Walking casually, aimlessly, they turned right down a street opposite the undertaker's on West Street. Dr. Harper said: "Are we being followed, do you think?"

Bruno said: "Watched, I don't know. Shadowed, no."

Inside two or three hundred yards the street deteriorated into a winding country lane. Soon afterwards it came to a stout wooden bridge which spanned a slow-flowing and obviously very deep river, some thirty feet in width with ice already forming at both edges. Bruno examined the bridge with some deliberation, then hurried to catch up with an impatient Harper, whose circulation was clearly not geared to cope with the subfreezing temperature.

Immediately beyond the bridge the road was swallowed up by what appeared to be virgin pine forest. Less than a quarter of a mile further on the two men came to a large semicircular glade lying to the right of the road.

"The helicopter," Dr. Harper said, "will land here."

Dusk was falling when Bruno, clad in his best street clothes, returned to Wrinfield's office. Only the owner and Maria were there.

Bruno said: "Okay if I take my fiancée for a coffee, sir?"

Wrinfield smiled, nodded then got back to looking worried and preoccupied again. Bruno helped the girl on with her heavy Astrakhan coat and they walked out into the thinly falling snow.

Maria said crossly. "We could have had coffee in the canteen or in your living room. It's very cold and damp out here."

"Nagging and not even married yet. Two hundred yards, is all. You will find that Bruno Wildermann always has his reasons."

"Such as?"

"Remember our friends of the other night who followed us so faithfully?"

"Yes." She looked at him, startled, "You mean—"

"No. They've been given a rest—snow has an adverse effect upon both marcelled hair and bald heads. The lad behind us is about three inches shorter than you, with a cloth cap, torn coat, baggy trousers and scuffed shoes. Looks like a skid-row graduate but he's not."

They turned into a café that had obviously abandoned hope a generation ago. In a country where the cafés seemed to specialise in smoke and minimal lighting, this one had really touched rock bottom. One's eyes immediately started to smart: a couple of guttering candles would have provided an equal level of illumination. Bruno guided Maria to a corner seat. She looked around her in distaste.

"Is this what married life is going to be like?"

"You may look back on this as one of your happiest days." He turned round. The Chaplinesque figure had slumped wearily into a chair close to the door, produced a ragged paper from somewhere, and sat there dispiritedly with his elbow on the table and a grimy hand to his head. Bruno turned back to Maria.

"Besides, you must admit there is a certain wild Bohemian charm to the place." He put his finger to his lips, leaned forward and pulled up the collar of her Astrakhan coat. Nestling deep in the fold of the collar was a small shining metal device no bigger than a hazelnut. He showed it to her and she stared at him wide-eyed. "Order up for us, will you?"

He rose, crossed to where their shadow was sitting, seized him unceremoniously by the right wrist, pulled it away from his head and twisted sharply, an action that gave rise to a sudden yelp of pain from the man but no reaction from the few other customers who were presumably accustomed to such diversions to the point of boredom. Nestled in the man's hand was a tiny metal earphone attached to a wire. Bruno followed the wire to a small metal box, hardly larger than the average cigarette lighter, which was tucked away in a breast pocket. Bruno put those items in his own pocket and said: "Tell your boss that the next person who follows me will be in no condition to report back again. Leave."

The man left. Bruno went back to his table and showed the trophies. He said: "Let's try it." He lifted the tiny meshed metal oval to his ear. Maria turned her mouth towards the collar of her coat.

She murmured: "I love you. Truly. Always."

Bruno removed the earphone. "It works just fine, although it doesn't seem to know what it's saying." He put the equipment away. "A persistent lot, aren't they. But so very, very obvious."

"Not to me. I think you should be doing my job. But did you have to let him know we were on to him?"

"They know anyway. Maybe now they'll stop shadowing me and let me move around in peace. Anyway, how could I talk to you with that character invading my privacy."

"What is there to talk about?"

"My brothers."

"I'm sorry. I didn't mean—*why* were they taken, Bruno?"

"Well, for one thing, it's given that hypocritical, twisting, sadistic liar—"

"Sergius?"

"Are there any other hypocritical, twisted, sadistic liars around? He had the perfect excuse to fingerprint every man in the circus."

"How will that help him?"

"Apart from giving him a feeling of power and making him feel very clever, I don't know. It doesn't matter. They're my hostages to fate. If I step too far out of line things will happen to them."

"Have you talked to Dr. Harper about this? You can't risk their lives, Bruno. You just can't. Oh, Bruno, if I lose you and they're lost and all the others in your family gone—"

"Well, really, you are the biggest crybaby I've ever met. Who on earth picked you for the CIA?"

"So you don't believe this story about the kidnapping?"

"Love me?" She nodded. "Trust me?" She nodded again. "Then don't discuss anything I discuss with you with any other person at all."

She nodded a third time. Then she said: "Including Dr. Harper?"

"Including Dr. Harper. He has a brilliant mind, but he's orthodox and doesn't have the Central European mentality. I'm not brilliant, but I'm unorthodox and I was born right here. He might not care for some improvisations *I* might care to make."

"What kind of improvisations?"

"There you are. The perfect wife. How come that red stain on your handkerchief? How should I know what improvisations? I don't even know myself yet."

"The kidnapping?"

"Rubbish. He had to have a story to explain their disappearance. You heard him say he knew who a couple of the gang were but could prove nothing? If Sergius knew them he'd have them in Lubylan in nothing flat and he'd have the entire truth out of them five minutes before they died in screaming agony. Where do you think you are—back home in New England?"

She shivered. "But why the threats? Why say they'd

cut off your brothers' fingers? Why ask for that money?"

"Background colour. Besides, liberally rewarded though Sergius may be for his nefarious activities, fifty thousand bucks in the hip pocket gives a man a very comfortable feeling of support." He looked at his untouched coffee in distaste, put some money on the table and rose. "Like some real coffee?"

They returned to the exhibition hall looking for transport to the train, which was almost immediately arranged. As they moved out again into the darkness and the cold they met Roebuck coming in. He was pinched-looking, bluish and shivering. He stopped and said: "Hi. Going back to the train?" Bruno nodded. "A lift for your tired and suffering friend."

"What are you suffering from? Been swimming in the Baltic?"

"Come winter, all the cab-drivers in this town go into hibernation." Bruno sat silently in front on the way to the station. When they alighted at the siding opposite the passenger coaches Bruno sensed as much as felt something being slipped into his jacket pocket.

After the coffee, sweet music and sweet nothings in Bruno's living-room, Maria left. Bruno fished out a tiny scrap of paper from his pocket. On it Roebuck had written: "4:30. West entrance. No question. My life on it." Bruno burnt the note and washed the ashes down the hand-basin.

8

It was during the last performance on the following night—it was officially billed as the opening night, although, in fact, there had already been two performances, a free matinee of school children and a somewhat shortened version of the full show in the afternoon—that the accident happened. Such was the rapturous enthusiasm among the huge audience that the effect was all the more shocking when it came.

The Winter Palace had not one empty seat left, and over ten thousand applications for tickets, made in advance over the previous two weeks, had had to be regretfully refused. The atmosphere at the beginning was gay, festive, electric in anticipation. The women, who gave the lie to the Western concept of Iron Curtain women being habitually dressed in belted potato sacks, were dressed as exquisitely as if the Bolshoi were visiting town—which indeed it had done, though not to so tumultuous a welcome—and the men were resplendent in either their best suits or in bemedalled uniforms. Sergius, seated next to Wrinfield, looked positively resplendent. Behind the two of them sat Kodes and Angelo, the latter tending slightly to lower the whole tone of the atmosphere. Dr. Harper, as ever, sat in the front row, the ever-present black bag unobtrusively under his seat.

The audience, suitably primed by all the wildly enthusiastic reports that had preceded the circus, were prepared for magnificence and that night they got it. As if to make up for the absence of The Blind Eagles—a broadcast announcement before the start of the performance had regretted that two members were indisposed, what Sergius didn't want to get into the papers didn't get into the papers—the performers reached new heights that astonished even Wrinfield. The crowd—there were eighteen thousand there—were entranced, enthralled. Act merged into act with the smooth and flawless precision for which the circus was justly famed and each act seemed better than the one that had preceded it. But Bruno that evening surpassed them all. That night he was not only blindfolded but hooded as well and his repertoire on the high trapeze, helped only by two girls on the platforms who handled the two free trapezes in timing with the strict metronomic music of the orchestra, had an almost unearthly magic about it, a sheer impossibility that had even the most experienced circus artistes riveted in a stage halfway between awe and outright disbelief. He climaxed his act with a double somersault between two trapezes—and his outstretched hands missed the approaching trapeze. The heart-stopping shock throughout the audience was a palpable thing—unlike the crowds at many sports ranging from auto-racing to boxing, circus audiences are always willing the performers to safety—and equally palpable was the sigh of incredulous relief when Bruno caught the trapeze with his arched heels. Just to show that there was no fluke about it, he did it all over again—twice.

The crowd went hysterical. Children and teen-agers screamed, men shouted, women cried in relief, a cacophony of noise that even Wrinfield had never heard before. It took the ringmaster three full minutes and repeated broadcast appeals to restore a semblance of order to the crowd.

Sergius delicately mopped his brow with a silk handkerchief. "No matter what you pay our young friend up there, it must always be only a fraction of what he is worth."

"I pay him a fortune and I agree with you. Have you ever seen anything like that?"

"Never. And I know I never will again."

"Why?"

Sergius cast about for an answer. He said: "We have an old saying in our country: 'Only once in a lifetime is a man permitted to leave himself and walk with the gods.' Tonight was such a night."

"You may be right, you may be right." Wrinfield was hardly listening to him, he turned to talk to an equally excited neighbour as the lights dimmed. A millimetric parting appeared between the upper and lower parts of Sergius's mouth—one could not call them lips. Sergius was permitting himself yet another of his rare smiles.

The lights came on again. As usual, in the second part of his act, Bruno used the low wire—if twenty feet could be called low—strung across the cage, open at the top, where Neubauer was, as he liked to put it, conducting his choir—putting his dozen Nubian lions, an unquestionably savage lot who would permit nobody except Neubauer near them, through their paces.

For his first trip across and back the cage on his bicycle and with his balancing pole, Bruno—without the normal burden of having to carry his two brothers—obviously found it almost ridiculously easy to perform the acrobatic balancing feats which in fact few other artistes in the circus world could emulate. The crowd seemed to sense this ease, and while appreciating the skill, daring and expertise, waited expectantly for something more. They got it.

On this next sally across the ring he had a different machine, this one with a seat four feet high, pedals clamped below the seat and a vertical driving chain four feet in length. Again he crossed and recrossed the ring, again he performed his acrobatic feats, although this time with considerably more caution. When he crossed for the third time he had the audience distinctly worried, for this time his seat was no less than eight feet in height, with a vertical drive chain of corresponding length. The concern of the audience turned to a lip-biting apprehension when, reaching the sag in the middle, both bicycle—if that strange contraption could any longer be called that—

and man began to sway in a most alarming fashion and Bruno had virtually to abandon any but the most elementary acrobatics in order to maintain his balance. He made it safely there and back, but not before he had wrought considerable changes in the adrenalin, breathing and pulse-rates of the majority of the audience.

For his fourth and final excursion both seat and chain were raised to a height of twelve feet. This left him with his head some sixteen feet above the low wire, thirty-six above the ground.

Sergius glanced at Wrinfield, who, eyes intent, was rubbing his hand nervously across his mouth. Sergius said: "This Bruno of yours. Is he in league with the chemists who sell sedatives or the doctors who specialise in heart attacks?"

"This has never been done before, Colonel. No performer has ever attempted this."

Bruno started to sway and wobble almost immediately after leaving the top platform but his uncanny sense of balance and incredible reactions corrected the swaying and brought it within tolerable limits. This time there was no attempt to perform anything even remotely resembling acrobatics. His eyes, sinews, muscles, nerves were concentrated on one thing alone —maintaining his balance.

Exactly halfway across Bruno stopped pedalling. Even the least informed among the audience knew that this was an impossible, a suicidal thing to do: when the factor of balance has reached critical dimensions—and here it already appeared to have passed that critical limit—only movement backwards or forwards could help to regain equilibrium.

"Never again," Wrinfield said. His voice was low, strained. "Look at them! Just look at them!"

Sergius glanced at the audience but not for longer than a fraction of a second. It was not difficult to take Wrinfield's point. Where audience participation is concerned a certain degree of vicarious danger can be tolerable, even pleasurable, but when the degree of danger becomes intolerable—and prolonged, as in this case—the pleasure turns to fear, a corroding anxiety. The clenched hands, the clenched teeth, in many cases the averted gazes, the waves of empathy washing across the exhibition hall—none of this was calculated to bring the crowds flocking back to the circus.

For ten interminable seconds the unbearable tension lasted, the wheels of the bicycle neither advancing nor going backwards as much as as inch, while its angle of sway perceptibly increased. Then Bruno pushed strongly on the pedals.

The chain snapped.

No two people afterwards gave precisely the same account of what followed. The bicycle immediately tipped over to the right, the side on which Bruno had been pressing. Bruno threw himself forward—there were no handle-bars to impede his progress. Hands outstretched to cushion his fall, he landed awkwardly, sideways, on the wire, which appeared to catch him on the inner thigh and the throat, for his head bent backwards at an unnatural angle. Then his body slid off the wire, he seemed to be suspended by his right hand and chin alone, then his head slid off the wire, the grip of his right hand loosened and he fell into the ring below, landed feet first on the sawdust and immediately crumpled like a broken doll.

Neubauer, who at that moment had ten Nubian lions squatting on a semicircle of tubs, reacted very quickly. Both Bruno and the bicycle had landed in the centre of the ring, well clear of the lions, but lions are nervous and sensitive creatures and react badly to unexpected disturbances and interruptions—and this was a very unexpected disturbance indeed. The three lions in the centre of the half-circle had already risen to all four feet when Neubauer stooped and threw handfuls of sand in their faces. They didn't sit, but they were temporarily blinded and remained where they were, two of them rubbing their eyes with massive forepaws. The cage door opened and an assistant trainer and clown entered, not running, lifted Bruno, carried him outside the cage and closed the door.

Dr. Harper was with him immediately. He stooped and examined him briefly, straightened, made a signal with his hand, but it was unnecessary, Kan Dahn was already there with a stretcher.

Three minutes later the announcement was made from the centre ring that the famous Blind Eagle was only concussed and with any luck would be performing again the next day. The crowd, unpredictable as all crowds, rose to its collective feet and applauded for a whole minute: better a concussed Blind Eagle than a dead one. The show went on.

The atmosphere inside the first-aid room was distinctly less cheerful: it was funereal. Present were Harper, Wrinfield, two of his associate directors, Sergius and a splendidly white-maned, white-moustached gentleman of about seventy. He and Harper were at one end of the room where Bruno, still on the stretcher, lay on a trestle table.

Harper said: "Dr. Hachid, if you would care to carry out your own personal examination—"

Dr. Hachid smiled sadly. "I hardly think that will be necessary." He looked at one of the associate directors, a man by the name of Armstrong. "You have seen death before?" Armstrong nodded. "Touch his forehead." Armstrong hesitated, advanced, laid his hand on Bruno's forehead. He almost snatched it away.

"It's cold." He shivered. "Already it's gone all cold."

Dr. Hachid pulled the white sheet over Bruno's head, stepped back and pulled a curtain which obscured the stretcher. Hachid said: "As you say in America, a doctor is a doctor is a doctor, and I would not insult a colleague. But the law of our land—"

"The law of every land," Harper said. "A foreign doctor cannot sign a death certificate."

Pen in hand, Hachid bent over a printed form. "Fracture of spine. Second and third vertebrae, you said? Severance of spinal cord." He straightened. "If you wish me to make arrangements—"

"I have already arranged for an ambulance. The hospital morgue—"

Sergius said: "That will not be necessary. There is a funeral parlour not a hundred metres from here."

"There is? That would save much trouble. But at this time of night—"

"Dr. Harper."

"My apologies, Colonel. Mr. Wrinfield, can I borrow one of your men, a trusted man who will not talk?"

"Johnny, the night watchman."

"Have him go down to the train. There's a black case under my bunk. Please have him bring it here."

The back parlour of the undertaker's emporium was harshly lit with neon strip lighting which pointed up the coldly antiseptic hygiene of the surroundings, tiled walls, marble floor, stainless steel sinks. Upended coffins lined one wall. In the centre of the room were three more coffins on steel-legged marble tables. Two of those were empty. Dr. Harper was pulling a sheet over the third. Beside him, the plump undertaker, a man with gleaming shoes and gleaming bald pate, virtually hopped from foot to foot, his professional feeling visibly outraged.

He said: "But you cannot do this. Straight into the coffin, I mean. There are things to be done—"

"I will do those things. I have sent for my own equipment."

"But he has to be laid out."

"He was my friend. I shall do it."

"But the shroud—"

"You will be excused for not knowing that a circus performer is always buried in his circus clothes."

"It is all wrong. We have ethics. In our profession—"

"Colonel Sergius." Harper's voice was weary. Sergius nodded, took the undertaker by the arm, led him some way apart and spoke quietly. He was back in twenty seconds with an undertaker three shades paler and with a key which he handed to Harper.

"The parlour is all yours, Dr. Harper." He turned to the undertaker. "You may leave." He left.

"I think we should leave, too," Wrinfield said. "I have some excellent vodka in my office."

Maria was in the office, forehead resting on crossed arms on the desk, when the men came in. She lifted her head slowly, peering through half-closed eyes as if not seeing too well. A concerned and troubled Dr. Harper was standing before her, an equally concerned Wrinfield and an impassive Sergius beside him: Sergius's facial muscles for conveying sympathy had atrophied over the years. Maria's eyes were red and puffy and glazed and her cheeks glistened. Wrinfield looked at the grief-stricken face and touched her arm awkwardly.

"Do forgive me, Maria. I had forgotten—I didn't know—we shall go at once."

"Please. It's all right." She dabbed at her face with some tissues. "Please come in."

As the other three men rather reluctantly entered and Wrinfield brought out his bottle of vodka, Harper said to her: "How did you know? I'm so terribly sorry, Maria." He looked at her engagement ring and looked away again. "But how did you know?"

"I don't know. I just knew." She dabbed at her eyes again. "Yes, I do know. I heard the announcement about his fall. I didn't come to see—well, because I was scared to come. I was sure that if he wasn't badly hurt he'd ask for me or you would have sent for me. But nobody came."

In an understandably strained silence and with considerable haste the men disposed of their vodkas and filed out. Harper, the last to leave, said to Maria: "I have to see to some equipment. I'll be back in two minutes."

He closed the door behind him. Maria waited for some moments, rose, glanced through the window, opened the door and peered cautiously out. There was no one in the immediate vicinity. She closed the door, locked it, returned to her desk, took a tube from a drawer, removed the cap, squeezed and rubbed some more glycerine into her eyes and face. She then unlocked the door.

Dr. Harper returned shortly with a suitcase. He poured himself another vodka, looked everywhere except at the girl as if uncertain how to begin. Then he cleared his throat and said apologetically: "I know you're never going to forgive me for this but I had to do it. You see, I didn't know how good an actress you might be. Not so good, I'm afraid. Your feelings do tend to show through."

"My feelings tend—you know that Bruno and I—" She broke off, then said slowly: "What on earth do you mean?"

He smiled at her, broadly although albeit somewhat apprehensively. "Dry your tears and come and see."

The first beginnings of understanding touched her face. "Do you mean—"

"I mean come and see."

Bruno pushed back the two covering sheets and sat up in his coffin. He looked at Harper without much enthusiasm and said reproachfully: "Weren't in too much of a hurry, were you? How would you like to lie in a coffin wondering when some enthusiastic apprentice is going to come along and start battening down the lid?"

Maria saved Harper the necessity of a reply. When Bruno had finally disentangled himself, he climbed stiffly down to the floor, reached inside the coffin, held up a limp, dripping linen bag and said: "And I'm soaking wet, too."

Maria said: "What *is* that?"

"A slight subterfuge, my dear." Harper gave a deprecatory smile. "An ice-bag. It was necessary to give Bruno the cold clammy forehead of the deceased. Ice, unfortunately, melts." Harper placed the case on the coffin and opened the lid. "And, alas, we now have to cause Bruno some more suffering: we have to transform him into a thing of beauty and a joy forever."

The transformation took all of twenty minutes. Harper had not necessarily mistaken his profession but clearly he would have been perfectly at home in the make-up department of any film studio. He worked swiftly and skillfully and obviously derived some satisfaction from his creative handiwork. When he was finished, Bruno looked at himself in a full-length mirror and winced. The light brown wig was just that too much long and straggly, the light brown moustache a soupçon too luxuriant: the vivid semicircular scar that ran from his forehead round the corner of his right eye almost to his nose was the result, clearly, of an encounter with a broken bottle: for clothes he wore a blue and white striped shirt, red tie, light brown suit with red vertical stripes, mustard socks and shoes of the same appalling colour. The rings on his fingers would appear to have had their source of origin either in a fair-ground stall or Christmas crackers.

Bruno said: "A thing of beauty, the man says. I could always hire myself out as a scarecrow." He bent a discouraging look on Maria, whose hand, discreetly covering her mouth, could not disguise the crinkling in her eyes. He looked back to Harper. "This makes me inconspicuous?"

"The point precisely. It makes you so conspicuous that no one will bother to take a second look at you—except for those who will do a double-take to convince themselves that their eyes weren't deceiving them in the first place. It's the anonymous, furtive, grey man slinking down alleyways that attracts suspicion. You are Jon Neuhas, a machine-tool salesman from East Germany. The passport and papers are in your inside pocket."

Bruno dug out his passport, a venerable-looking document that attested to the fact that his salesman's duties had taken him to virtually every Iron Curtain country, some of them many times. He looked at his picture and then again at himself in the mirror. The resemblance was quite remarkable.

He said: "This must have taken quite a time to prepare. Where was it made?"

"In the States."

"You've had it all that time?" Harper nodded. "You might have shown it to me earlier on. Given me time to get accustomed to the awfulness of it all."

"You would probably have refused to come." Harper checked his watch. "The last train in tonight arrives in fifteen minutes. A car is waiting for you about a hundred yards down the street from here, which will take you discreetly to the station, where you will make sure you are seen—you have just come off the train. This suitcase contains all the clothes and toilet gear you will require. The same car will then drive you up to a hotel where you made a reservation two weeks ago."

"You fixed all this?"

"Yes. Rather, one of our agents did. Our man, as you might say, in Crau. Invaluable. He can fix anything in this city—he ought to, he's a big wheel in the city council. One of *his* men will be driving your car tonight."

Bruno looked at him consideringly. "You certainly believe in playing a tight game, Dr. Harper."

"And I survive." Harper permitted himself a patient sigh. "When you've spent most of your adult life in a racket like this you will discover that, at any given time, the fewer people who know anything about anything, the greater the safety factor. Maria will hire a car in the morning. Two blocks west of here is an inn called the Hunter's Horn. Be there at dusk. Maria will be there shortly afterwards. She'll look in the doorway then walk away. You will follow her. You have a singular gift for sensing when you will be shadowed, so I have no worries on that score. Any change of plan or further instructions will be given you by Maria."

"You said your man in Crau could fix anything?"

"I did say that."

"Have him fix a few sticks of dynamite. Any explosive will do as long as it has an approximately ten-second fuse. He can fix that?"

Harper hesitated. "I suppose. Why do you want it?"

"I'll tell you in a couple of days and that's *not* because I'm doing a Dr. Harper and being all mysterious. I'm not quite sure myself but I'm developing an idea that it might help me to leave the Lubylan."

"Bruno." The dark anxiety was back in the girl's face again, but Bruno didn't look at her.

"I think there's a chance I might get in undetected. I don't think there's a chance in hell that I'll be able to get out undetected. I may have to leave in a very great hurry indeed and once the alarm is raised I'm sure the exits will be automatically sealed. So my best line of exit may well be to blast my way out."

"I seem to recall you saying that you had no wish to kill anyone. A dynamite blast could kill quite a few."

"I'll be as careful as I can. It may have to come to the inevitable choice—them or me. One hopes not. Do I get the bangers or not?"

"You'll have to give me time to think about that one."

"Look, Dr. Harper. I know you're in charge, but, here and now, you're not the person who matters. I am. I'm the person who's got to put his life on the line to get inside Lubylan—and out again. Not you. You're safe and sound in base camp and will disclaim all knowledge of anything if I get chopped. I'm not asking, not now, I'm demanding. I want that explosive." He glanced down in distaste at his clothes. "If I don't get it you can try on this suit for size."

"I repeat, I need time."

"I can't wait." Bruno hitched his elbows on the coffin. "I can wait all of five seconds. I'll count them. Then I'm taking this damned suit off and going back to the circus. I wish you luck in your break-in to Lubylan. I also wish you luck when you come to explaining to the police just how you made the trifling error of certifying me as being dead. One. Two. Three."

"This is blackmail."

"What else? Four."

"All right, all right, you can have your damned fireworks." Harper pondered then went on complainingly: "I must say this is a side of your nature I've never seen before."

"I'd never examined that damned Lubylan before. I've seen it now. I know my chances. Please have Maria take the explosives in her car tomorrow night. Does Wrinfield know that this was a charade tonight?"

"Of course."

"You took a chance bringing Sergius with you here."

"Apart from the fact that he insisted, I'd have taken a damned bigger chance if I hadn't. That would have been the one thing calculated to rouse his suspicions."

"And he's not? Suspicious, I mean?"

"The last thing that would occur to Colonel Sergius is that anyone would ever be misguided enough as to pick his parish as a place to commit suicide."

"Money?"

"In your other inside pocket."

"It's freezing outside."

"There's a nice warm coat in the car." Harper smiled. "You're going to love it."

Bruno nodded to the open coffin. "That?"

"Will be weighted and the lid screwed down during the night. We will bury you on Monday morning."

"Can I send me a wreath?"

"That would not be advisable." Harper smiled thinly. "You can always, of course, mingle discreetly with your mourners."

Forty minutes later Bruno was in his hotel room, unpacking, his eyes straying occasionally towards the nice warm coat that Harper had so thoughtfully provided. It was made of thick brushed nylon, in black and white wavy vertical stripes, and looked for all the world like a four-thousand-guinea chinchilla. Indisputably, it was the only one of its kind in Crau and, likely enough, for some hundreds of miles around, and the stir he had caused strolling through the lobby to the reception desk had been more than considerable: when the effect of his coat was added to the fact that he had had it carelessly flung open to reveal the sartorial rainbow of his suiting beneath it was understandable that hardly anyone had bothered to give his face a first glance, far less a second one.

Bruno put out the light, eased the curtains, opened the window and leaned out. His room was at the back of the hotel, overlooking a narrow warehouse-lined lane. It wasn't quite in total darkness but it wasn't far from it either. Less than four feet away were the steps of a fire escape, the easy and, in combination with the darkened lane, the perfect way to leave the hotel. Too easy, too perfect.

In line with Harper's advocated policy of non-concealment, Bruno went down to the hotel dining-room for dinner, carrying under his arm an East Berlin newspaper, dated that day, which he had found in his case. Harper was a man to whom the most insignificant detail could be of importance. Where he had obtained it Bruno had no means of knowing. His entrance did not cause any notable sensation—the citizens of Crau or visiting firemen were too well mannered for that. But the raised eyebrows, the smiles, the whispers were evidence enough that his presence had not gone unnoted. Bruno looked casually around. There was nobody in sight who looked remotely like a secret police agent, although there was little comfort in that: the best agents never did. Bruno ordered his meal then buried himself in his newspaper.

At eight o'clock the following morning Bruno was once more in the dining-room, again reading a paper but this time a local news sheet. The first thing that caught his attention was a large black-bordered box—the borders were half an inch thick—in the centre of the front page. From this he learnt that he had died during the night. The grief was profound for circus lovers the world over but nowhere, of course, as keenly felt as in Crau. There was much sentimentalising and philosophical sorrowing over the machinations of a strange fate that had brought Bruno Wildermann home to die. He was to buried at 11

A.M. on Monday. It was hoped that large numbers of the citizens of Crau would turn out to pay their last respects to their city's most illustrious son, the greatest aerialist of all time. Bruno took the paper back up to his room after breakfast, found scissors and cut out the black-bordered article, which he carefully folded and placed in an inside pocket.

Late that afternoon Bruno went shopping. It was a cold and sunny day and he had left his fur coat in his room. This he had done neither because of the weather nor because of any innate bashfulness. It was just too bulky to be carried inconspicuously, however well it might have been wrapped up.

This was the town that Bruno knew better than any in the world and he could have shaken off any shadower without even half thinking about it: it took him less than five minutes to know that he was not being followed. He turned down a side street, then into an even meaner street, little more than a lane, and entered the shop of a haberdasher for whom Savile Row must have lain on the far side of Paradise: even the best clothes it had for sale could not have qualified for the description of second-hand. The proprietor, an elderly stooped man whose watery eyes swam behind thickly pebbled glasses—although it seemed an extremely remote possibility that the oldster would ever be called upon to identify him Bruno doubted whether he could have identified members of his own family, if any—had a unique but eminently practical way of displaying the wares he had for sale. The articles of clothing were piled in untidy heaps on the floor, jackets in one pile, trousers in another, coats in another, shirts in another and so on. Ties were conspicuous by their absence.

When Bruno emerged it was with a bulky and exceedingly grimy brown paper parcel roughly tied with some frayed twine. He made his way to the nearest public conveniences and when he emerged his transformation was complete. He was clad in ill-fitting patched and ancient clothes, wholly disreputable, not the sort of person the average citizen would approach within yards of, far less associate with: the grimy crumpled beret was two sizes too large and fell over his eyes: the dark raincoat was irreparably stained, the trousers baggy beyond belief, the creased, once-navy shirt tieless and the heels of the scuffed shoes so worn down at the back that they lent him a peculiarly rolling gait. To complete matters he was surrounded by a powerful aura that afflicted people at a distance of several yards: to keep lice, fleas and other forms of wild life at bay, the haberdasher was a great believer in drenching every article of apparel with a disinfectant that was as vile-smelling as it was powerful.

Clutching his brown parcel under his arm, Bruno made his leisurely way across town. Dusk was beginning to fall. He took a short cut through a large park, a section of which was given over for use as one of the city's cemeteries. Passing by an opened iron gate in the high wall that surrounded the cemetery, he was intrigued to see two men busily digging by the light of a pair of storm lanterns. Intrigued, he approached the spot and as he did two men, standing in an as yet shallow grave, straightened up and rubbed clearly aching backs.

"You work late, comrades," Bruno said sympathetically.

"The dead wait for no man," the elder grave-digger said in a sepulchral voice, then, peering more closely, added: "Some of us have to work for a living. Do you mind standing to the other side of the grave?"

The light wind, Bruno realised, was .wafting his presence across the grave. He moved round and said: "And whose last resting place is this?"

"A famous American, though he was born and brought up in this town. I knew his grandmother well. A Wildermann, he is. He was with a circus—the circus—in the Winter Palace. Killed in an accident. It'll be a big day here on Monday with Johann and myself in our best suits."

"An accident?" Bruno shook his head. "One of those damnable buses, I'll be bound. Many's the time—"

The younger man said: "No, you old fool. He fell off a wire in the circus and broke his neck." He jammed his shovel into the sandy soil. "Do you mind? We have work to do."

Bruno mumbled his apologies and shambled away. Five minutes later he was in the Hunter's Horn, where he had to show his money to a nose-wrinkling waiter before being served coffee. After about fifteen minutes Maria appeared in the doorway, looked around, clearly failed to recognise anybody, hesitated and moved off again. Bruno rose leisurely and rolled his way towards the door. Once in the street he lengthened his stride without increasing his pace and within a minute he was only a few feet behind her.

He said: "Where's the car?"

She wheeled round. "Where on earth—you weren't —yes, you were!"

"You'll feel better shortly. Where's the car?"

"Round the next corner."

"Any car follow you?"

"No."

The car was a nondescript battered black Volkswagen, one of hundreds similar in the town: it was parked under a street lamp. Bruno got in behind the wheel, Maria in the passenger seat. She sniffed in disgust.

"What on earth is that dreadful smell?"

"Me."

"I appreciate that. But—"

"Just disinfectant. A very powerful one, but still a disinfectant. You'll get used to it. Quite bracing, really."

"It's awful! Why on earth—"

"Disguise," Bruno said patiently. "You don't actually think this is my preferred mode of dress? I think that Dr. Harper underestimates Colonel Sergius. I may be Jon Neuhas, a citizen in good standing from a friendly satellite country, but I'm still an East German. I'm an outsider—and you can bet Sergius has every outsider tabbed from the moment he's within twenty miles of Crau. He will know—if he wishes—within ten minutes of any stranger checking in to any hotel in Crau. He'll have a complete description of me. I have the documentation so he won't give me a second thought. But he'll give a second thought if a respectable sales representative for a major firm is found in a sleazy dump like the Hunter's Horn or parked indefinitely in the shadow of the Lubylan. Don't you think?"

"Agreed. In that case there is only one thing to do." She opened her handbag, extracted a small eau-de-cologne aerosol, sprayed herself liberally then squirted the contents over Bruno. When she had finished Bruno sniffed.

"The disinfectant wins," he announced, and, indeed, instead of the cologne having a neutralising effect it had a compounding effect. Bruno lowered the windows and hastily moved off, his eye as much on the rear-view mirror as on the road. He twisted and turned through the darkened streets and alleyways until any tail car there might have been must have been irretrievably lost. As they drove, they briefly rehearsed the plans for the Lubylan break-in on the Tuesday night. Then Bruno said: "Got the stuff I asked for?"

"In the trunk. Not what you asked for—Dr. Harper's contact couldn't get that. He says you're to be very careful with this stuff—it seems you've only to look at it and it will explode."

"Good God! Don't tell me he's got me nitroglycerine?"

"No. It's called amatol."

"That's all right, then. It's the detonator he'll be worried about. Fulminate of mercury, isn't it?"

"Yes, he said that."

"Seventy-seven grains. Very temperamental stuff. It

will have a length of RDX fuse and a chemical igniter."

"Yes. He did say that." She looked at him curiously. "How come you're an expert on explosives?"

"I'm not. I read about it some years ago and just sort of filed the information away."

"Must be quite a filing cabinet you've got in there. This instant and total recall bit—how's it done?"

"If I knew that I'd be making a fortune out of it instead of fooling my life away on a trapeze. Now, there's something else I want. First a large eight-by-eight—preferably—sheet of rubber matting or hide leather."

She took his hand and said: "What do you want that for?" Her eyes told him that she knew.

"What do you think? To throw over that damned electrified fence of course. A tumbler's mat would do fine. Also I require a rope with a padded hook. I want to see them both as soon as possible. Ask Dr. Harper to arrange for those things and have them put in the trunk of the car. Would you like to have lunch with me tomorrow?"

"What?"

"I want to see that stuff."

"Oh, I'd love to." She inhaled deeply. "No, I wouldn't. Not if you're wearing those clothes. Anyway, no half-decent restaurant would let you through the front door."

"I'll change."

"But if we're seen together—in daylight, I mean—"

"There's a charming little inn in a charming little village about ten miles from here. Nobody will know us there and nobody will be looking anyway:

I'm dead. Which reminds me. It's less than an hour since I was talking to a couple of grave-diggers."

"We are being humorous again, are we?"

"Fact. Very interesting."

"In the Hunter's Horn?"

"In the cemetery. I asked them who it was for and they said it was for me. Well, the American who fell off the wire. It's not everyone who's privileged enough to watch his own grave being dug. They were making a very neat job of it, I must say."

"Please." She shivered. "Must you?"

"Sorry. That wasn't funny. I just thought it was. Now, you'll go to this village—it's called Kolszuki—by car and I'll go by train. We'll meet at the station there. We might as well go now and check the train time-tables at the Crau station. You'll have to get clearance from Dr. Harper, of course."

On a very Spartan metal table in a very Spartan and largely metal office, the spools of a tape-recorder revolved. On either side of the table sat Colonel Sergius and Captain Kodes. Both had headphones to their ears. In addition to the phones Sergius had a cigar, vodka and as close to a beatific smile as he was ever likely to achieve. Captain Kodes, too, was permitting himself the luxury of smiling broadly. Angelo, discreetly seated in a far corner, although he had neither phones nor vodka, was also smiling. If the Colonel was happy, that made him happy too.

Bruno returned from consulting the time-tables inside the Crau station. He said: "There's a very convenient train for lunch. Meet me at the Kolszuki station at noon. You won't have any trouble in finding it—there aren't more than fifty houses in the village. Know where this place is?"

"There's a map in the glove compartment. I've checked. I'll be there then."

Bruno drove up the main street and parked the Volkswagen just opposite the lane abutting on the southern side of Lubylan. The lane was not deserted—there were two trucks and a car on the south side of the lane, obviously parked for the night. It was a measure of the confidence in their security arrangements of those within Lubylan that they raised no objections to vehicles parking in such close proximity. Bruno made a mental note of this: there is no objection to the night-time parking of trucks in the south lane.

Bruno said: "Now don't forget to tell Dr. Harper everything we discussed tonight. And don't forget that, for the benefit of any innocent passers-by, we're just a couple of lovers lost in each other's eyes. Darling, darling Maria. That's for practice."

"Yes, Bruno," she said primly. "We'll be married soon, Bruno."

"Very soon, my love." They relapsed into silence, their eyes fixed on the lane, Maria's all the time, Bruno's most of the time.

In the headquarters of the Secret Police, Colonel Sergius was making harsh croaking noises in his throat. He was not choking on his vodka. Colonel Sergius was laughing. He gestured that Angelo should pour him another vodka then indicated that Angelo should help himself also. Angelo refrained from crushing the bottle in his surprise, smiled his wolfish smile and swiftly complied before Sergius could change his mind. This was without precedent, an epoch-making night.

Bruno turned suddenly, put his arms around Maria and kissed her passionately. For a moment she stared at him, dark eyes open in astonishment and surmise, let herself relax against him then stiffened as an authoritative rat-tat-tat came on her window. She broke from Bruno's arms and swiftly wound down the window. Two large policemen, complete with the customary guns and batons, were bent down peering into the car. Uniforms and weapons apart, however, they bore no resemblance to the popular conception of the Iron Curtain policemen. Their expressions were genial, positively paternal. The larger of the two sniffed suspiciously.

"Very strange smell in this car, I must say."

Maria said: "I'm afraid I've just broken a phial of perfume. A drop is nice—but a whole bottle—well it *is* a bit strong, I must say."

Bruno, stammering slightly and with his voice sounding acutely embarrassed, said: "What is it, Officer? This is my fiancée." He held up Maria's beringed left hand so that there should be no doubt about it. "Surely there's no law—"

"Indeed not." The policeman leaned a confidential elbow on the window-sill. "But there's a law against parking in a main street."

"Oh! Sorry. I didn't realise—"

"It's the fumes," the policeman said kindly. "Your mind must be all befuddled."

"Yes, Officer." Bruno smiled weakly. "Is it all right if we park behind those trucks?" Hopefully, he indicated the vehicles in the south lane.

"Certainly. Don't catch cold now. And, comrade?"

"Officer?"

"If you love her so much, why don't you buy your fiancée a bottle of decent perfume? Needn't be expensive, you know." The policeman beamed and walked away with his colleague.

Maria, remembering her momentary yielding to Bruno, said in a cross voice: "Well, thank you. For a moment there I thought you had found me irresistible."

"Always use your rear-view mirror. It's just as important when you're stationary as when you're driving."

She made a face at him as he pulled the car into the south lane.

The two policemen watched them park. They moved out of eyeshot of the car. The larger man pulled a walkie-talkie microphone from his breast pocket, pressed a button and said: "They're parked in the south lane by the Lubylan, Colonel."

"Excellent." Even with the metallic distortion and the fact that his speech was interrupted by a series of whooping gasps—laughter was an unaccustomed exercise for him—Sergius's voice was unmistakable. "Just leave the love-birds be."

It took Bruno and Maria minutes only to establish that there were indeed ground-level guards. There were three of them and they kept up a continuous peripheral patrol, each making a full circuit of the

Lubylan in turn. At no time was any guard in sight of the other two. As sentries, they were a degree less than enthusiastic. Not for them the continually roving, probing eye, the piercing scrutiny of all that lay in their path of vision: with downcast gaze and trudging steps they gave the impression of thoroughly miserable men, huddled against the cold and living only for the moment of their relief. There had been night-time sentries patrolling the Lubylan for ten, perhaps twenty years, and probably no untoward incident had ever occurred: there was no conceivable reason why it ever should.

From the two watch-towers they could see, the south-west and south-east ones, searchlights flashed occasionally and erratically along the tops of the perimeter walls. There was no discernible predetermined sequence to the switching on and off of the searchlights: it appeared to be a quite random process, its arbitrary nature dependent on the whim of the guard.

After twenty minutes Bruno drove off to the public convenience he had patronised earlier that evening. He left the car, kissed Maria goodbye as she moved into the driver's seat, and disappeared into the depths. When he emerged, the grimy parcel with the old clothes and the amatol tucked under his arm, he was clad in his original sartorial glory.

Precisely at noon on the following day Bruno was met by Maria at Kolszuki station. It was a beautiful, cloudless winter's day, crisp and clear and sunny, but the wind off the plains to the east was bitingly cold. On the twenty-minute journey out Bruno had passed the time of day studying his own highly coloured obituary in the Crau Sunday paper. He was astonished at the richness and variety of his career, the international acclaim that followed him wherever he went, the impossible feats he had performed before heads of state the world over: he was particularly touched to discover how kind he had been to little children. It contained just enough fact to make it obvious that the reporter had actually been interviewing someone in the circus, a person clearly possessed of a deadpan sense of humour. That it wasn't the work of Wrinfield he was sure: Kan Dahn appeared much the most likely culprit if for no reason other than the fact that he was the only person mentioned in the article apart from Bruno. The article, Bruno reflected, augured well for the morrow: the turn-out at the cemetery at 11 A.M. promised to be a remarkable one. Bruno carefully cut the piece out and put it together with the previous day's black-bordered obituary.

The inn Bruno had in mind was only two miles away. One mile out, he pulled into a lay-by, got out, opened the boot, gave a cursory examination to the tumbler's mat and the padded hook attached to a rope, closed the boot and returned to his seat.

"Both mat and rope are just what I wanted. Just let them stay there until Tuesday night. You have this car rented until then?"

"Until we leave here on Wednesday."

They pulled off the main road, went some way up a narrow lane, then pulled up in the cobble-stoned court-yard of what looked to be a very ancient inn indeed. The head waiter courteously escorted them to a corner table and took their order. As he was finishing, Bruno said: "Do you mind if we sit by that corner table." Maria looked her surprise. "It's such a lovely day."

"But of course, sir."

When they were seated, Maria said: "I can't see any lovely day from here. All I can see is the back of a broken-down barn. Why the new table?"

"I just wanted my back to the room so that no one could see our faces."

"You know somebody here?"

"No. We were followed from the station by a grey Volkswagen. When we stopped at that lay-by he passed us by but then pulled into a side turning and waited until we had passed him, then he tucked in behind us again. Where he's sitting now he's directly facing our previous table. He may well be a lip-reader."

She was vexed. "It's supposed to be my job to see those things."

"Maybe we should swap jobs."

"That's not very funny," she said, then smiled in spite of herself. "I somehow don't see myself as the daring young girl on the flying trapeze. I can't even stand on a first-floor balcony, even stand on a chair, without getting vertigo. Fact. See what you're letting yourself in for?" The smile faded. "I may have smiled, Bruno, but I'm not smiling inside. I'm scared. See what else you're letting yourself in for." He said nothing. "Well, thanks anyway for not laughing at me. *Why* are we being followed, Bruno? Who could possibly know we were out here? And who is the person they're following—you or me?"

"Me."

"How can you be so sure?"

"Did anyone tail you out here?"

"No. I've listened to your lectures on driving mirrors. I spend more time looking backwards than forwards now when I'm driving. I stopped twice. No one passed me."

"So it's me. And nothing to worry about. I detect Dr. Harper's fell hand in this. It's what I take to be the old CIA mentality. Never, never trust anyone. I suspect half the members of espionage and counter-espionage services spend a good deal of their time watching the other half. And how is he to know that I'm not going to go native and revert to my old Crau sympathies? I don't blame him. This is a very, very difficult situation indeed for the good doctor. A hundred against one that that lad behind us is what it pleases Harper to call his man in Crau. Just do me one favour—when you get back to the circus train, go see Dr. Harper and ask him straight out."

She said doubtfully: "You really think so?"

"I'm certain."

After lunch they drove back to Kolszuki station with the grey Volkswagen in faithful if distant attendance. Bruno stopped the car outside the main entrance and said: "See you tonight?"

"Oh yes, please." She hesitated. "Will it be safe?"

"Sure. Walk two hundred yards south of the Hunter's Horn. There's a café there with the illuminated sign of the cross of Lorraine. God knows why. I'll be there. Nine o'clock." He put his arm round her. "Don't look so sad, Maria."

"I'm not sad."

"Don't you want to come?"

"Oh yes, yes, yes, I want to spend every minute of the day with you."

"Dr. Harper wouldn't approve."

"I suppose not." She took his face in her hands and looked deep into his eyes. "But have you ever thought that now is all the time there may be?" She shivered. "I can feel someone walking over my grave."

"Nobody's got any manners any more," Bruno said. "Tell him to get off." Without looking at or speaking to him again she let in the clutch of the car and moved off: he watched her until she had disappeared from sight.

Bruno was lying on the bed in his hotel room when the phone rang. The operator asked if he was Mr. Neuhas and when Bruno said he was she put the caller through. It was Maria.

"Tanya," he said. "What a pleasant surprise."

There was a pause while she apparently adjusted to her new name, then she said: "You were quite right. Our friend admits responsibility for what happened at lunch-time."

"Jon Neuhas right as ever. See you at the appointed time."

By 6 P.M. that evening the full darkness of night had already fallen. The temperature was well below freezing, a faint wind was stirring and patches of slowly drifting cloud occasionally obscured the three-quarter moon. Most of the sky was bright with twinkling frosty stars.

The lorry park outside the truck-drivers' pull-up, three miles south of town, was filled almost to capacity. From the long low single-storey café bright yellow light and the sound of juke-box music: the café was being heavily patronised, drivers entering or leaving at fairly regular intervals. One driver, a middle-aged man enveloped in the numerous swathes of his breed, emerged and climbed into his vehicle, a large and empty furniture van with two hinged rear doors and securing battens running along both sides. There was no partition between the driver and the body of the van: just that single seat up front. The driver turned the ignition, the big diesel thudded into life but before the driver could touch brake, clutch or gear he was slumped forward over his wheel, unconscious. A pair of giant hands reached under his armpits, plucked him from his seat as if he were a puppet and deposited him on the floor of the van.

Manuelo applied adhesive to the unfortunate driver's mouth and then set about fixing a blindfold. He said: "I am grieved that we should have to treat an innocent citizen in this manner."

"Agreed, agreed." Kan Dahn shook his head sadly and tightened the last knot on their victim's wrists. "But the greatest good of the greatest number. Besides," he said hopefully, "he may not be an innocent citizen."

Ron Roebuck, who was securing the man's ankles to one of the parallel securing battens, did not appear to think that the situation called for any comment. There were lassos, clothes-lines, heavy twine and a large coil of nylon rope—the most conspicuous of all and by far the heaviest and thickest: it was knotted at eighteen-inch intervals.

At 6:15 P.M. Bruno, magnificently attired in what he privately thought of as his pierrot's suit and the magnificent pseudo chinchilla, left the hotel. He walked with the unhurried measured gait of one for whom time is not a matter of pressing concern: in fact he did not wish to disturb the fulminate of mercury in the six explosive devices that were suspended from his belt. The voluminous nylon coat concealed those perfectly.

As befitted a man with time on his hands, he wandered at apparent random, following what would otherwise have been thought to be a devious twisting route. He spent a considerable amount of his time in stopping and apparently examining goods in shop-windows, not omitting the side windows at shop entrances. He finally sauntered round a corner, quickened his pace for a few steps, then sank into the dark shadow of a recessing doorway. A dark rain-coated man rounded the same corner, hesitated, hastened forward, passed by where Bruno stood concealed, then sagged at the knees, momentarily stunned, as the edge of Bruno's right hand caught him below his right ear. Bruno held him upright with one hand, went swiftly through his pockets with the other and came up with a snub-nosed automatic. The safety catch clicked off.

"Walk," Bruno said.

The hijacked furniture van was about halfway down the south lane abutting on the Lubylan, the last of five parked trucks. Bruno saw it at once when he halted, arm apparently cordially in arm with his erstwhile shadow, at the corner of the main street and the south lane. Bruno had deemed it prudent to halt because a guard was coming up the other side of the lane, machine-gun shoulder-slung. From his general appearance the weapon was the last thing on his mind. Like the guards of the previous night he wasn't walking with a brisk military step, he was just trudging along, wallowing in the unplumbed depths of his own frozen miseries. Bruno dug his automatic deeper into his companion's side, just above the hip-bone.

"Call out and you're a dead man."

Clearly, the idea did not appeal to the prisoner. The combination of fear and the cold gave him the impression of one who was frozen stiff. As soon as the guard had turned the corner into the main street—he did not have the appearance of one who was about to glance back suspiciously over his shoulder—Bruno marched his captive down to the line of parked trucks: once safely abreast these they were hidden from the sight of anyone on the other side of the lane.

Pushing the man in front of him Bruno moved out cautiously between the third and fourth parked trucks and glanced to his right. A second guard had just appeared round the south-east corner and was on his way up the south lane. Bruno retreated to the pavement. There was no guaranteeing that his captive would not suddenly screw his courage to the sticking point and, moreover, it was now safe, because free from observation, to have an unconscious man on his hands, so Bruno repeated the earlier blow, although this time with considerably more force, and eased the man to the ground. The guard passed unwittingly by the other side. Bruno hoisted his captive to his shoulder and carried him to the rear of the van just as one of the doors opened: someone had been keeping a good watch through the windscreen. Kan Dahn had the unconscious man inside in a second and Bruno followed.

"Is Roebuck on his way? To get that little toy for me from the train. And the cassettes?"

"On his way." Kan Dahn jumped down, followed by Manuelo, who hid behind the end of the van. Kan Dahn lay down in the middle of the lane, produced a bottle of scotch from his pocket, poured a liberal amount over his face and shoulders and lay still, the bottle still clasped in his hand. His arm covered his face.

A guard came round the south-east corner and saw Kan Dahn almost immediately. He stood stock still for a moment, looked around warily, saw no danger and broke into a run towards the prostrate man. As he approached he unslung his machine-pistol and advanced slowly and cautiously, the barrel trained on the massive bulk. At fifteen feet it was unthinkable that he should miss. At twenty-five feet it was equally unthinkable that Manuelo should miss. The hilt of the knife caught the guard squarely between the eyes and Kan Dahn, courteously breaking his fall, had him inside the van in five seconds.

In another ten seconds Manuelo had retrieved his knife and retreated into his former hiding position while Kan Dahn resumed his recumbent position. Such was Bruno's faith in the two that he did not even bother to watch the painful proceedings but concentrated instead on the process of immobilising gagging and blindfolding the prisoners. Within six minutes there were five men lashed to the side of the furniture van, completely helpless and silenced, three of them already conscious but none of them able to do anything about their circumstances. The people of the circus are pastmasters in the art of tying knots: their lives too often depend on this very expertise.

The three men left the van. Kan Dahn had a pair of canvas shoes in a pocket and carried a finely chiselled but massive crow-bar; Bruno carried a pocket flash, three bound poles slung from his shoulder, and a polythene wrapped and very peculiar packet in his pocket; Manuelo, in addition to a variety of throwing knives, carried a pair of rather fearsome-looking and heavily insulated wirecutters. The amatol explosives Bruno had left behind in the van.

They walked eastwards along the lane. Occasionally the moon shone through and their presence there was readily to be seen by anyone with eyes to see. Even so, they had no option other than to carry on as unobtrusively as they could—although it was questionable whether any close observer would have found anything unobtrusive about the crow-bar, wire-cutter and poles. By the time they had reached the power station, some three hundred yards distant from the prison side of the Lubylan, the moon had slid behind some barred cloud again. There were no guards to be seen or heard, and the only form of protection appeared to be a heavy steel mesh mounted on ten-feet-high hollow steel tubes, with one cross-railing at the top and one six feet up. The top railing was liberally festooned with very unpleasant barbed wire.

Bruno took the crow-bar from Kan Dahn, pressed one end firmly into the earth and let the other fall against the mesh, at the same time taking two prudent backward steps. There was no pyrotechnical display, no blinding coruscation of arcs, sparks and flashes. The fence was not electrified nor had Bruno for a moment thought it would have been. Only a madman would put two thousand volts through a fence at ground level; but Bruno had had no guarantee that he wasn't dealing with madmen.

Manuelo began to snip his way through the mesh.

Bruno took out his red pen and thoughtfully pushed down the end button. Kan Dahn looked at him curiously.

"Left it a bit late to write your last will and testament?"

"A toy Dr. Harper gave me. Fires anaesthetic darts."

One by one they stooped and passed through the hole Manuelo had made. Five paces they took and then they discovered that the lack of human guards was compensated for by the presence of canine ones in the form of three Doberman pinschers that came at them out of the gloom. Manuelo's knife flickered forward in an underhand throw and the leaping dog died in mid-air, the blade buried to the hilt in its throat. The dog jumping for Kan Dahn's throat found itself with one iron forearm under its lower jaw and the other behind its ears: one effortless twist and the vertebra snapped. The third dog did succeed in knocking Bruno down but not before the steel dart had lodged in its chest. The dog landed heavily, rolled over twice and lay still.

They advanced to the power house itself. The door was made of metal and was locked. Bruno put his ear to the door and moved away quickly: even on the outside the high speed whining of turbines and generators was an assault on the eardrums. To the left of the door and about ten feet up was a barred window. Bruno glanced at Kan Dahn, who stooped, caught him by the ankles and hoisted him effortlessly: it was like going up in a lift.

The power house was deserted but for one man seated in a glass-enclosed control room. He was wearing what Bruno at first took to be a pair of headphones: they were, in fact, ear-muffs for excluding sound. Bruno returned to earth.

"The door, please, Kan Dahn. No, not there. The handle side."

"Designers always make the same mistake. The hinges are never as massive as the securing bolts." He inserted the chisel edge of the crow-bar between the door and the wall and had the door off its hinges in ten seconds. Kan Dahn looked at the bent crow-bar in some vexation, grasped it in his hands and straightened it out as if it were made of putty.

It took them no more than twenty seconds, making no attempt at concealment, to reach the door of the control box. The duty engineer, facing rows of breakers and gauges, was no more than eight feet away, completely oblivious to their presence. Bruno tried the door. This too was locked. Bruno looked at the two men. Both nodded. With one scything sweep of his crow-bar Kan Dahn removed most of the glass from the door. Even the ear-muffled engineer could not have failed to hear the resulting racket, for when Kan Dahn shattered a sheet of plate glass he did it *con brio*. He swung round in his swivel chair and had only the fleeting fraction of a second to register the impression of three vague silhouettes outside the control room when the haft of Manuelo's knife caught him on the forehead.

Bruno reached through the hole and turned the key. They went inside and while Kan Dahn and Manuelo immobilised the hapless engineer Bruno scanned the metal labels on the breakers. He selected a particular one and yanked the handle down through ninety degrees.

Kan Dahn said: "Sure?"

"Sure. It's marked."

"If you're wrong?"

"I'll be barbecued."

Bruno sat in the engineer's vacant chair, removed his shoes and replaced them with the pair of canvas shoes he used on the high wire. His own shoes he handed to Kan Dahn, who said: "You have a mask, a hood?"

Bruno looked at his red and brown suit and mustard socks. "If I wear a mask they won't recognise me?"

"You have a point."

"For me, it doesn't matter whether I'm recognised or not. I don't intend to hang around when this lot is over. What matters is that you and Manuelo and Roebuck are not recognised."

"The show must go on?"

Bruno nodded and led the way outside. Curious to see the duration of the effect of the anaesthetic darts, he stooped and examined the Doberman, then straightened slowly. It appeared that Dobermans had nervous systems that differed from those of humans: this Doberman was stone cold dead.

There were several pylons, each about eighty feet high, inside the compound. He made for the most westerly of those and started to climb. Kan Dahn and Manuelo left through the hole in the compound mesh.

The pylon presented no problem. Dark though the night was—the moon was still behind cloud—

Bruno climbed it with no more effort than the average person would have encountered with a flight of stairs in daylight. Reaching the top cross-bar, Bruno unslung the bound poles, undid the bindings, which he thrust into his pocket, and screwed the three pieces solidly together: he had his balancing pole. He stooped and reached out to touch, just beyond the retaining insulator, the heavy steel cable that angled off towards the south-east corner of the Lubylan. For a moment he hesitated then fatalistically concluded that hesitation would serve no purpose. If he had switched off the wrong breaker then at least he would never know anything about it. He reached down and caught the cable.

He'd switched off the right breaker. The cable was ice cold to the touch but, all importantly, it was not ice-sheathed. There was some wind, but it was slight and fitful. The cold was close to numbing, but this was not a consideration to be taken into account: by the time he'd covered that interminable three hundred yards he'd be, he knew, covered in perspiration. He waited no longer. Balancing his pole, he made his gingerly way along the insulator anchoring wire and stepped out on to the power cable.

Roebuck took a couple of steps down towards the track, craned forward and peered cautiously fore and aft, saw no one in sight, descended the remaining steps then left the train at a measured pace. Not that he had not the right to leave the train whenever he wished, nor even to be seen with what he had then, two canvas sacks clipped together at their tops and slung over his shoulders, for those were the containers he habitually used to transport his ropes and the metal pins he used as targets in his act: what might have aroused a degree of passing curiosity was that he had left the circus train at a point four coaches distant from where he had his own quarters.

He climbed into the small Skoda he'd arrived in and parked it a hundred yards short of the Lubylan. He walked briskly on until he came to a small lane. He turned in here, crossed through a gate in a fence, jumped for and pulled down the spring extension of a fire-escape and climbed quickly until he'd hauled himself on to the roof. Crossing to the other side of the roof was akin to hacking one's way through the Amazonian jungle. Some arborealist whom Roebuck, in his total ignorance of Central European horticultural matters, presumed to have been of some distant English extraction, had seen fit to plant, in earth-filled tubs or troughs, shrubs, bushes, conifers extending to the height of twenty feet and, incredibly, two transverse and immaculately trimmed privet hedges and one lateral one that lined the edge of the roof overlooking the main street. Even in this egalitarian society the passion for privacy was not to be denied. This was, in fact, the same roof garden that Dr. Harper had remarked on their first trip from the station to the Winter Palace.

Roebuck, a latter-day Last of the Mohicans, parted the lateral hedge and peered across and up. Across the street and about fifteen feet above the elevation where he stood was the watch-tower at the south-west corner of the Lubylan. In size and shape it was very much like a telephone box, metal or wood for the first five feet then glass above. That it was manned by only one guard was clear, because a light was on inside the tower and Roebuck could clearly see the solitary occupant. Suddenly, a remote-controlled searchlight, mounted about two feet above the top of the tower, came to life, stabbing along the western perimeter of the roof, but depressed so that it would not blind the guard in the north-west tower. The light died, then came on again, this time playing along the southern perimeter, then again faded. The guard appeared to be in no hurry to put out his light. He lit a cigarette, then lifted what appeared to be a hip flask to his mouth. Roebuck hoped that the light would remain on: as long as it did the guard's night vision was virtually useless.

The curving spikes of the electrified fence were on a level with the base of the watch-tower. The distance, allowing for the angled increase of height, was about forty-five feet. Roebuck stepped back from the hedge, blessing the person whose sense of privacy had driven him to such horticultural lengths, removed the coil of rope from his shoulders and took about eight loops in his right hand. The free end of the rope had already been made into a running noose. The rope itself, hardly as thick as the average clothes-line, looked as if it might be fit for tying up a parcel but no more than that. It was, in fact, made of steel-cored nylon with a breaking strain of fourteen hundred pounds.

He parted the hedge again and peered down. Kan Dahn and Manuelo were standing, apparently chatting aimlessly, at the corner of the main street and the south lane. The main street was empty of all life, except for passing cars, which were of no concern: not one driver in a thousand ever looks upwards at night.

Roebuck stood up on the parapet, swung the rope once round his head and on the second circle let it go. With what seemed a childishly simple inevitability, the rope snaked outwards and upwards and the loop settled over precisely the two spikes he had chosen. Roebuck did not attempt to draw the noose tight; he could easily have pulled it off the outward-curving spikes. He gathered up all the remainder of the rope and threw it across the street to land precisely at the feet of Kan Dahn and Manuelo. They picked up the rope and disappeared along the south lane: the rope tightened and settled down on the base of the spikes.

The first half of the journey along the power cable towards Lubylan Bruno accomplished without too much difficulty. The second part taxed all his powers, his innate ability, his reaction, his superb sense of balance. He had not appreciated that there was such a sag in the cable nor that he would be faced with so steep an upward climb: nor had he bargained for the increasingly frequent gusts of wind. They were slight enough, to be sure, but to a man poised in his precarious position even the sharp increase of five miles an hour in wind speed could have been lethal. As it was it was strong enough to make the cable sway in a highly disconcerting fashion. Had there been the most infinitesimal coating of ice on the wire he could never have made it. But make it he did.

The cable was clamped into a giant insulator held in place by two anchoring wires attached to the wall. Beyond the insulator, the cable looped upwards through another insulator in the base of a heavy-switched breaker covered by a plastic hood. To switch off that breaker would nullify the danger that might be caused by someone discovering the power-station break-in and switching on the circuit that Bruno had already broken: but that twin-pronged switch, sunk though it almost certainly was in a bath of oil, might make enough noise on release to alert the guard in the south-east watch-tower, no more than ten feet distant. Bruno decided to leave it for the moment.

He unscrewed the balancing pole, bound it together and suspended it from an anchoring wire, unlikely though it was that he would be using it again. Getting over the fence of those outward-curving spikes would be no problem. It was only about three feet above his head, and all he had to do was to hoist himself up to the top of the breaker and almost literally step over. But here was also the moment of greatest danger—the first time he would be completely exposed to observation.

He threw a loop of rope over a spike, hoisted himself up until he was standing on the breaker, his head at least four feet above the top of the spiked fence. The massive flat-topped wall was at least thirty inches thick. A five-year-old who didn't suffer from vertigo could have toddled around the top perimeter with ease; but the same five-year-old would have been suicidally open to the repeated and irregular probings of the watch-tower searchlights along the perimeter walls.

And, just at that moment when he was about to step over the curved spikes of the steel fence, a searchlight bloomed into life. It came from the north-east tower and the beam traversed the length of the east perimeter wall he had been about to mount.

Bruno's reflex action was instantaneous. He crouched below the top level of the wall, holding on to the loop of the rope to keep himself from toppling outwards. It seemed very unlikely that the guard would pick up any object so small as the tiny bight of the rope round its anchoring spike, and so in the event it proved. The searchlight beam moved away through ninety degrees, briefly traversed the north wall then died. Five seconds later Bruno stood on top of the wall.

Five feet below on the opposite side was the roof of the detention block. The entrance to the watch-tower had to be from there. Bruno lowered himself to the roof and made his crouching way along to the base of the tower.

A flight of eight angled wooden steps led up to the tower platform. As Bruno glanced upwards a match inside the tower flared and he had a glimpse of a figure with a fur hat and turned-up collar of a great-coat lighting a cigarette. Bruno unscrewed the cover of the gas pen and soundlessly mounted the stairs, putting his left hand on the door. He waited until the guard drew heavily on his cigarette, opened the door without undue haste, aimed the pen at the red glow and pressed the clip.

Five minutes later he arrived, via the detention block roof, at the north-east watch-tower. His stay there occupied him no longer than had his brief sojourn at the first tower. Leaving the second guard there as immobilised and silenced as the first, he made his way back along the east wall, lowered himself down to the breaker and gently pressed down the lever. The muffled thud could not have been heard more than a few feet away, for as he'd guessed the switch had been immersed in a bath of oil. He returned to the south-east tower, peered over the south wall and flashed his torch three times in rapid succession, then pressed it on and left it on. A recognition flash came from the south lane below.

Bruno doused his light, produced a considerable length of weighted cord from a capacious pocket and lowered it. He felt pressure come on the end followed by a gentle tug and immediately started reeling in the cord. In very short order indeed he had in his hands the other end of the rope that Roebuck had succeeded in attaching to the spikes at the south-west corner of Lubylan. He pulled it taut but not too taut—the steel core of the nylon ensured that the sagging factor would be negligible—and fastened it securely. He now had a rope that ran the full length of the outside of the southern wall, three to four feet below the base of the spikes. For an aerialist and high-wire specialist it was as good as a public highway.

It was a fifty-yard trip to the south-west tower and he made it in under three minutes. With the rope to walk on and the base of the curved spikes for support it was, for Bruno, a ridiculously easy passage. Once, but then only very briefly, he had to duck low when the searchlight of the watch-tower he was approaching traversed the south wall, but there was never any danger of discovery. And within a minute of his arrival at his destination a third guard had lost all conscious interest in the immediate future.

Bruno pointed his torch down and signalled four times, this to let those waiting below know that he had arrived but to wait. There was still the final guard to be disposed of, the one in the north-west tower. It could well have been that the guards merely traversed their searchlights when and if the whim took them, or there could have been some concerted arrangement, however irregular that may have been. In any event, he could not afford to arouse any degree of suspicion.

He waited until the remaining guard had made a couple of perfunctory traverses with his searchlight, dropped down to the roof of the research building—like its eastern counterpart it was five feet below the level of the wall—and made his silent way across. Clearly the guard had had no suspicion at all. Bruno made his way back to the south-west watch-tower, flashed his torch twice and lowered his weighted cord again. A minute later he was securing a heavy knotted rope to the base of the spikes. He flashed again, waited a few seconds and gave the rope an experimental tug. It was bar-taut. The first of his companions was on his way up. Bruno peered downwards to try to identify the climber, but the gloom was too deep to make positive identification: from the bulk of the shadowy figure it looked like Kan Dahn.

Bruno embarked on a more careful examination of the roof. There had to be an access hatch for the watch-tower guards, for there was no such vertical access in or near the towers themselves. He located it almost at once by a glow of light emanating from a partially covered hatchway close to the inner edge of the roof, about halfway between the north and south walls. The hatchway cover, vertically sided, curved through an arc of ninety degrees, whether to obscure the light from above, which seemed unlikely, or to give protection against the weather to the hatch below, which seemed more probable. Bruno hitched a cautious eye round the corner of the cover. The light came from a heavily meshed square of plate glass set in a hinged trap-door. Looking down, Bruno could see only a part of the bleak room below but what he could see was enough. There were four guards there, fully clothed, three of them lying, apparently asleep, on hinged canvas bunks, the fourth, his back to Bruno and facing an open door, playing some sort of solitary card game. A vertical steel ladder ran from the floor of the room to the side of the trap-door.

Gingerly, Bruno tried the hatch, but it was locked, probably bolted from below. The place might not, as Harper had said it was, be guarded like Fort Knox, but they certainly took every precaution against the most unlikely occurrences. Bruno moved away and looked down over a low parapet into the courtyard. There were no immediate signs of the guard dogs Harper had mentioned, but that did not preclude the possibility of their lurking in one of several archways he could see, but that didn't seem likely: Dobermans are inveterate prowlers. And there was no movement or sign of life in the glass-enclosed elevated passageway that joined the two buildings on the fifth-floor level.

When Bruno returned to the south-west tower Kan Dahn was already there. The ninety-foot climb hadn't even altered his rate of breathing. He said: "How was the trip across?"

"A good performer always quits at the top. I can't ever top that, so I've just quit."

"And not a soul to see you. Alas, life's little ironies. I mean, with an audience there, we could have cleaned up twenty thousand bucks tonight." He appeared in no way surprised by Bruno's decision. "The watch-tower guards?"

"Asleep."

"All?" Bruno nodded. "So there's no rush?"

"There's no time to hang around either. I don't know when the reliefs come on duty."

"7 P.M. seems an unlikely hour."

"Yes. But we haven't come all this way to take what looks even like a ghost of a chance." He turned as first Roebuck and then Manuelo appeared in rapid succession. In contrast with Kan Dahn they appeared to be experiencing some difficulty with their breathing. Roebuck, the double canvas bag still slung over a shoulder, said: "Thank God we go down that rope instead of up when we leave."

"We don't leave that way."

"We don't?" Roebuck paled beneath the tan. "You mean there's another way? I'm not sure if I'm looking forward to that."

Bruno said soothingly. "A Sunday walk, that's all. Now, access. There's only one way in from the roof and that's locked."

Kan Dahn said: "A door?"

"A trap-door."

Kan Dahn brandished his crow-bar. "Poof! No trap-door."

"There are guards in the room below. One, at least, is wide awake." He led the way halfway along the west perimeter wall, knelt, caught hold of a curved spike and leaned out over the main street. The others did the same.

"I know the geography of this place. That first window down—I want to get in through there."

"That first window down," Roebuck said, "has got big thick iron bars protecting it."

"It won't have in a little while." Bruno knelt upright and produced the plastic packet from his pocket. He unrolled this to reveal two small polythene-wrapped packages. "For iron bars, the ultimate persuader. Turns them into a form of putty near enough."

Roebuck said: "What kind of hocus-pocus is this?"

"No hocus, no pocus. You can apologise at your leisure. Every professional magician worth his salt knows about it. You can soften and bend practically any metal by smearing it with this stuff—oddly enough, with reasonable care, it doesn't affect the human skin. The plastic inside this polythene contains an acid that eats into the interstices between the molecules of metal and softens it up. There's an Israeli magician who says that given time and enough of the stuff he could bend a Sherman tank. Here we have only two bars."

"How long does it take to work?"

"Five minutes should be enough. I'm not certain."

Manuelo said: "Burglar alarms?"

"Those I can fix."

Bruno tied a double bowline, slipped his legs through them until they reached the top of his thighs, secured a bight round his waist and eased himself out and over the curving spikes. He lowered himself to the full extent of his arms while Kan Dahn took a turn of the rope round a spike; then he exchanged his grip on the spikes for one on the rope, and Kan Dahn eased him down.

With the rope round his thighs and waist, his feet on the window-sill and one hand grasping an iron bar, Bruno was as safe as a man in a church. There were four bars on the window, each pair about eight inches apart. He removed the two cylinders of plastic compound from his pocket, opened them halfway and, careful not to remove the polythene covering, wrapped the plastic round the middle of the two centre bars, closing and smoothing the polythene round each in turn so that the compound was again completely sealed off. He climbed the few feet up the rope to the metal fence: Kan Dahn reached down, caught him under the armpits and lifted him easily over the wickedly out-curving spikes.

He said: "Five minutes. Manuelo, you'll come down with Kan Dahn and myself. Roebuck will stay here. And watch that canvas bag of yours—that's the last thing we can afford to lose at this stage of the game. Could I have the wire-cutters, please, Manuelo?"

Kan Dahn slipped into a double bowline, secured a bight round his waist, belayed the rope round three spikes—probably a sensible precaution for a man of his massive weight—and lowered himself down to the window ledge. He clenched a massive fist round each of the central bars and began to pull them apart. The contest was brief and unequal. The bars bent as if made from some inferior putty, but Kan Dahn wasn't content with just making a gap: he leaned some more on the bars and both came free from their anchorages. He handed them up to the roof.

Bruno joined Kan Dahn by means of a separate rope. Arrived opposite the window, he used his flash and peered through the glass. It appeared to be a perfectly innocuous office, bleakly furnished with metal cabinets, metal tables and padded metal seats. It certainly offered no hint of danger.

While Kan Dahn held the torch Bruno produced a roll of brown paper, unrolled it and pressed one side against a pane of glass. That side was clearly adhesive. He waited a few seconds then struck the centre of the glass quite firmly with the heel of his fist. The glass came away and fell into the room, making practically no noise at all. Bruno took the torch from Kan Dahn and, holding both torch and wire-cutters in the same hand, thrust his head and one of his arms through the hole he had made. He located the unconcealed alarm wires at once, severed them, reached up and opened the window catch and pushed the lower window upwards. Ten seconds and both he and Kan Dahn were inside the room: another ten and Manuelo had joined them. He was carrying Kan Dahn's crow-bar with him.

The office door was unlocked, the corridor beyond deserted. The three men made their way along until they came to an open door on the left. Bruno signalled to Manuelo to move forward. He did so and, holding a knife by the blade, cautiously showed an inch of the hilt round the edge of the jamb. Almost at once came the sound of discreet tapping on the glass of the hatch-cover above, enough to alert the card-playing soldier but not enough to disturb the three sleeping men. The guard at the table looked up questioningly, and then it was over. The hilt of Manuelo's knife caught him over the ear and Kan Dahn caught him before he even had time to strike the ground. Bruno picked up one of several guns stacked in a ramp and covered the three others with it. The last thing he wanted or intended to do was to use it, but the three men were not to know that and a man waking from his sleep is not going to argue with a Schmeisser machine-pistol. But they kept on sleeping soundly even when Kan Dahn unbolted the trap-door to allow Roebuck —and his canvas bag—down into the guard-room. Bruno took out his gas pen and advanced upon the three sleeping guards: Roebuck, armed with a suitable amount of rope, followed him.

They left the four guards there, securely bound and taped, three of them even more deeply asleep than they had been a few minutes previously. They bolted the trap-door, a probably unnecessary precaution, locked the guard-room door behind them and removed the key. Bruno said: "So far, so good." He hefted the Schmeisser he had borrowed from the guard-room. "Let's call on Van Diemen."

Kan Dahn paused in the passageway and looked puzzled. "Van Diemen? Why do we have to attend to him first—or at all? You know where his offices and laboratories are. Why don't we go straight in there now, find out the papers you want—you're quite sure you'll recognise those—"

"I'll recognise them?"

"Then fold our tents and steal away into the night. Like the Arabs, you know. A classy job, smooth, slick and noiseless. That's what I like."

Bruno looked his disbelief. "What you would like is to crack every skull in the Lubylan. I can give you four reasons for not doing it your way and then no arguing—the change of the guard may be due at any moment. Time is not on our side."

"The change of guard is all nicely asleep in the guard-room."

"That may not be the change of guard. They may have to report to some kind of H.Q. at change-over. There may be an officer who carries out a routine inspection. I don't know. Reason one: what we want may be in his private quarters. Reason two: we may be able to persuade him to tell us where the papers are. Reason three: if his filing cabinets are locked—and it would be astonishing if they aren't—we may make quite a noise in opening them up and his quarters are right next door. But reason four is most important. You should have guessed." From their expressions it was apparent that no one had guessed. "I'm taking him back to the States with me."

"Taking him back—" Roebuck looked his incredulity. "You've been through too much. It's your mind."

"Is it? What the hell's the point in taking the papers back home and leaving him here? He's the only man who knows those damned formulas or whatever they are—and all he'd do is just sit down and write them out again."

Roebuck said in slow comprehension: "You know, that had never occurred to me."

"Hadn't occurred to a lot of other people either, it would seem. Very odd, isn't it? Anyway, I'm sure that Uncle Sam can always find him a nice congenial job."

"Such as supervising the development of this damnable anti-matter?"

"From what I've heard of Van Diemen, he'd die first. He's a renegade, you know that. It must have taken some awfully compelling political and ideological reasons for him to defect from West Germany to here. He'd never co-operate."

"But you can't do this to a man," Kan Dahn said. "Kidnapping is a crime in any country."

"True. But better than death, I would have thought. What do you want me to do? Have him swear on the Bible—or any handy Marxist treatise that we can lay hands on—that he'll never again reproduce any of those formulas? You know damned well that he'd never consent to that. Or just leave him in peace to write his memoirs—all about how to construct this hellish weapon?"

The silence was very loud.

"You haven't left me much choice, have you? So what would you have me do? Execute him in the sacred name of patriotism?"

There was no immediate answer to this because he'd left them without the option of an answer. Then Kan Dahn said: "You have to take him back home."

10

Van Diemen's door was locked. Kan Dahn leaned on it and it was no longer locked. It crashed back against its hinges and Bruno was the first in, Schmeisser levelled—it had occurred to him, not, fortunately, too belatedly, that, without some recognisably offensive weapon, they were at a distinct disadvantage—a wandering guard, seeing them apparently unarmed, would be sorely tempted to cut loose with whatever weapon *he* might possess.

The startled man, propped on one elbow and rubbing sleep from his eyes, had a lean aristocratic face, grey hair, grey moustache and grey beard: he looked the exact antithesis of the mad scientist of popular conception. His unbelieving eyes switched from the intruders to a bell-push on his bedside table.

"Touch that and you're dead." Bruno's voice carried utter conviction. Van Diemen was convinced. Roebuck advanced to the bell-push and sliced the flexible lead with the wire-cutters.

"Who are you? What do you want?" Van Diemen's voice was steady, seemingly without fear: he had about him the look of a man who has suffered too much to be afraid of anything any more.

"We want you. We want the plans of your anti-gravity invention."

"I see. You can have me any time. Alive or dead. To get the plans you'll have to kill me first. They're not here anyway."

"You said the last two sentences the wrong way round. Tape his mouth and tie his hands behind his back. Then we look. For papers, keys, perhaps even one key."

The search, which lasted perhaps ten minutes and left Van Diemen's quarters in an indescribable shambles, yielded precisely nothing. Bruno stood in momentary indecision. For all he knew, time might be running out very fast indeed.

"Let's try his clothes."

They tried his clothes. Again they found nothing. Bruno advanced on the bound and gagged figure sitting up in bed, regarded him thoughtfully for a moment, then reached down and gently lifted the gold chain he wore round his neck. No crucifix for Van Diemen, no Star of David, but something that was probably even more precious to him than those could have been to Catholic or Jew: dangling from the end of the chain was a bright and intricately cut bronze key.

Two whole walls of Van Diemen's main office were lined with metal filing cabinets. Fourteen in all, each with four sliding drawers. Fifty-six key holes. Roebuck was unsuccessfully trying his thirtieth. Every pair of eyes in the office looked at him intently. All except Bruno's. His did not leave Van Diemen's face, which had remained expressionless throughout. Suddenly there was a tic at the corner of his mouth.

"That one," Bruno said.

That one it was. The key turned easily and Roebuck pulled the drawer out. Van Diemen tried to throw himself forward, which, if an understandable reaction, was a futile one, for Kan Dahn had one massive arm around him. Bruno advanced to the drawer, started leafing quickly through the files. He picked out one sheaf of papers, checked the other files, double-checked them and closed the drawer.

Roebuck said: "Yes?"

"Yes." Bruno thrust the files deep inside the inner pocket of his garish suit.

Roebuck said complainingly: "Seems like a bit of an anticlimax."

"I wouldn't worry about that," Bruno said encouragingly. "The climax may still be to come."

They descended to the eighth floor. Van Diemen had his mouth taped and hands bound behind his back, for the prison staff lived there and it seemed highly likely that Van Diemen might have wished to call attention to their presence. There were no guards here, either asleep or awake, and no reason why there should have been: guards were expendable but Van Diemen's papers were not.

Bruno headed directly for the door at the foot of the stairs. It was not locked and neither were the filing cabinets inside, and again there was no reason why any of them should have been. Bruno began opening filing drawers in swift succession, extracting files, leafing through them rapidly and discarding them in turn by the elementary process of dropping them on the floor.

Roebuck looked at him in some puzzlement and said: "A moment ago you were in one God Almighty damned hurry to get out. What place is this anyway?"

Bruno looked at him briefly. "You forget the note you passed me?"

"Ah."

"Yes, ah. '4:30. West entrance. No question. My life on it.' They keep the prison records here."

Bruno offered no further explanation to anyone. Suddenly he appeared to find what he wanted, a highly detailed schematic diagram with rows of names printed on one side. He glanced briefly at it, nodded in what appeared to be some satisfaction, dropped it to the floor and turned away.

Roebuck said: "We are doing our mentalist bit again?"

"Something like that."

They eschewed the elevator, walked down to the fifth floor, and crossed to the detention block by way of the glass-enclosed passageway. There was an admitted element of risk in this, but slight: the only people who might reasonably have been expected to have a watchful eye on that goldfish bowl corridor were the watch-tower guards and they were in no condition to have their eyes on anything.

Bruno halted the others as they reached the closed door at the far end of the passageway. "Wait. I know where the guard-room is—just round the corner to the left. What I don't know is whether the guards will be patrolling."

Roebuck said: "So?"

"There's only one way to find out."

"I'll come with you."

"No. Nobody's recognised you yet. I don't intend that anyone shall. Don't forget that true trouper Roebuck is performing tonight. And Kan Dahn. And Manuelo. And not forgetting, of course, Vladimir and Yoffe."

Manuelo looked at him in something approaching stupefaction.

"Your brothers?"

"Of course. They're here. Where else do you think they would have been taken?"

"But—but the ransom demands?"

"Courtesy of the Secret Police. So my brothers can perform with impunity. Nobody's got anything against them. How can they? They were just pawns, hostages for my good conduct. And do you think the police are going to admit they abducted them and sent ransom demands? Now that *would* cause an international uproar."

Manuelo said complainingly: "You do play the cards pretty close to the chest."

"It's one of the better ways of surviving."

"And how are you going to survive any longer?"

"I'm getting out of here."

"Sure. No problem. You just flap your arms and fly away."

"More or less. Roebuck has a little gadget in that bag of his. I just operate it and a whirligig should be here in about twenty minutes."

"Whirligig? Helicopter? From where, for God's sake?"

"American naval vessel lying offshore."

There was no ready answer to this. Then Roebuck said: "Very, very close to the chest. That means that you're the only one of us who's leaving?"

"I'm taking Maria. The police have recorded tape evidence that she's up to her ears in this."

They stared at him in complete incomprehension.

"I think I forgot to mention. She's a CIA agent."

Roebuck said heavily: "Very, very, very close. And how do you propose to get her?"

"Go up to the circus for her."

Kan Dahn shook his head sadly. "Quite, quite mad."

"Would I be here if I weren't?" He depressed the top knob of the black pen, slipped off the safety catch on his machine-pistol and cautiously eased open the door.

It was a prison just like any other prison, rows of cells on four sides of the block, passageways with four-feet-high railings bordering the deep well that ran the full vertical height of the building. As far as Bruno could see there was no one on patrol, certainly not on that fifth floor. He moved out to the railing, glanced up and then down the fifty-foot drop to the concrete below. It was impossible to be certain, but there appeared to be no one on patrol, nor could he hear anything. And prison guards, especially military guards, are not noted for the lightness of their steps.

Light came from a glass-fronted door about twenty feet to his left. Bruno pussy-footed his way towards it and peered in. There were two guards and two only, seated one on either side of a small table. Quite clearly they weren't expecting any senior officers or NCOs around on a tour of inspection, for they had a bottle on the table and a glass apiece. They were playing the inevitable cards.

Bruno pushed the door open. Both men turned their heads and looked down the uninviting muzzle of the Schmeisser.

"On your feet."

They complied with alacrity.

"Hands behind your necks. Close your eyes. Tight."

They wasted no time over this either. Bruno pulled out the gas pen, squirted it twice, then whistled softly for the others to join him. While they were immobilising the two guards, Bruno inspected the rows of numbered keys hanging on the guard-room wall.

On the seventh floor, Bruno selected the key numbered 713 and opened the cell door. The two brothers, Vladimir and Yoffe, stared at him in open disbelief, then rushed out and hugged him wordlessly. Bruno pushed them smilingly aside, selected more keys, opened 714 then 715 and 716 in succession. Bruno, standing outside 715, smiled without mirth at his two brothers, companions and Van Diemen, who had moved up to join him.

He said: "A rather nice touch, don't you think, to lock all the Wildermanns up together?"

The three doors opened almost simultaneously and three people made their way, two with very faltering footsteps, out into the passageway. The two who could not walk too well were old and stooped and grey, one who had been a man, the other who had been a woman, their prison faces lined with suffering and pain and privation. The third figure had been a young man but was no longer young, except in years.

The old woman stared at Bruno with dull lack-lustre eyes. She said: "Bruno."

"Yes, mother."

"I knew you would come some day."

He put his arm round the frail shoulders. "I'm sorry I took so long."

"Touching," Dr. Harper said. "How very very touching."

Bruno removed his arm and turned round unhurriedly. Dr. Harper, using Maria Hopkins as a shield, had a silencer pistol in one hand. Beside him, smiling wolfishly, Colonel Sergius was similarly armed. Behind them stood the giant Angelo, whose preferred form of weapon was a giant lethal club the size of a baseball bat.

Harper went on: "We're not interrupting, are we? I mean, you weren't thinking of going someplace?"

"We had that in mind."

"Drop that machine-pistol," Sergius ordered.

Bruno stooped, placed it on the ground, then, as he came upright, moved with lightning speed, grabbed Van Diemen and held him before him as a shield. With his other hand he got the red dart pen from his breast pocket, depressed the knob, and pointed it over Van Diemen's shoulder at Harper's face. At the sight of the pen Harper's face widened in fear and the finger tightened on the trigger of the silenced gun.

Sergius, no longer smiling, said viciously: "Drop that. I can get you from the side." Which was an accurate observation but, unfortunately for Sergius, he had transferred his attention to Bruno while he was speaking, a period of about two seconds, and for a man possessed of the cobra speed and accuracy of Manuelo two seconds was a laughably long time. Sergius died unawares, the knife buried to the haft in his throat.

Two seconds after that both Van Diemen and Harper were on the floor, Van Diemen with the bullet intended for Bruno buried in his chest, Harper with the dart buried in his cheek. Angelo, his face contorted in fury, made an animal noise deep in the throat and leapt forward, his huge club swinging. Kan Dahn, moving forward even more quickly, and with astonishing agility for a man of his immense bulk, avoided the downward blow, wrenched the club from Angelo and tossed it contemptuously to one side. The struggle that followed was as titanic as it was brief; and the sound of Angelo's neck breaking was that of a rotten bough shearing under the woodman's axe.

Bruno put one arm round the violently trembling girl, the other round the stunned, terrified and uncomprehending old woman.

He said: "*Fine. Terminé*. It's all over and you're all safe now. I think we should leave this place now. You won't really mind will you, Father?" The old man gazed at the prostrate figures and said nothing.

Bruno went on, to no one in particular: "About Van Diemen I'm sorry. But perhaps it's best. He'd really no place left to go."

Kan Dahn said: "No place?"

"In his world, yes. In mine, not. He was completely amoral—not immoral—in devising so fiendish a weapon. A totally unheeding, irresponsible man. I know it's a very cruel thing to say, but the world can well do without him."

Maria said: "Why did Dr. Harper come for me? He kept saying something about his transmitter and tapes being missing from his railway compartment."

"Yes. It had to be something like that. Roebuck here stole them. Can't trust those Americans."

"You don't trust me very much. You don't tell me very much." There was no reproach in her voice, just a lack of understanding. "But perhaps you can tell me what happens when Dr. Harper comes to."

"Dead men don't come to. Not on this planet, anyway."

"Dead?" She had no emotions left to register.

"Those darts were tipped with lethal poison. Some form of refined curare, I should imagine. I was supposed to kill some of their own men. Fortunately, I had to use it on a guard dog. Now a very dead guard dog."

"Kill their own men?"

"It would have looked very black for me—and America—if I'd killed some of the guards here then been caught red-handed. Their own men. People like Harper and Sergius are men without hearts, without souls. They'd shoot their own parents if it served their personal political ends. It was also slated, incidentally, that you should die. I had, of course, been instructed not to use the dart gun on Van Diemen on the pretext that he had a weak heart. Well, God knows he's got a weak enough heart now—Harper put a bullet through it." He looked at Maria. "You know how to operate the call-up on the transmitter—Roebuck has it in his bag there?" She nodded. "Right, send the signal now." He turned to Kan Dahn, Roebuck and Manuelo. "Bring my folks down slowly, will you? They can't hurry. I'll wait below."

Kan Dahn said with suspicion: "Where are you going?"

"The entrance is time-locked, so someone must have let them in. Whoever that was will still be there or thereabouts. You're all still in the clear. I want you to stay that way." He picked up the Schmeisser. "I hope I don't have to use this."

When the others joined him on the ground floor some five minutes later, Bruno had already done what he had to do. Kan Dahn surveyed the two bound, gagged and for the moment unconscious guards with considerable satisfaction.

"By my count that's making thirteen people we've tied up tonight. It's certainly been an unlucky number for some. So it's up, up and away."

"Indeed." He asked of Maria: "You made contact?"

She looked at her watch. "It's air-borne. Rendezvous in sixteen minutes."

"Good." He looked and smiled at Kan Dahn, Manuelo, Roebuck, Vladimir and Yoffe. "Well, it's the van for us while you five make your own discreet way back to the Winter Palace. *Au revoir* and many thanks. See you all in Florida. Have a nice night at the circus."

Bruno helped his elderly parents and youngest brother into the back of the van, climbed into the front with Maria and drove off towards the rendezvous with the helicopter. He stopped the van about thirty yards beyond the wooden bridge spanning the narrow, fast river. Maria looked at the trees closely crowding on both sides.

"*This* is the rendezvous?"

"Round the next corner. In a clearing. But I have a little chore to attend to first."

"Inevitably." She looked and sounded resigned. "And is one allowed to ask what it is?"

"I'm going to blow the bridge up."

"I see. You're going to blow the bridge up." She registered no surprise and was by now at the stage where she wouldn't have lifted an eyebrow if he'd announced his intention of razing the Winter Palace to the ground. "Why?"

Carrying his clutch of amatol explosives, Bruno descended from the van. Maria followed. As they walked on to the bridge Bruno said: "Hasn't it occurred to you that when they hear the chopper's engine—and you can hear a chopper's engine an awfully long way away—the police and army are going to come swarming out of town like enraged bees? I don't want to get stung."

Maria was crest-fallen. "There seems to be an awful lot of things that don't occur to me."

Bruno took her arm and said nothing. Together,

they walked out to the middle of the bridge, where Bruno stooped and laid the charges together between two struts on the side of the bridge. He straightened and surveyed them thoughtfully.

Maria said: "Are you an expert on *everything?*"

"You don't have to be an expert to blow up a wooden bridge." He produced a pair of pliers from his pocket. "All you require is one of those to crimp the chemical fuse—and, of course, the sense to walk away immediately afterwards."

He stood there thoughtfully and she said: "Well, aren't you going to crimp the fuses, then?"

"Two things. I only crimp one fuse: the other charges will go up through sympathetic detonation. And if I blow up the bridge now then the angry bees would be out here immediately, perhaps with enough time to figure out a way to cross the river or find a nearby bridge. We wait till we hear the chopper, blow up the bridge, drive round to this glade in the woods and use the van's headlights to light up the landing area."

She said: "I can hear the helicopter now."

He nodded, stooped again, crimped a fuse, took her hand and ran off the bridge. Twenty yards beyond the bridge they turned round just on the moment that the explosion came. The noise was a very satisfactory one indeed, and so was the result: the centre of the bridge, a flimsy structure at best, simply disintegrated and fell into the river below.

The transfer to the helicopter and the flight back to the ship went without a hitch, the pilot hedge-hopping all the way to keep below the radar screen.

In the wardroom Bruno was being apologetic to a rather stormy Maria.

"I know I fooled you and I'm sorry. But I didn't want you to die, you see. I knew from the beginning that most of our conversations were being recorded. I had to make Harper think that the break-in was going to be on Tuesday. He was all set to get us that night and that meant that he would have got to you too."

"But Kan Dahn and Roebuck and Manuelo—"

"No risk. They were in it from the beginning."

"Why, you close, devious—but something must have put you on to Harper in the first place?"

"My Slav blood. Nasty suspicious natures we Slavs have. About the only place that wasn't bugged was the circus office back in the States. The electronic snooper that Harper brought in was an accomplice of his: this was designed to throw suspicion on the circus. If there was no internal circus contact then it *had* to be Harper. Only four people were really privy to what was going on—your boss, Pilgrim, Fawcett and Harper. Your boss was above suspicion, Fawcett and Pilgrim were dead. So, Harper. Aboard ship, Carter, the purser, wasn't there to make sure that my cabin wasn't bugged—he was there to make sure that it was. So was yours."

"You have no proof of this."

"No? He was in correspondence with Gdynia and he had fifteen hundred dollars in his cabin. New dollars. I have the serial numbers."

"That night he met with the accident on deck—"

"Kan Dahn was the accident. Then Harper told me he had keys for Van Diemen's offices. He must have thought me a simpleton. You'd have needed a hundred skeleton keys to cover every lock. He'd keys for one reason only—he'd access to Van Diemen's keys. And he kept asking me about my plans for entry. I kept saying I'd play it by ear. So eventually I gave him all my plans—a tissue of lies—by giving them to you in your cabin. You may remember Harper suggested your cabin as a rendezvous. And, of course, I didn't trust you either."

"What!"

"I didn't *distrust* you. I just didn't trust anyone. I didn't know you were clean until you insisted that Harper had personally appointed you to this job. If you had been in cahoots, you'd have said your boss did."

"I'll never trust *you* again."

"And why were we followed by the Secret Police everywhere. *Someone* gave them the tip-off. When I knew it wasn't you, there wasn't anyone else very much to suspect."

"And you still expect me to marry you?"

"I'll have to. For your own sake. After you've resigned, that is. This may be the day of women's lib, but I think all this is a bit too lib for you. Do you know why Harper picked you—because he reckoned you were the person least likely to give him any trouble. He was right. My God, it's never even occurred to you how Harper managed to drag Fawcett inside the tiger's cage without being savaged."

"Well, since you're so clever—"

"He anaesthetised the tigers with a dart gun."

"Of course. Maybe I should retire at that. You don't make many mistakes, do you?"

"Yes. A major one. One that could have been fatal for many people. I assumed that the red dart gun was the same as he'd used on the tigers. It wasn't. It was lethal. If it hadn't been for that Doberman pinscher—ah well, it was fitting that he died at his own hand, so to speak. Hoist on his own petard or those who live by the sword die by the sword or something like that."

"One thing—among, seemingly, many others—I don't understand. This business of you having to take Van Diemen prisoner. Surely Van Diemen's almost certain ability to reproduce the formulas would have been foreseen by the CIA back in Washington?"

"It was foreseen. It was intended that I kill him with the lethal red pen. If not, Harper—who probably carried a vest pocketful of red pens—was slated to attend to him on Tuesday night, the supposed time of the break-in. He would have got off with it—he was as cunning as he was brilliant—and there would have been no one to testify against him. I would have been dead."

She looked at him and shuddered.

He smiled. "It's all over now. Harper told me a fairy story about Van Diemen's heart condition and insisted that I use the black gas pen against him. The need to use either did not arise. It was Harper's—and, of course, his masters'—intention that Van Diemen should survive. As I said, Harper died by his own hand—and Van Diemen by Harper's. Harper is totally responsible for the deaths of both Van Diemen and himself."

"But why—*why* did he do it?"

"Who knows? Who will ever know? A dedicated

anti-American? A million dollars on the nail? The motivation—or motivations—of a double agent lie beyond comprehension. Not that it matters now. Sorry, incidentally, that I jumped on you that night in New York—I had no means of knowing whether my family was alive or dead. You know, of course, why Harper sent us out to the restaurant that night—so that he could have my stateroom bugged. Which reminds me—I must send a telegram to have Carter arrested. And Morley—Harper's bogus electronics friend who bugged my stateroom on the train. And now, I have a delicate question for you."

"And that is?"

"May I go to the men's room?"

So he went to the men's room. There he extracted from his inside pocket the papers he had taken from Van Diemen's filing cabinet. He did not even look at them. He tore them into tiny pieces and flushed them down the toilet.

Captain Kodes knocked on the circus's office door and entered without invitation. Wrinfield looked up in mild surprise.

"I'm looking for Colonel Sergius, Mr. Wrinfield. Have you seen him?"

"I've just arrived from the train. If he's inside he'll be in his usual seat."

Kodes nodded and hurried into the large exhibition hall. The late night performance was in full swing and, as usual, it was a capacity house. Kodes made his way along to the section of the seats opposite the centre ring, but there was no sign of Sergius. For a few moments he stood there irresolute then instinctively, almost inevitably, his eyes followed the gaze of ten thousand other pairs of eyes.

For long moments Kodes stood stock still, as if petrified, his mind at first blankly refusing to accept the evidence of his eyes. But his eyes were making no mistake. What he was witnessing was the impossible but the impossible was indubitably there: two of The Blind Eagles were going through their customary hair-raising trapeze act.

Kodes turned and ran. As he went through the exit he was met by Kan Dahn, who greeted him in genial fashion. It was questionable whether Kodes saw him. He burst into Wrinfield's office, this time without the benefit of knocking.

"The Blind Eagles! The Blind Eagles! Where in God's name have they come from?"

Wrinfield looked at him mildly. "Their kidnappers released them. We notified the police. Didn't you know?"

"No, I damn well didn't know!" Kodes ran from the office and into his car.

Ashen-faced and stunned, Kodes stood on the seventh floor of the Lubylan detention block. The shock of finding gagged and bound men both at the open entrance below and in the guard-room had been shattering enough: but nothing could have prepared him for the sight of the three dead men lying there, Sergius and Van Diemen and Angelo.

A sure instinct led Kodes to the undertaker's emporium. He was hardly conscious of the fact that the lights were on in the front office. They were also on in the back parlour. He made his way to the coffin that had been so briefly occupied by Bruno, and slowly removed the lid.

Dr. Harper, hands crossed on his chest, looked curiously peaceful. The hands held the large black-bordered box that had been cut from the paper that had announced Bruno's death.

The Admiral leaned back in his chair in his Washington office and stared in disbelief as Bruno and Maria entered.

"God! That suit!"

"Beggars can't be choosers." Bruno surveyed his suit without enthusiasm. "Chap in Crau gave it to me."

"He did? Anyway, welcome home, Bruno. And Miss Hopkins."

"Mrs. Wildermann," Bruno said.

"What the devil do you mean?"

"Holy matrimony. They give you a special licence for people in a hurry. We were in a hurry."

The Admiral contained his near-apoplexy. "I have the outline of the past few days. The details, please."

Bruno gave him the details and when he had finished the Admiral said: "Magnificent. Well, well, it took a long time before we could put it all together. Van Diemen and your family."

"A long time."

Maria stared from one to the other in puzzlement.

The Admiral said briskly: "And now. The plans."

"Destroyed."

"Naturally. But your mentalist mind isn't."

"My mentalist mind, sir, has gone into a state of total shock. Amnesia."

The Admiral leaned forward, his eyes narrowing, his hands tightening on the desk. "Repeat that."

"I destroyed them without looking at them."

"You destroyed them without looking at them." It was a statement not a question. His voice was very quiet. "Why?"

"What did you want, sir? Another mutual balance of terror throughout the world?"

"Why?"

"I told you why. Remember? I hate war."

For long moments the Admiral looked at him without enthusiasm, then he slowly relaxed, leaned back and astonished them both by laughing.

"I've a damned good mind to fire you." He sighed, still smiling. "But you're probably right on the whole."

Maria said blankly: "Fire him?"

"Didn't you know? Bruno has been one of my top, and certainly most trusted, agents for the past five years."

About the Author

ALISTAIR MacLEAN is known throughout the world as one of today's top storytellers. His previous bestsellers include *Bear Island, Caravan to Vaccares, Puppet on a Chain, Force 10 from Navarone,* and *The Way to Dusty Death.* As well as being highly successful novels, *Ice Station Zebra, The Guns of Navarone, Where Eagles Dare,* and *Breakheart Pass* were also made into motion pictures.